GREENEBRIAR'S GARBAGE

There is More Than Trash in a Garbage Dump

A novel by S. M. Drake

WESTBOW
PRESS
A DIVISION OF THOMAS NELSON
& ZONDERVAN

Copyright © 2014 S. M. Drake.

All rights reserved. No part of this book may be used or reproduced by any means, graphic, electronic, or mechanical, including photocopying, recording, taping or by any information storage retrieval system without the written permission of the publisher except in the case of brief quotations embodied in critical articles and reviews.

This is a work of fiction. All of the characters, names, incidents, organizations, and dialogue in this novel are either the products of the author's imagination or are used fictitiously.

WestBow Press books may be ordered through booksellers or by contacting:

WestBow Press
A Division of Thomas Nelson & Zondervan
1663 Liberty Drive
Bloomington, IN 47403
www.westbowpress.com
1 (866) 928-1240

Because of the dynamic nature of the Internet, any web addresses or links contained in this book may have changed since publication and may no longer be valid. The views expressed in this work are solely those of the author and do not necessarily reflect the views of the publisher, and the publisher hereby disclaims any responsibility for them.

ISBN: 978-1-4908-4242-4 (sc)
ISBN: 978-1-4908-4241-7 (e)

Library of Congress Control Number: 2014911319

Printed in the United States of America.

WestBow Press rev. date: 12/18/2014

ACKNOWLEDGEMENT

Thanks so much to my friends and family who read, corrected and gave their opinions for this first novel of a series.

Writers spend many long lonely hours with their new friends, the characters they create. Sometimes we need an additional pair of eyes to read what has been written.

I appreciate the time and efforts by those who read my story: Barbara, Bruce, Carole, Frank, Gary, Harvey, Jason, Joyce, Leona, Lisa, Richard and SuZan.

A very special thanks is given to Lynda Money and Becky Smith who met with me week after week after week for final editing, and to Debbie who helped me format the book

Please accept my sincere apology if I forgot to mention you.

Thank you fellow author, Cosette Riggs, for the front and back cover designs, your continued support and the hours you spent to put everything together.

You may contact me at sandeedrake1@gmail.com
Check out my website smdrake.com, available 12/1/14

"Experience is not what happens to a man; it is what a man does with what happens to him" from Texts and Pretexts: An Anthology with Commentary. By Aldous Huxley. Published 1932

MAIN CHARACTERS

Sally and Seth Williams	Temporary president of HOA
sons, Grant, Garrett	
Lisa and Nate Bennett, son Brett	Sally's friend
Alicia and Barry Butchikas	neighbors next door
children, Alexander, Andromeda, Aldebranne, Andrew	
Vera and Vladmir Kiselev	sell house to Williams family
Jeff Crawford, sons Casey and Cody	cleaning crew
Lonnie and Hank Balliteria	Doug's former girlfriend and her husband

Homeowners Association Board of Directors (HOA))

Board Members ('77-79)	Temporary Board ('78-79)
President: Steve Smith	Sally Williams
Vice Pres.: Paul Hoffman, wife Patsy	continues in this job
Secretary: Suzanne Jones	Leah Lansing
Treasurer: Connor Pawlowich	Chris Kolanos
Block Captain: Andrea Czolowski	Alexandra Hyatt
Clubhouse/pool: Doug Pulchowoski	Emil Galloway
wife, Marlene, sons Jordan, Josh	
Clubhouse/rental: Mary Jane Trumps	Karen Murray
Grounds maintenance: Brian Murphy,	Mike Smith
wife Anna, daughter Gail;	
her friends, Becky Ingalls, Jenny Erthner	
Membership/Newsletter: Ellie Dobrowolski	Patty Breslford
Social Activities: Ingrid Fielding	Nancy VandeVenter
HOA lawyer, Daniel Gibson	

CHAPTER ONE
DEATH

Error, Error . . .

The numbers on the tape of the adding machine seemed to jump off the page, screaming: 'can't you see the mistake?' Paul punched the figures in again and hunched over the machine. *This just can't be right,* he thought. Suddenly a realization hit him as beads of perspiration rolled down his creased forehead. Not only was Doug over budget, he had overspent by hundreds of dollars.

"Paul, dinner is ready."

"I'll just finish up here, Patsy," he called out to his wife. "Give me five more minutes." His jaw tightened as he looked out the window to see the last of the fall leaves on their maple tree.

After I finish dinner I'll tell Patsy I have a new project to work on tonight and then maybe I can figure out this mistake. He could have left out some numbers, or maybe he forgot to write down a specific receipt amount.

He took out the box of receipts, looking in Doug's notebook where all purchases were dutifully recorded. As Paul perused Doug's notes, he realized this would take longer than five minutes. He closed the spiral pad, stood up to stretch and walked into the kitchen where he smelled a mouth watering aroma of lasagna, his mother-in-law's favorite recipe. Then he remembered: *tonight is my turn to clean up and lasagna turns the sink orange, a time consuming mess.*

Paul, a volunteer board member of the homeowners association, had been elected Vice President. This past year, 1978, he had been on a committee which involved renting the clubhouse for family members whose dues were current if they wanted to host a party. He also had been on Doug's committee (pool and clubhouse maintenance)

Three mornings a week, a preschool for families living in the subdivision, used this clubhouse which also had a large swimming pool and patio area.

In this south suburb of Chicago, the town of Eden had land flat as a pancake. Everyone joked about the name of this HOA, Greenebriar, wondering who would have picked this name, since there were no briar bushes anywhere.

"Patsy, is there any way we could swap cleaning and cooking for a couple of nights? I've found an error in the receipt book and I need to get this cleared up with Doug before the next board meeting. Remember, the annual meeting is only two weeks away." He looked at her hopefully and grinned.

"Paul, you promised me this volunteer position wouldn't take very much of your time. After most of the Board resigned in June, I knew you'd be busy for a while getting the new board set up, but then I thought you'd have more time for us." With her fingers, she combed back her short blond hair and unbuttoned the top two buttons of her blue striped blouse, fanning her flushed face with the other hand after she took the lasagna out of the hot oven.

"I really don't think this is fair," she said with a sigh. "I work all day too, and now you want to change the schedule." Patsy looked up at him with concern. "I spent most of the week-end fixing the meals for my nights to cook because I had such a busy schedule ahead of me and now at the last minute you want to change." She gave him the silverware and looked at him with a tense face.

"Seems as though you are somewhere else mentally; what gives?" She shoved her hands into deep pockets of her black slacks, waiting the obligatory five minutes for the food to set before she cut into the noodles.

"Never mind. I'll clean up the kitchen. Is there a babysitter lined up tomorrow afternoon for the boys?"

"What? Don't you remember?" She sat down and let out a long, slow breath. "You said you'd be able to get off work early and be home by 3:30. Paul, what's going on? This schedule has been set for over two weeks now." Her freckled face showed exasperation as she bent her small five foot two frame to cut the lasagna.

"Sorry, I forgot." He picked up his day planner from the kitchen desk. "Yes, I see now. I penciled in to be home tomorrow afternoon, so don't worry. I'll be here." He took off his loafers and placed them under his chair, and then pulled his blue oxford shirt out of his navy slacks.

"Let's eat; the smell is driving me crazy," Paul grinned. "Are the boys out back?" He patted his ample stomach, knowing this would not be a low calorie dinner.

"No, don't you remember what happens every Thursday night? They had a Cub Scout meeting and then pizza. We talked about this on Sunday." Her voice rose in pitch. She stopped cutting and looked up at him with concern.

"Well yes, I did forget, so sue me." Paul said with a frown.

"Don't get angry with me because you forgot. You were the one who suggested we write everything down each Sunday night and talk about our plans for the week." She sat down and tapped her perfectly polished red fingernails on the table.

Paul knew he'd better get in control quickly. He wasn't ready to share Doug's budget problems now. He took in a deep breath and said, "You're right, Patsy. Sorry. This board member stuff is taking more time than I imagined. I'll set up a meeting with Doug on Saturday morning." He sat down and took a large gulp of wine.

"There is a party at the club house tomorrow night. Afterward I'll have to check on the condition of the place before their deposit money is returned." He walked over to Patsy and gave her a hug. She pulled away and finished cutting the lasagna.

A few days later, a bright sun rose into a cloudless sky on Saturday morning. At the home of the temporary association president, Sally Williams, the phone rang and she picked it up with a frown. *Who would be calling this early?*

"Hi Lisa, can't this wait until our afternoon walk?"

"Are you telling me no one has called you?"

"No one called; what happened?" Sally asked.

"Brace yourself, Sally. This won't be your best early morning news."

"O.K., Lisa. Lay it on me. What newsworthy item do you have up your sleeve-full-of-gossip?"

"This isn't gossip I'm telling you; this news is unreal." Her voice almost whispered, "Doug is dead. The cleaning crew found him this morning when they arrived to clean up after last night's party. He had been there all night."

"What, dead?" Sally almost yelled into the phone. "I just talked with him last night; he's perfectly healthy." She stared out the back window in disbelief. "How could he just drop dead?" Slowly she sat down in one of the kitchen chairs.

"You talked to him last night, in the clubhouse? I can't believe the police haven't called you yet. I mean, you are the president of our board."

The rest of the conversation passed in a jumbled blur. *How could her best walking buddy Lisa know about this first?* Sally felt a little annoyed, yet glad her husband Seth still had his pilot training in Atlanta and would be gone until the end of this stressful year, 1978. Last spring he told her he didn't think she should undertake such a time consuming volunteer job. Sally quickly remembered another conversation about six months ago when she told him of the drastic dilemma at the last board meeting when everyone walked out after resigning, leaving her and Paul to pick up the pieces. She had been voted in as temporary president.

"Do you think Doug had any health problems we don't know about?" Lisa asked. "His neighbors let the board know how displeased they were when they built their family room addition."

"Really don't have a clue. I remember some discussion about his addition, but he had all the required architectural house plans and it passed." She stood up and walked over to the wall phone and finished the conversation.

"Thanks for letting me know. I'd better get off and prepare some sort of statement in case I do get a phone call." She hung up quickly, pushing her auburn bangs off her forehead, creased with concern for Doug and his family.

Looking back at the last year as a board member and now as president, Sally remembered Doug's behavior at some of the monthly board meetings. Could this have been a sign of ill health and did this have something to do with his death? He did not follow some of the requirements set up in their by-laws. Maybe these were clues showing stress from his job or family situation. Did he have problems at work and money issues?

"Some people aren't made of money," he would always reply when an increase would be discussed.

The ten board members had a difficult task keeping a balanced budget when a lot of the contractors raised their fees each year. There did not seem to be a choice—they had to raise the monthly dues. These people were elected by the homeowners at the annual meeting the third week in November, and one of their main jobs included spending wisely for the upkeep of the grounds. Greenebriar was a pristine subdivision of over 200 earth tone colored homes, and well manicured lawns (all homeowner requirements), about two hours south of Chicago in Eden, a small town. There were four other HOA subdivisions in this town, Bluebriar, Redbriar, Whitebriar and Yellowbriar. This was supposed to be a safe and wonderful place to raise a family.

Sally and Seth had been given only one house hunting trip from Transcontinental Airlines, (Trans Air), Seth's employer, to find a new place and this subdivision seemed perfect.

"Could I have misunderstood those arguments when Doug continued on and on, month after month when his spending had been questioned?" She spoke out loud, while looking out the bedroom window.

Someone would eventually call her. She fixed her hair and put on her makeup. *I'll write up something right now to describe what a devoted and hard-working board member Doug had been. Maybe I'll say something simple like, he'll be missed. I wonder if we'll be able to get more work done now without all his interruptions.* She walked into the hallway and called out, "Boys, time to get up."

The door-bell rang. She walked into Grant's room and looked out his window. A police car was parked in her driveway. She was startled as her youngest son, Garrett came up behind her and asked, "Mommy, why is there a police car in our driveway?"

"Dear, I don't know why he is here, but I'll find out. Get your brother up and have your cereal. You can go downstairs and watch cartoons for an extra thirty minutes."

The doorbell rang again. She called as loudly as she could, "Just a minute."

I can't believe my knees are shaking; this just can't be happening. At least Seth isn't here to say I told you so. She finished dressing as quickly as she could and threw on a clean sweatshirt, pulled on her jeans and stuffed her feet into her fluffy blue slippers, walking downstairs to open the oversized metal door. A tall clean cut young man in a crisp blue uniform stood on her doorstep. Her hands shook as she held onto the cold brass handle.

"My name is Sam Gregorczyk from the Eden police. Are you Sally Williams?" She nodded her head. "I need to ask you a few questions. Did you know a Doug Pulchowski?"

"Yes, he's one of our board members. You said 'did'; what happened?" She tried to keep her voice calm.

He took off his gloves and hat and looked at her with regret. His brown short hair looked so professional, trimmed just right, every image of a policeman. "A cleaning crew found him dead inside the clubhouse about 7:30 a.m. Looks like blunt force trauma."

Perfectly plucked brown eyebrows rose on her creased forehead. "I just talked with him last night. He called me to say there had been complaints about noise outside the clubhouse and he was going over there." She gripped the door handle tighter, trying hard to control her breathing as her hands shook.

"Did he say anything specific about the noise? Do you know who was having the party?" He shivered a little in the early morning cold.

"No, he didn't and I don't know who had the party, but I can find out." She noticed him shiver. "Would you like to come inside?

"Yes, thanks. I do have more questions," he said as he walked into the entrance. "Someone from the cleaning staff gave me your name as did Doug's wife, Marlene. Is Karen Murray the person who does the booking?"

"Yes, she's the one. Come on upstairs. Would you like something hot to drink, coffee, tea, hot cider?" She remembered she had banana bread too in case he'd want to eat something.

"You have cider? Great."

He followed her up the short staircase to a large rectangular living room. They turned right and walked through the dining room, almost bumping into Grant and Garrett who carefully carried their cereal bowls. "We won't spill anything, Mom," they said with broad grins. They walked out of the kitchen and downstairs to their family room.

Sally filled the copper kettle for tea and put it on the stove. She then took out fresh cider from the 'fridge, and put it in the ghastly green micro-wave.

"Officer, how many people have you talked to this morning besides the cleaning crew?"

"Only Mr. Crawford's cleaning crew and Mrs. Pulchowski."

She fixed her tea, gave him his warm cinnamon and clove scented cider and put some banana bread on a plate, placing two napkins next to the bread.

"Thanks Ma'am, this smells good." He put his large hands around the warm mug, and then picked up a piece of bread, his blue eyes shining with delight at the chance to sit down and eat.

Sally took a sip of tea and recalled the conversation with Doug the previous evening. The phone rang and Lisa started firing questions as rapidly as she walked. Almost every afternoon they took a brisk walk around the inside of the neighborhood.

"Not now Lisa -- don't you see the police car in my driveway? I'll call you later, or if you can wait, I'll save everything for our afternoon walk, O.K.?" She caught her breath and looked back at her un-expected guest.

The cinnamon scent from the heated cider reminded her of the last party at the clubhouse where the Smyths presided over Halloween games. October suddenly seemed a long time ago.

The officer took a bite of the banana bread, and unbuttoned his jacket. His short brown hair stood up straight, like the crew cut of yesteryear. He took a sip of the cider and pulled out a small notebook and pen. "What time did Doug call you, Mrs. Williams?"

"Please call me Sally. My boys stayed up late to finish a movie we rented. It could have been about nine-thirty."

"What was the problem?" He started writing.

"Actually, we talked about the board meeting coming up this Tuesday and he had another call on his second line. When he came back, he told me a neighbor complained about the noise level of the party and he thought he'd go over and see what was going on." She took a bite of bread and chewed slowly, savoring the banana flavor and crunchy walnuts. "I think he said the music was too loud."

"Anything else you can remember? Was he upset about having to go over there? His long thin fingers gripped the pencil tightly.

"Yes. Some parties get loud if people are out by the pool. There are two speakers mounted on the outside wall of the clubhouse. He probably had better things to do on a Friday night."

Sam drained his cup of cider. "Well, I guess this will do for now. If you hear anything else or remember something, please don't hesitate to call me," Sam said as he gave her a card with his precinct phone number. He put the pad in his jacket pocket.

"Thanks for stopping by, Sam, and giving me the information you have so far. There are over 200 homeowners who live here and tons of children who play at the playground next to the clubhouse. I know they won't be very happy with this terrible news." She stood up slowly and put both cups in the sink.

"You certainly understand, Mrs. Williams, we'll have to close down the area until the lab can get over there and dust for fingerprints." He put his pen inside his top pocket.

"Don't worry, Sam. The pool is closed for the season, but we are having our next board meeting Tuesday night. Only the pre-school meets in the mornings." She thought for a minute. "We can cancel the pre-school if necessary."

"I'll be in touch. We should be done in three days. Thanks again for the cider." He stood up, put on his hat and followed her out of the kitchen.

"Of course, glad I could be of some help." Sally said as she closed the door. She leaned against it as she breathed a sigh of relief, wondering how Marlene handled this horrible news.

"Mom, can we get ready now?" Her older son Grant called out from the basement, "We have hockey at 10:30."

"What? I don't know if we'll be able to go. I had planned to take you to Sunday school, stay for church and go out for lunch. Just a minute, I need to make a phone call." She breathed in deeply, trying to calm her frazzled nerves.

Sally realized she had never made a condolence call before and wondered what she could say to Marlene. As she walked through the dining room and back into the kitchen, the phone rang.

"Well, I'm dying of curiosity."

"Not funny. I really can't talk now, Lisa. The boys have scheduled ice for hockey practice at 10:30 and I had planned to go to church since I thought their time was this afternoon. I need to call Marlene first and say something." Her fingers tapped tautly on the table. "Any suggestions?"

"First, take a deep breath and sit down." For once, Lisa spoke quite calmly. "Listen carefully now. Today isn't Sunday, it's Saturday. Just tell Marlene you talked with the police, you're sorry about this tragic event and ask her what we as a homeowners group can do."

"What? Saturday?" Sally sat down and looked at the calendar on the wall. She closed her hazel eyes momentarily and pushed her bangs off her forehead. "Guess I'm a little frazzled with this news. I'll have to talk to you this afternoon when we come back from hockey unless you and Brett want to come with us."

"I've told you before, no son of mine is going to play hockey. Thanks again, but we're going to the mall. Nate won't be home 'til later tonight, so I don't have to cook dinner. Are we still on to walk?"

"Just a second; let me check the schedule. Dang it. Grant is right. Practice is from 10:30 to 11:30. I must have confused today's schedule with tomorrow." She put her head down on the table balancing the phone against her shoulder. "I can't believe Doug is dead. The policeman said he was killed. This is just too much for one day and it's not even nine a.m." She took a deep breath.

"The boys have practice tomorrow morning too, so there'll no Sunday school or church again. All the mothers should band together and get the practice time changed to Saturday." She took another deep breath. "Would you like to you meet us for lunch?"

Lisa, always one for eating out asked, "Is fast food o.k.?"

"No, the boys will be really hungry after skating so let's go to the diner across from the mall. I'll want them to take a shower, so we'll need an extra 15 minutes."

"Great. We'll see you about 12:30 then. Bye and good luck."

She walked over to the railing, leaned over and called downstairs to tell the boys their plan for the day.

"Grant, you were right about the time. I mixed up the days. Lisa wants us to meet her and Brett for lunch after practice. Please get dressed and put your gear in the trunk as soon as possible. I need to make a phone call, and then I'll tell you why the policeman was here."

As she walked down the short hall, Sally had to compose herself for a minute. Talking with the police officer had not been her favorite way to start a Saturday morning.

She had difficulty imagining someone so angry at Doug they would murder him. First, she walked slowly into the bedroom and sat down in her rocking chair to change from her fuzzy slippers to her favorite leather loafers. Then, she breathed in and out slowly. She walked over to her closet and took off her garnet and gold Florida State sweatshirt and put on a red striped blouse and navy sweater. She tucked the blouse in her jeans and grabbed a dark brown leather belt.

You can do this. Sally walked over to the phone on her nightstand to make the condolence call.

CHAPTER TWO
DISCOVERY

Earlier the same morning, at the clubhouse, Jeff unloaded his truck and called to his twins, Casey and Cody, to get the vacuum, mop, buckets and other cleaning supplies to start their cleaning job at Greenebriar's clubhouse. Jeff, the sole owner of Crawford's Cleaning Crew, rarely worked on Saturdays. He was actually doing this job as a favor to one of the soccer dads he'd met and talked to on occasion during the Saturday morning games.

He became acquainted with Mark Beals when his youngest son began playing AYSO with Richard Beals. As often was the case, the dads were standing on the sidelines watching the game as their boys ran up and down the short field and their wives cheered.

For nine year olds, they were strong runners and both boys seemed to have picked up the game rules quickly when they started playing several years ago.

Jeff, like a lot of dads, had become involved in soccer when his older sons, Casey and Cody, brought home a flier from school about seven years ago telling of a starter soccer program. When the head honcho called the Crawford home that fateful night, the statement was something like this: "Mr. Crawford, you are the last dad on the list of boys signed up for this team. If you don't coach, there will be no team."

As Jeff liked to embellish the story, ". . .and so started a fantastic friendship with me and the fascinating game of soccer." His afternoons were devoted to practicing with the team. The chief coach, a British fellow, helped him often until he felt Jeff had the knowledge from the free training classes and confidence to work alone.

By starting this cleaning job at 7:30 a.m., they could finish and be ready for the morning games at the season finale, a local tournament. The older boys seemed to enjoy working with their dad, since earning extra spending money was an incentive for them. They were driving now and needed cash, not only for gas and insurance, but dates with "cool chicks." Because Jeff knew the party had been a large one, he encouraged the boys to find a couple of friends who'd help so they could be done in less than two hours and still get to the fields in time to start their games.

Pete and Brenden, the friends who agreed to help clean up, were the first to arrive at the clubhouse door. They both turned around at the same time. Pete said, "The door is already open Mr. Crawford."

As the other three came up to the door, carrying the rest of the equipment, Jeff looked surprised at the opened door. He took off his Blackhawks hat, and scratched his graying black hair. "Wait a minute guys, the door should have been locked; let me go inside and call Mr. Beals."

He walked into the darkened entryway, took a dime out of his worn jeans and used the pay phone to call Mark. "Are you positive you left the door locked? Let me look around first and see what I find." Jeff walked up the stairs and entered the large eating area off the kitchen. He saw paper goods piled into trash cans and a couple of overturned chairs, but otherwise the room looked alright. Then he went back downstairs and walked into the living area. A lamp lay on the floor, broken, and a couple of the couch cushions were piled in front of a reclining chair, which had been left in the reclining position.

He walked around the back of this couch toward another group of chairs and saw a pair of legs extending past the couch. They were still, not moving at all. He gasped and opened his mouth in shock as he called out, "Boys, I don't think we'll be working today; start taking the equipment back to the truck."

"What do you mean, dad?" Casey asked as he walked into the living room area, scratching his blond streaked hair.

"Boys, I mean it. Take the stuff outside. Don't come in any further!" His voice level raised about two octaves.

"Holy crap Mr.Crawford," exclaimed Brenden as he walked toward the body. His green eyes opened wide, surprised by the sight. "What happened?"

The other boys came into the room as Jeff motioned for them to go out with a strong sweep of his arm, pointing toward the entry door. Ever so slowly, Jeff peeked around the couch. A man lay sprawled on the floor, his head partly covered in blood. There was a large jagged cut on the side of his head. No movement of any kind came from the body and there was a small pool of almost dried blood forming a small perfect circle under his grey face, his left side facing up. Jeff carefully placed his fingers on the man's wrist and felt no pulse.

"Boys, I told you to leave now; this isn't something for you to see. Cody, call the police." His voice sounded shaky to his son.

"Dang, Mr. Chapman; is he dead?" Brenden walked into the room and stood next to Pete, their eyes open wide in shock. "I've never seen a dead person; this is way too creepy." He took off his Cubs hat, looked up and then made a sign of the cross on his chest. "I think I will wait outside. Come on guys."

"Wow; this is gross. I'm coming," Pete exclaimed, stuffing his shaking hands into his jeans pockets.

Cody walked slowly back into the living area, trying not to look at the still body and focus on his dad's face. "The police are on their way, Dad. They said not to touch anything and for us to wait outside."

An eerie silence overcame the entire work crew as they walked carefully out of the room. Jeff left the door ajar. They sat on the wrought iron bench next to the front door. For a few minutes no one spoke.

"Dad, how long do you think we'll have to stay? Do we really have to wait for the police?" Cody took off his Cubs ball cap and ran his shaking fingers through his blond curly hair.

"I just might throw up," Casey added, looking a little green. He closed his blue-grey eyes. "Our game isn't until eleven-fifteen, but we both volunteered to referee a game at ten."

They were fraternal twins, although their friends said many times it was hard to tell them apart.

"What should we do?" Casey asked, looking more worried now. "Seeing a dead person has really creeped me out. How can we get this picture out of our heads?"

"Guys, I know this is tough. I remember seeing my first dead body in Vietnam and there are nights when I still see him, motionless on the muddy ground. You'll have to be strong for a while; maybe the priest can talk to you later." He tightened his mouth and knitted his shaggy brows together. "For now, we really can't do anything until the police arrive; I'll be sure to tell them you need to go and you didn't touch anything."

His face scrunched up with concern. "I'm real sorry you boys had to see this, so, listen up for a minute. Don't go shooting off your mouth to the others at the field later, o.k.? You have what some might consider juicy gossip right now, but silence is absolutely necessary. I'm sure the police won't want this spread all around the soccer field before they identify the man and notify his family. Will each of you swear to me you won't tell a single soul?"

"Sure dad," said Casey and Cody, nodding their heads.

"We're cool. Don't worry about us," Brenden answered while looking at Pete who also nodded his head in agreement.

As the sun rose into a cloudless sky and without any prompting from Jeff, the twins looked upward saying a small prayer out loud for the dead man before making a sign of the cross. "Guess you guys didn't go to catechism for nothing," Jeff remarked with a sad smile.

In less than 10 minutes, a patrol car pulled into the parking lot next to the clubhouse. A tall thin young man wearing a crisp blue uniform walked up to them as another police car pulled into the parking lot. He took off his hat and extended a hand.

"Morning. My name is Sam Gregorczyk. Before we go inside, would you tell me exactly what happened from the moment you arrived?"

As he talked, two officers from a second police car arrived and went inside the clubhouse.

Jeff told him exactly what happened and then each of the boys proceeded to tell their version. After some direct discussion, the boys and Jeff were allowed to leave under strict instruction from Sam.

"Do not mention this to anyone until you get a call from me. I'm not sure how long it will take to notify next-of-kin after identification."

Sam went inside and observed the two other officers who carefully removed a wallet from the dead man's rear pants pocket. One lifted up a corner of the man's denim jacket and held it up while the second officer removed a worn black leather wallet. They handed the wallet to Sam and took off their gloves. He had just put on a pair of rubber gloves. Carefully, he opened the wallet and looked for some type of identification.

Officer Zibokowski asked the next question. "Is he a local, Sam, or does he live elsewhere?"

Sam looked at the address and closed his eyes for a moment. He realized he knew the victim and wondered immediately if this could this be tied to what happened last spring. "His name is Doug Pulchowski; he lives just around the corner, at 4131 Boulder.

The third policeman said out loud, "Should we get the phone book in the entryway by the pay phone and look up his phone number?"

"I don't need the book guys, I know this man." Sam leaned against the wall, trying to gain a little composure, his face sad. His blue eyes looked quite troubled. He closed them for just a few seconds as scenes flashed across his mind remembering conversations with Doug on his backyard discovery last April. Until the forensics team arrived, everyone agreed on blunt force trauma as a cause with this body dead for several hours and no weapon nearby.

Sam looked at his watch, trying to guess how Marlene would have handled her husband never coming home last night. He wondered why Doug had been here: as a guest or a board member following another complaint? He would have to make a difficult drive over to their house, knowing no one would want to get this kind of news so early on a Saturday morning.

CHAPTER 3
DILEMMA

A year and a half earlier, July, 1977

A cool summer had been in full swing for a month, yet the heat in this real estate closing room became unbearable quickly. The buyer's real estate lawyer slammed his portfolio closed with such force the sellers, Vladimir and Vera Kiselev actually jumped a little. The buyers, Seth and Sally Williams, wondered what problem could have come up so suddenly. The realtors looked at each other with concern. Everyone was just about to sign the final papers to transfer the split level house in Greenebriar to the buyers, who had moved to Illinois from Irving, Texas.

"Where are your papers for proof of payment for your HOA, (homeowner association) dues? Looks like you are in arrears over 6 months." He looked at the buyers, a frown on his disgruntled face. "We can't close without this paid in full and verified." Gerald Gephardt, lawyer for the buyers, looked toward the sellers with what he thought was justified anger, his grey eyebrows tightly knitted.

"Homeowner dues? What are you talking about Gerald? Are we moving into some type of mini town?" Sally asked, her hazel eyes showing concern, as her eyebrows scrunched closer together.

"Didn't your real estate agent tell you about the HOA?" Gerald asked with surprise, looking at his buyers, and then their realtor. His dark brown eyes blinked rapidly.

"I sure don't remember anything about dues. Amanda, did you forget to tell us something important?" Seth looked at their real estate agent, his reddish-brown eyebrows raised in surprise. "Can we still buy this house?"

Amanda's creased forehead and downturned mouth showed her concern.

"Well, first there are covenants and restrictions which define how you care for your property and house. Then there are monthly dues which must be paid for the upkeep of the common grounds, pool and clubhouse. I don't know if we'll be able to close today or not." Amanda answered sheepishly, wondering if this deal would fall through. She slipped her feet out of her black heels and took off her black suit jacket, feeling a little warm.

"Oh no," Seth muttered under his breath as he looked from his realtor to his lawyer with disdain. "Gerald, I have only three days off, and the movers are supposed to be here tomorrow. I bid for this schedule specifically; I'm the number one pilot for this month. I can't leave Sally and the boys to supervise the unloading and unpacking." He showed his exasperation with a higher pitch in his voice with each spoken word. "What can we do to finish this now?"

"You don't have to do anything just yet." Then he looked sternly at the sellers and their realtor. "The ball is now in your court, Mr. and Mrs. Kiselev. What do you propose?"

"Well, I didn't know anything about papers for proof of payment. Our realtor never said anything about this. I sure didn't remember we were behind in our dues." He looked at his wife and his realtor with an exasperated look. "Vera, you're in charge of the bills, what happened here?" Vera ran her beautifully manicured pink fingernails through her short white blond hair. Vladimir looked at his real estate agent, a little more exasperated now. "Nikolai, did you forget something important?"

Vera seemed upset too as she looked at her husband and said, "I don't remember either, except . . . we did get some type of letter a while back from the homeowner's treasurer and I was going to call. With all of the people coming to look at the house, the quick sale, the packing and all the other stuff I had to do, I just forgot." She wrung her hands nervously.

The two real estate agents looked at one another, their frowning faces showing concern. An uncomfortable silence hung in the air. Finally Gerald said: "Why don't the four of you step outside the office for a few minutes and we'll see what we can do to have the closing today."

He spoke with authority and a stern voice. He stood up, pointing his buyers toward a carved wooden door.

The four stood uncomfortably outside in the waiting room. No one spoke. Ten long minutes later, the door opened and Gerald called everyone back inside the office. "We have come to an agreement, if buyers and sellers can agree."

Almost at the same time, Seth and Vladimir asked, "What?"

The seller's realtor shuffled some papers and then looked up at them, a look of contempt and concern on his sallow face. His grey hair, slicked back, seemed to stick more closely to his round head. He loosened his blue and yellow checkered tie, and wiped his sweating brow with a neatly folded handkerchief he took out of his shirt pocket.

"There are three things you must do, Vladimir. Pay your dues right now, sign a note saying a copy of the current covenants and restrictions will be given to the buyers tomorrow before 5 p.m. and get a letter from the treasurer of the homeowner's association to verify you are paid in full. As long as you agree to all three, then we can proceed."

"All right," Vladimir responded with a sad smile. "How much do we owe?" He took out a worn leather wallet from his green knit slacks and starting counting his bills.

Gerald looked at the seller with disdain and said, "$150 in cash or we don't close today." Looking like a distinguished court-room lawyer in his grey striped suit, he loosened the knot on his red and grey striped tie and waited for an answer.

With a pained expression on her face, Vera looked at her husband knowing she only had fifty dollars in her wallet. She said to him in almost a whisper, "How much cash do you have? I have fifty dollars." This was partly her mistake and she felt worried the closing wouldn't happen today.

"Then we are set," he said with a cheerful tone, taking off his dark framed glasses and touching his thinning brown moustache. "I happen to have a hundred dollars on me, so we'll have enough. We'll sign whatever you want, and as soon as we leave, I'll call the treasurer to get the paperwork you need."

The Williams looked at their agent. With a stern tone, Seth asked, "Why didn't you tell us about this homeowner's stuff?"

Amanda Martin looked sheepishly at both buyers and finally answered the question asked of her minutes before. Her black rimmed eyeglasses slipped forward on her bright red hair and her green eyes closed momentarily as her long, painted eyelashes fluttered. She said as plainly as possible: "I'm really sorry. I completely forgot about the dues. This is equally my fault, but we can solve this if you'll accept cash and the note of promise for receipt of the papers and the dues." Her facial expression showed worry from her creased forehead as she said, under her breath. "You can make this work today."

Sally and Seth looked at each other, wondering if buying in a HOA would make any difference to them. Neither knew what paying monthly dues or following specific rules would mean.

"I still want this house, Seth. What do you want to do?"

Since the furniture arrival couldn't be stopped, they decided, after a quick discussion, to close the sale, figuring they would deal with the association problems after they moved into their house.

The next morning, nothing moved quickly enough for Seth and Sally. The boys were awakened at seven and told to dress as fast as possible if they wanted to eat breakfast at their favorite fast food restaurant, McDonald's, even though Sally knew three-year-old Garrett might need a little help putting on his shirt and shoes. He wanted so much to be self-sufficient, like his six-year-old brother Grant. The pouring rain put a damper on having a quick bite to eat as they didn't have umbrellas or raincoats. Everyone scurried down the hallway of their motel and into the car to drive across the street for pancakes.

As the boys continued to slop each bite of pancake into gobs of syrup, Seth set up the morning plan. Sally would write down what was going into each room so the movers could unload and place the furniture and boxes in the right place. They had always lived in a ranch style home and this split level would pose a few logistical problems for their furniture. She sipped her tea and took one last bite of her Egg Mc Muffin.

"Boys, you each have a coloring book, crayons, puzzles, reading books and soccer ball. Since it is raining so hard, you'll probably have to forgo playing soccer in our back yard. How about we put you in your new bedrooms to read and color until most of the stuff in unloaded?" Seth spoke calmly, yet letting them know he wasn't kidding. "We really need your cooperation on this one."

"Dad, don't I get to pick out my room since I'm the oldest?" Grant asked. He took off his Rangers ball cap to scratch his light brown hair. He smiled as his mom noticed once again how the freckles on his cheeks continued to multiply.

"This is the first time I'll get my own room, and I know which one I want."

Sally rolled her eyes as she continued to scribble, glad to have Seth there to settle this potential argument with the boys. She really didn't think Garrett would mind as she guessed Grant would want the bigger room.

"Yes, you are correct, young man. We did agree you could pick out your room. We should get there before the movers, so you guys hurry and finish eating." He explained, "We have less than an hour's drive to get there. I asked your mom to be our navigator with the map I bought yesterday."

Garrett dropped some syrup on his new Cubs t-shirt and then another couple of drops on his jeans. He looked over to his parents with an opened mouth and wide eyes. "Sorry, Mommy. I tried to hurry."

Seth dabbed the syrup with a napkin and they cleaned off the table, throwing the empty plates and plastic utensils into the trash container. Then they quickly ran out into the rainstorm, practically jumping into the car. Sally took out a map from her purse even before she put on her seat belt. She started to say which road to take when Garrett remembered a really important item on their list before taking a road trip. He forgot to use the potty.

"Can't you wait 'till we get there?" Seth asked.

"No, Daddy, have to go now!" His voice rose in desperation.

Seth opened his door, whirled around to open the back door, grabbed Garrett, put him under his arm, and ran back out into the rain.

After they left, Sally asked Grant if he had to go, too, and he said he was sure he could wait until they arrived at their house. "I want to use our new bathroom first," he said with a broad grin.

They managed to follow the directions to get on Interstate 294 southeast, heading to Indiana when they saw a sign for 45, south.

"Sally, do you have any change? I forgot about this toll. We should have taken the other road." A scowl crossed his face.

"Yes, I have change. The toll is only forty cents. The other road would have taken so much longer with all the traffic lights."

After stopping to throw in the toll charge, everyone seemed to settle down. Even though the boys were coloring quietly, Sally sensed an excitement as they drove toward their new neighborhood in a homeowner's association, of all things. As she continued to scribble down notes, she pondered what an HOA would mean to them. She started to speculate about what control they would be giving up to maintain their house, only the second one they had owned. She wondered who would be taking care of all the work to maintain such a place. Did an outside staff run the association or did the homeowners themselves have some control? *Maybe this is something I could do, she thought.*

CHAPTER FOUR
NEIGHBORS

Shortly after they left the interstate, Sally followed the directions she had written down to Eden; they drove down a side road, with houses to their left. The Greenebriar sign towered above the entrance road. They turned into the subdivision and followed the long, winding street.

"Here we are boys. Seth turn left here and then right onto West Dover Drive."

"Mom, look. There's a big moving van in front of a house down the block. Is this our house?" Looking hesitantly at the moving van, Grant pushed his face up and over the front seat, looking intently at his mom. "Yes, this is ours. Look across the street boys; is this park big enough for you?"

They pulled into the driveway and Seth opened the door as quickly as possible, practically falling into a large, heavy man who walked up to the car. After introductions were made, Seth told Sally to unlock the house and get the boys settled into their rooms while the movers opened the truck and started the unloading process.

As they walked up the stairs to a large cement porch, a manila envelope had been propped up next to the bottom railing. The letters CCR were printed in the corner. "Great" Sally muttered and a scowl crossed her freckled face. "Our rules to live here have arrived."

Sally walked down the hallway before the boys ran inside and up the short flight of five stairs to find their bedrooms. When the doorbell rang, she yelled down, "Come in." She asked Grant which room he wanted and heard a feminine voice call out, "Hello?"

Sally went back into the living room and looked down into the entry. A petite woman with long auburn curls and a freckled face smiled up at her. Two little blonde haired girls, each hanging onto a tanned leg, and a toddler in her arms, who struggled to get down, presented a welcoming picture. They wore cut-off jeans, t-shirts and sandals.

Greenebriar's Garbage

"Hi, I'm Sally Williams. We moved here from Irving, Texas.

"Welcome to the neighborhood. My name is Alicia Butchikas and I live next door. We've been waiting to see if your children might want to come over and play while you unload. These are my daughters, Andromeda, Aldebranne and my son, Andrew. Our older son, Alexander, is in summer school."

Sally, trying to digest the names, turned as the boys came into the room. "Boys, this is our neighbor, Mrs. Butchikas. This is Grant and Garrett." Turning back to them, she asked, "Would you like to go next door and play while we unload?"

They both nodded.

"This is an unexpected surprise, Alicia. You are so thoughtful and I really appreciate your offer. Say 'hi' to my husband Seth on your way out. Thanks again"

"No problem. Don't worry about lunch. They can stay all afternoon."

They left as the first load of boxes came up the stairs. With surprising haste, the movers had everything unloaded in a little over four hours. Since it was now almost one, Seth asked, "Where are we going for lunch?"

"No clue. The boys were invited for lunch by our neighbor; did you get a chance to meet her?"

"Missed our first visitor, too. Guess I'll meet her later. Let's go, I'm starvin'." He grinned as they closed and locked the front door.

They left to drive around the corner to a local diner Alicia suggested. Over lunch, they talked about her children's names.

"Where on earth did they find those names?" asked Seth.

"While you are gone on your trip tomorrow, I'll sure find out. I have several questions to ask her about living here."

The first trauma came for Sally the next morning after Seth left on his four day trip. Talking on their kitchen phone, after cleaning up from a breakfast of cereal, English muffins and grape juice, she asked her neighbor about the neighborhood rules.

"What do you mean I must get permission before we can paint our house, Alicia?" Sally almost laughed out loud. "How can someone else tell me what color I can use?" She twisted the telephone cord nervously worried now about these CCRs. and what control they would present.

"One of the major restrictions here is for all the houses to have a uniform look. By saying only earth-tone colors, the board of directors is just following the rules in the codes, covenants and restrictions made by the original owner of this land."

Alicia frowned, wondering how many others moved here without knowing about these rules.

"Didn't your lawyer and realtor explain this to you before your closing?" Alicia's voice sounded perplexed, as though everyone knew this information.

Sally had called to invite her for lunch as a thank you. This was only the second day in their new home, and the unpacking was on going. Before Seth left on his four-day trip, he asked his overwrought wife to get referrals for painting their faded green house.

Listening intently to Alicia, Sally put the phone up to her ear and held it in place with her shoulder as she finished putting the dishes into the horrid green dishwasher. She hoped they could buy a new one when they came back from their vacation in early August.

"Well, our closing was actually the first indication about this association. Our realtor never told us anything about dues or rules." Sally scrunched her eyebrows remembering the complexities of closing on their house.

"The owners were delinquent in their monthly dues, and they had to pay cash-on-the-spot. Our lawyer is the one who told the sellers they must give us a copy of association rules if they wanted to close."

"You were really lucky to even close," Alicia said with a shocked tone. "When we bought, we had to see a copy of the codes and know the amount of monthly dues before we could present an offer. Our realtor told us he had lost a few closings when people found out about a homeowner's association."

Sally made pb and j sandwiches for the children, wrapped them in waxed paper and set them in the equally horrid green refrigerator, continuing to balance the phone on her shoulder. Then she put the copper teapot on the stove to boil water for tea. "Have you read these codes, Alicia? I don't know if I want to go through over 15 pages of rules right now." She sighed and took out tea bags from the cabinet. "I really wish we had known this before, 'cause we might have found another house."

Alicia said she'd bring over her copy of the codes after she checked on Andrew, down for a morning nap. They could continue this discussion over lunch. Sally hung up and hurried to fix chicken salad. About an hour later, the gregarious group arrived. Grant, talking to the girls, turned to her with a partial sentence: ". . . half starved, Mom." She served the children their food at the kitchen table. She and Alicia sat at the dining room table, copies of the codes in one hand, a fork in the other.

"Could you explain briefly about all these rules and the board of directors? I mean, what hold do they have over us, legally?" Sally shuffled her papers to get them in some sort of order.

"Well, they do have a legality which we don't have on our side of this equation. There have been homeowners who have gone to court and lost and then had to pay a lot of money for lawyers as well as court costs." Alicia frowned and took her papers out of a manila folder. "I've never known any of these people personally, but I sure have heard stories floating around. I really don't know enough to explain anything to you since neither Barry nor I have ever read all of the codes and we've lived here three years."

The phone rang. Grant called out, "It's Dad. Can I talk first?"

"Excuse me for a minute." Sally pushed her chair away from the table and walked into the kitchen to take the call.

"Hi, Seth. I'm talking to Alicia right now about all the rules for living here. I just found out we have to get permission to paint our house and the color must be approved."

"You'd better be kidding," he said in exasperation. "I'll call you later to find out all the details. Sure hated to go back to work and leave you to finish unpacking. Just miss you guys." Sally gave each of the children a bowl of applesauce and a cookie. She walked back into the dining room, worried about getting their house painted.

"With all the legal stuff, I wonder if I should talk to one of those people on this board of directors you keep talking about, Alicia. We have only a short time left before school starts and we're going on vacation for two weeks in early August. Maybe I'll wait 'till we get home and the boys are in school." She took a last bite of salad and grinned at her new neighbor. "I sure do appreciate your help these past few days. Can you get me the phone number of someone to call about paint colors?" She stood up to take their plates into the kitchen.

"I just remembered something, Sally." Her eyes widened and one could almost see the light go off in her head. "We have a block captain who is supposed to welcome you here, give you phone numbers of all the board members and explain the CCRs to you. If no one comes by in a couple of days, let me know." She stood up and pushed her chair in. "Thanks for lunch, just delicious."

After they left, Sally told the boys what she'd be doing and asked them to play quietly or finish unpacking their boxes of toys.

"I'll even take you out to McDonald's for dinner if you behave." She smiled, knowing this would be the key to cooperation.

She decided to call the elementary school first, figuring there would be more information to write down. The school district office secretary gave Sally all the information for sign up and told her the dates for the start of the '77-'78 school year. Grant would have to ride a bus for 25 minutes and needed his name on a list to get on the route. As she started dialing the phone number for a private preschool for Garrett, the doorbell rang. She went downstairs to answer and felt pleased with the introduction.

"Hi. I'm Jessica Jankowski, your block captain. Do you have a few minutes to talk about the subdivision rules?"

Sally opened the screen door while saying, "Of course. Come on in. This is perfect timing since I have some specific questions I hope you can answer."

They walked upstairs and went into the living room where Jessica pulled out several sheets of paper and replied, "I always wait at least a couple of days for our new homeowners to get unpacked. Maybe you should start first with your questions, Sally."

"Terrific." She motioned Jessica toward a chair. "We didn't know we were moving into a homeowner's association until closing. Unfortunately, there were several important items not explained to us, like monthly dues and getting permission to paint our house. Can you start with these two?" Sally walked back into the dining room to pick up the papers Alicia had left for her to read, came back and sat on the loveseat. She took off her loafers and put her feet under folded legs to get comfortable.

For over an hour Jessica explained as best she could all the major rules and then gave Sally papers with the list of approved earth tone colors and the written explanation of the monthly dues. The activities included block parties at the clubhouse, summer tennis tournaments, the women's bowling league and a preschool for three and four year olds at the clubhouse. When she finished, Sally knew she could contact any board member for specific questions. The list also gave a brief description of each person's duties and the job title.

"Thanks so much for waiting a couple of days. See you later." As she closed the door, she thought about Jessica's appearance; her casual style of navy blue shorts and a white blouse, tucked in with a wide belt and perfectly styled hair and makeup reminded her of a model. She was pencil thin and her white blonde hair had the latest shades of blond streaks in just the right places as to appear 'natural'. She knew this hair style was the current 'in' look with a longer back, shorter sides and teased top. Sally's faded jeans and red t-shirt made her feel a little out of style. She went up into the kitchen and called Alicia to ask about the pre-school.

"Well, I've never used it since I think the girls are too young for school. But the private school I told you about is supposed to be quite good. Just depends on how far you want to drive." Sally heard her let out a long sigh and wondered why she didn't want her girls to go to preschool. "Tinley Park Christian School has a good reputation although it's a little pricy for me. The Methodist preschool here in Eden, is less expensive. I can give you names of people who have sent their kids to both."

"Thanks a lot Alicia." Sally felt relieved knowing there was a choice of schools for Garrett. "Is your husband home for dinner tonight? I've promised the boys we can go to McDonalds for dinner; can you come?"

"Yes, he's home. Alexander has a baseball game and since his team is in the semi-finals, we'll have to take a rain check." Alicia paused before asking, "Hey, why don't you come on over to see the game after you have eaten? The park where the baseball games are played is on the same street as the restaurant, just a few blocks south."

"I'll ask the boys to see if they are interested."

Sally spent the next half hour calling the two preschools and asking her list of questions. The Christian School in Tinley Park wanted an interview with Garrett; however the earliest they could see him would be in two weeks. The one in Eden said they would send an application.

Later, after dinner and the baseball game, Sally read the boys their nightly bedtime story. Grant asked if he could play baseball. She told him they would discuss this when his dad came home. After they were tucked in, they said their prayers. She went into the kitchen to put on the water for a cup of tea when the phone rang; it was Seth. She turned on the gas flame as she listened to Seth say "My flight has been delayed and I won't be home later tonight, but tomorrow afternoon."

She felt agitated and her response showed this feeling as her voice rose in pitch. "Not again Seth. What's wrong?" She shook her head and leaned against the counter, dipping her blackberry tea bag into her cup of hot water. He told her the toilets were leaking and the plane couldn't take off until they were fixed. The mechanics didn't have the part in stock so he'd have to spend the night in Atlanta.

"Can we save the painting topic until you get home then? I need to talk to you about Grant's latest idea." She put a teaspoon of honey in her tea and sat down in one of the kitchen chairs, suddenly feeling very tired. Then she brought up the baseball team idea. Seth seemed pleased Grant was willing to make such a commitment. He didn't want to wait, so she then told him about the required application for painting the house.

"What do you mean, fill out an application?" His voice rose in pitch as he finished the question. "You are telling me someone else has to approve what color we paint our house? I don't like this one bit. Do we have any other options?"

After Sally told him in detail what Jessica said, he calmed down a little bit after hearing the choices. His favorite color, beige, in five different shades, was listed. They agreed she would fill out the application and go through the proper channels to have everything approved. After they hung up, she took out the blackberry brandy and poured a small shot into her cup of tea. She went back into the living room, taking her latest Mary Higgins Clark book off the bookshelf and settled in for a quiet night of mystery.

The next morning as Sally cooked dinner for Seth's arrival, the phone rang. She felt relieved to hear the Christian School had a cancellation and would be able to interview Garrett at ten thirty this morning if they could come. She called Alicia immediately to see if Grant could stay there while they drove over to Tinley Park. She finished the dinner and did two loads of wash before they left. She changed into navy slacks and a light blue striped blouse and made sure Garrett had on clean shorts and a shirt which matched. He liked to pick out his own clothes and didn't quite understand about not mixing plaids with stripes.

On the way to the interview, Sally dropped off her application to paint the house to the director in charge of grounds. No one answered the door, so she left the paper under the welcome mat.

After arriving at the school, Sally filled out their application and waited while Garrett went inside to interview with the principal. Fifteen minutes later, she was called in while he sat at a small table with coloring books and crayons.

The principal introduced herself. "I'm Janet Jankovic. Welcome to our school. We would be pleased to have Garrett as a student. He spoke well for a three year old and answered all my questions correctly." She then pushed her blue pearl eyeglasses up onto short curly red hair and stood up to shake Sally's hand, barely reaching her shoulders, even in heels.

"My secretary will give you the rest of the necessary papers. He will need a physical exam and have all his immunization records copied for our files." Sally asked what the charge would be and could she sign up for the bus with the secretary.

"This is a private school, Mrs. Williams. We do not provide bus transportation. I do know there are two other families in your subdivision who carpool." She was told a list would be given to her after the initial payment. As the principal came around her desk, Sally was reminded of her father, a career military man, by the way this woman stood and her authoritative manner. She picked up her purse and said, "I'll discuss this with my husband when he comes home and we'll let you know our decision in a couple of days."

"We usually have a waiting list by the first of August so I would suggest you decide as soon as possible. Thank you for coming in."

She closed the door and Sally went over to the secretary's desk to get the rest of the papers. As they walked outside, Sally realized she'd have to put everything on hold until Seth returned. On the drive home, Garrett volunteered some details of his interview.

"Mom, guess what she asked me? I knew the colors, the sounds of the alphabet and all the shapes she showed me. She said I was smart." His blue eyes sparkled as he grinned. "Can I go here, please? He folded his little hands as if to pray. "Please?"

Sally, perceptive in observing her son's behavior, tousled his strawberry blond hair and said, "Don't you want to see the other school? One of them is much closer and we wouldn't have such a long drive." She reached over to turn down the radio volume.

"When can we go?" he asked, reaching down to the floor to pick up his Texas Rangers ball cap. "Can the girls come too?"

"Maybe we can go tomorrow morning. I'll call as soon as we get home. I don't know about the girls coming; we'll have to ask their mom." She knew Alicia's answer already and wondered if her mind could be changed.

When they arrived home, Grant came over from next door and

wondered out loud about lunch. The phone rang as they came upstairs so he hurried into the kitchen.

"It's dad," he said, a broad smile across his freckled face. "He'll be home in three hours. He can't talk now." He hung up the phone. "Can we have macaroni and cheese for dinner, Mom?

"I wanted Sloppy Joes," Garrett said with a determined grin. He knew this was one of his dad's favorites.

"Well you boys are in luck. I had planned both for dinner tonight. I know after eating restaurant food for three days he'd want something he really likes." She took some bread from the bread drawer and pulled out a knife from the silverware drawer. "How about bologna for lunch? Go wash up please. I'll have everything ready in about five minutes."

As the boys left the kitchen, Sally realized she and Seth had a lot to talk over with the private school issue and the house painting requirements. She wondered what kind of mood he'd be in today and hoped his morning flight had no more problems.

CHAPTER 5
ADJUSTMENT

After Seth came home, unpacked and settled in with a beer, they walked into the living room. Sally brought up the painting and baseball. They agreed someone should read the codes to make sure they knew what was expected of them before they did any work on fixing up the house. She knew this might cause a little problem, so she took a deep breath, folded her hands to remind herself to go slowly and leaned back into the soft cushion of the couch.

"I would like you to volunteer to read this stuff. I have done so much already this week, finishing the unpacking and getting the information for the boys to start school. With you gone, everything seems to always fall on me." She adjusted her position on the couch, and continued. "Besides finding new doctors, a dentist and all the stores we'll need, I still must plan, shop, cook and clean up for three meals a day. Then there is always laundry. We need to find a church too." Her facial expression appeared a little conflicted after naming all her things to do. "When you come home, you need a day to rest and a day to get ready. This only leaves one day to get stuff done." She pushed her bangs off her forehead and waited for his answer.

The boys came into the living room from their bedrooms. Grant asked, "When's dinner, Mom?"

Sally looked at him: *this wanting to know what's to eat will never change so just relax, and answer quietly.* "Your dad needs to unwind just a little and we have to talk about baseball and painting our house right now. Please go downstairs and watch your afternoon cartoons for about 30 minutes and then I'll heat up everything."

As soon as they left, Seth mustered up his courage and said with a sneer, "Oh, I don't pull my weight around here. Is that what you are saying?" He drank a long swallow of beer and started to say something when Sally cut him off.

"Of course I don't mean that; why do you always change what I say? Everything was much easier in Texas when the boys were younger and didn't have so many demands on what we do each day. Now they both will be in school and I'll have more stuff to do. One of the major things will be to carpool." She sighed and looked at her watch.

"Checking your watch already? Is this conversation going on too long for you? Fine, I'll read the codes." He sighed then rolled his eyes, almost showing defeat. "Let's eat, I'm starving." He took another long drink from his beer can and said, "I'm going downstairs to be with the boys until dinner."

As he left, Sally felt glad for the few minutes alone. She knew the dinner was already made and only had to be heated up, so she walked to the dining room and opened the hutch, pulling out a bottle of Merlot to have with their dinner. In the kitchen she remembered how much she wanted to change the avocado colored appliances and wondered if they would be able to afford to replace all of them. She opened the wine and set the table.

The boys were jubilant during dinner, sharing every possible thing they did while Seth was gone. They were happy and bubbling with excitement. Sally was glad to be able to ponder the next day's plans while they dominated the conversation. She already had two lunches and dinners planned while Seth was home.

As she cleaned off the dinner dishes with Grant's help, another great idea popped into her head. "Seth, would you give the boys their baths and read their stories tonight?" She forced her voice to be calm and not demanding.

"Please Dad?" Garrett chimed in immediately. The boys and Seth just stood there looking at her as though this was an unusual question. He nodded his head and they left walking to the bathroom.

After cleaning the kitchen, Sally walked into the bedroom to find the folder with all her vacation plans. She knew they would be camping on their way to Flagstaff and had found some places along the way she wanted the boys to see. Her two favorite choices were Mt. Rushmore,

South Dakota and Four Corners, a place out west where four states boundaries meet.

Before Seth took his job flying with Trans Air, they had lived near Flagstaff where he worked for the Forest Service as a civil engineer. After he had accepted the flying job, they moved to Irving, Texas. Seth decided they should buy some land he had found while surveying in-between Williams and Flagstaff. Now their summer plans always included a trip to check on the property and plan their vacation home.

"I win." She heard Garrett exclaim loudly from downstairs. She knew they were playing one of his favorite games, Chutes and Ladders, a challenge for him because he had just learned to sit still long enough to play a board game.

She checked her watch and waited a minute, wondering if she should be the one to say bedtime. Then she heard Seth say, "Time for your bath," so she continued to look through her vacation folder. The phone rang and she called out, "I'll get it."

"May I speak to Sally Williams?" A distinctive, masculine New England accent asked this question. "Yes, who is calling?"

"My name is Brian Murphy and I'm the director in charge of property maintenance. I have your application here and just needed to check a few things with you. When were you going to have your house painted and what is your second color choice?"

Sally took a deep breath and asked, "Does this make a difference? We just moved here and are trying to understand the codes for this neighborhood." Seth and the boys came into the kitchen

"Sally, who is it? The boys wanted a glass of juice before their baths."

"Someone from the board about painting the house," she whispered as she covered the mouthpiece of the phone.

"Let me speak to him," as he walked toward the phone.

Sally gave him the phone and ushered the boys out and down the hall to the bathroom.

"Why don't you get undressed while I start to fill up the tub?" she asked.

"Isn't Dad going to give us our bath?" Garrett asked

"Yes, I'm sure he will as soon as he gets off the phone." She tested the water, put in a little bubble bath and went in to their bedrooms to make sure they were putting their clothes into the hamper. By the time they were ready, the tub was almost filled and each carefully put one foot in to make sure the temperature was just right.

Seth came into the bathroom saying "I'm glad this is settled. Now all we need to do is get some referrals for painting and we can get started."

Sally walked back into the kitchen to make her nightly cup of tea and brought her vacation folder with her. As she read, she listened with contentment as Seth bathed the boys, dressed them and started their story and helped them say their prayers. She looked through her pictures of Mt. Rushmore and Four Corners sipping her blackberry tea with a drop of lemon honey.

About fifteen minutes later, Seth came into the kitchen, and she asked him if he wanted a cup of tea. He agreed and asked if they could go downstairs to talk about painting and baseball. "Don't forget about our vacation plans," Sally added. "I have the folder right here with all the information."

He shrugged his shoulders and pursed his lips, which reminded her Seth wasn't always eager to talk about vacation plans. His idea of a great vacation was to be home for more then three days in a row doing things he enjoyed, such as finishing his model airplane.

Downstairs in the dark paneled family room, she settled into the overstuffed armchair and waited for him to start the conversation. He sat on the sofa and looked at her, his mouth corners turned down and his eyebrows knitted. "I really want to be more involved with the boys; you know I do, but. . ."

"Wait just a minute," Sally interrupted. "Are we going to have another disagreement or can we talk about all the stuff we need to decide before you leave?"

Once again the phone interrupted their conversation. Sally answered and heard another male voice ask for Seth.

"Hello. Yes this is Seth Williams. Crew scheduling? Today is my off day; why are you calling?" His voice rose in pitch and he hit the table with his open hand. Sally knew all was not well. "Of course I know I'm on reserve this month; I'm on vacation in four days. What? Are you sure?" He hit the table again, with a little more force.

He slammed down the phone and plopped back onto the couch, stretching his 6'2" frame so his long legs covered the coffee table and his size twelve feet hung over the side. He rolled his blue eyes in disgust, closed them and wiped the back of his hand across his forehead. "I've been assigned a trip for tomorrow, not my regular on- call for a trip." He put his head back onto the couch and closed his eyes. "I have to go. Get this, check in is 10 am. I'm just under the minimum for sleep."

"What do you mean an assigned trip? Can they do this to you on your days off?" Sally was upset, knowing she'd have to pack everything for their vacation, alone.

"When they are short-handed and the number one reserve pilot is already called, the next person on the list has to go. Since this trip is assigned, I'll get more pay. Why didn't you ask who was calling? You could have said I'm not here."

Sally was dumbfounded as she looked at Seth. "Are you saying this is my fault?'

He collected himself and softened his voice a little, "No, just thinking out loud. From now on we must have a plan so this doesn't happen again. I picked this month's schedule so I could go right into vacation without another trip." With a depressed look and concern on his forehead, he stood up and walked to the stairs. "Sorry. I'm going up to get a shot of cognac."

"I know this move hasn't been easy for you either dear, with barely enough time for you to settle down, much less settle in. Don't worry; I'll get the list written down and we can go over plans for packing your first night out. Where are you going on this trip?"

"I'll get the schedule and let you know." He walked out slowly, head down.

Sally let out a long sigh and realized any confrontation wouldn't help anyone. She thought of how much she'd have to do during these three days, feeling a tinge of relief knowing it could get done as long as there was a plan and everything would be written down so she could check and re-check the list. She decided to go upstairs, get ready for bed and give Seth a big hug.

CHAPTER 6
ACCIDENT

The next morning everyone helped Seth pack. Sally made bacon and eggs; the boys were thrilled to have Saturday's breakfast during the week. Even though they were a little upset at his leaving, this was his job; everyone talked about having time together during their vacation. After he left, the boys asked if they could go next door to play with the girls. Sally called Alicia to check, told her what happened and asked for referrals for a painter, doctor, and dentist. Alicia said she'd look for some names, so Sally decided to make her list for their vacation. About an hour later, she decided to get the boys and take them out to lunch. She changed from sweats and put on a clean pair of red shorts, a red, white and blue t-shirt and red sandals.

At the exact minute her hand turned the handle of the front door, there was a loud screech of tires. When Sally opened the large metal door, she heard girl's voices and a chilling cry. She stepped quickly onto the front porch, gripped the railing and stared in shock at the sight before her.

Three teen-age girls stood by the front of a stopped car, yelling at each other while Grant, Garrett, Aldebranne and Brett, a new playmate from across the street, stood frozen in place on the sidewalk. In front of the blue sedan, sprawled on the pavement, still and silent lay Andromeda, blood trickling from her head.

Sally yelled out loudly. "I'm going to call for help."

Alicia had just come out onto her lawn, screaming, "No, No."

Sally grabbed the screen door handle, pushed the front door with all her might, and ran inside, taking the stairs two at a time. In the kitchen she dialed the number, practically yelling to the voice on the other end. "Need an ambulance immediately at 2830 W. Dover Dr. in Eden, Greenebriar. A child has been hit by a car. Please hurry."

She waited just long enough for the voice to repeat the information then dropped the receiver, pulled open the freezer door, grabbed the container of ice while opening a drawer to get a kitchen towel. She dumped the ice into the towel and ran out of the kitchen, down the stairs and outside. Her head pounded and her heart beat ever so loudly as she raced to the street, her fingers now numb from holding the ice so tightly.

"Move away girls," she almost yelled. Another car had stopped and Sally observed an older man and heavy set woman hovering over Andromeda. The woman tried to hold Alicia back while the man felt for a pulse.

The children continued to cry and two of the teens hit the side of the car and walked in circles. "I told you to slow down," the tallest girl cried out. Her red curls bounced around her frantic face. The blond, who sobbed non-stop didn't look up or respond.

"I can't believe you didn't stop when you saw the ball roll into the street."

Alicia broke away from the woman and ran to help her daughter, crying out loud "No, no." Large sobs gurgled out of her mouth. She too picked up a limp arm and felt for a pulse. Sally gave the man her towel with ice and walked back to the curb to hug each one of the other three children, now sitting on the lawn crying. Brett's mom, Lisa, had already crossed the street and taken him home.

"Just sit here with me for a minute. She held her boys shaking hands and looked at their panic filled faces. Aldebranne, who continued to cry, blubbered. ". . .her hurt bad." Sally let go of their hands and picked her up, stroking her check, talking quietly. "Don't worry dear, the ambulance will be here soon and she will get help." Her shaking legs gave way as she sank to the ground and looked at the still silent, stone faced little girl sprawled on the street.

A blaring siren caught everyone's attention. A large red and white ambulance turned the corner sharply, and then slowed down. A police car drove up from the opposite direction and stopped abruptly behind the blue sedan. All three girls turned back to look at two police officers get out of their patrol car. Everyone watched in silence as the paramedics took control of the situation.

Sally stood up and motioned for the children to go up to Alicia's front porch to sit down. They looked stoic, as though in a trance. She felt like the next movements appeared to go in slow motion:

--- paramedics checking for a pulse,

--- lifting the motionless body to a stretcher,

--- carefully placing her into the truck,

--- taking Alicia's arm, putting her inside,

--- closing the back door, driving off, siren screaming '. . . Get out of our way.'

"Let's go inside and get something to drink at our house while we wait," Sally said to the children who continued to cry. Their faces showed concern, fear and panic, all bundled into a very sad look. They walked quietly up the front porch stairs, silent as floating ghosts.

One of the policemen called out as Sally walked away. "We'll need a statement from you Ma'am." He pushed his hat back on his head and nodded to her.

Grant asked the next question so quietly, Sally hesitated before she answered. They were sitting at the kitchen table, each looking at a glass of lemonade. She wiped her forehead with the back of her right hand and pulled down a paper towel to wipe off the excess sweat.

"Mom, is she going to die?" His eyes filled with tears. He stood up and walked over to her, grabbing her waist and squeezed.

Garrett's mouth dropped open and his eyes widened as he hugged his little friend. "No, Mommy." He let go of her as she burst into tears.

"I don't know. If her head injury is really bad, they could operate. There might only be a concussion, so she'll just need to stay there for a while. I'm going to say a prayer right now for her recovery. Let's hold hands." They stood in a circle in the quiet kitchen: "God, please take care of Andromeda. Be with her mom, the doctors and nurses who will take care of her. Amen."

Everyone walked into the living room and sat on the couch except Sally, who looked out the window into a peaceful back yard. An eerie quiet settled in the room until the phone rang several minutes later. They all jumped off the couch.

"Sally, this is Alicia" Her voice sounded so sad; she spoke slowly. "Andrew is still sleeping in his crib. Will you go over and get him?" Her voice seemed to strain to get the words out clearly.

"I'll go over right now. How's . . .?" She didn't finish because Alicia cut in.

"She's in the operating room right now. Her dad is on his way over. I'll have to call you back; thanks so much." Sally heard her start to cry as they hung up.

She looked at three fearful faces. "She is in the operating room. We forgot Andrew, so please stay here while I go over and get him."

Luckily he slept soundly in his crib; the entire ordeal lasted less than fifteen minutes. Sally picked him up carefully, taking his blanket, teddy bear and a couple of diapers. He didn't wake up until she put him on Garrett's bed. The boys came in and asked if they could watch him for a while since Aldebranne continued to sob.

Sally went back into the living room, picked her up and sat in the rocking chair. She was asleep in a few minutes.

Grant came in a little later and asked his famous question, said a little more slowly than usual. "What's for lunch, Mom? I'm hungry."

After they ate, the boys asked if they could go back to their rooms. Sally took Andrew downstairs while she looked for Garrett's playpen. Then she remembered they sold it. She called Lisa, Brett's mom to ask if she had one. "Why don't you just go back to Alicia's and get theirs."

"Thanks . . . guess I'm not thinking straight." She sat down in the overstuffed chair and let out a long breath as she looked at the dark paneling, which mirrored her feelings: afraid, upset and worried of the outcome.

"They are operating as we speak. How's Brett?"

"After lunch he fell asleep on the couch. I just can't believe this happened. Did you see the accident? What were those girls thinking?" Lisa's voice rose in pitch with each question.

"Slow down. I didn't see anything. Since I have Alicia's other children, I've had my hands full with their needs. We'll have to go outside and watch out for the bus and be ready when Alexander comes home from summer school." Sally felt very tired and realized she needed to hang up and re-group so she could be ready for Alex. She wondered how a twelve year old brother would handle such news..

By 3:45 p.m. she called the children to ask if they'd like to go outside and wait for Alex. As soon as they were on the porch Garrett yelled, "There's the bus."

All three waved to the bus driver as Alexander came down the stairs, crossed the street and walked over to them. His sister was the first to run toward him, her long blond hair flying behind her. "Andromeda hurt," she cried out, wiping new tears from her already swollen eyes.

The concern on his freckled face was genuine. He took off his Chicago Cubs hat, ran his fingers through his thick black hair and took off his backpack.

"How bad, Mrs. Williams? Tell me now," he said, walking toward them, picking up Andrew and giving him a hug. Grant and Garrett stood by their mom, concerned and solemn. Everyone walked inside, silent as a sleeping baby. The phone rang and everyone looked at her, afraid of who would be telling them bad news.

Her hands shook as she picked up the phone. "Hi, Seth." She sat down in one of the chairs breathing a sigh of relief. "We are having a really tough day. I though you were Alicia."

Briefly she told him what happened, while five pair of concerned eyes looked at her, filled with questions. "It's Mr. Williams." She asked if he could call back later.

"Grant, get the cookies and napkins, please." She opened the 'fridge and picked up the apple juice, closed the door and reached over to open the cupboard door. She then took out the brightly colored Tupperware plastic cups and gave them to Alexander. Everyone walked into the dining room. Each had a cup of juice and a peanut butter cookie. When they finished eating, she asked, "Grant will you take everyone downstairs while I talk to Alexander? You can watch your cartoon show."

She motioned Alex into the kitchen and sat down. He came in slowly still eating his cookie. He put his glass of juice on the table and looked a bit more concerned.

"Thanks for your patience. I'll come right to the point. This morning your sister was hit by a car in front of your house."

He gasped and scrunched his eyebrows, "Is she. . .?"

Sally took a bite of the chocolate kiss on the peanut butter cookie to give her a minute before explaining this difficult and upsetting story.

"She's in the operating room right now, and we are waiting to hear."

Even though he was six years older than his sister he took the news hard, tears welling up in his green eyes. He put his head in his hands then slowly lay his cheek flat onto the blue flowered placemat. When the phone rang a few minutes later, he jumped.

"Hi Lisa. How's Brett? No, we haven't heard anything. Thought you'd be Alicia. All I know is she's in the operating room." Lisa sounded worried too. "Yes, I'll call you as soon as I hear."

She reached over to give Alex a comforting pat on his shoulder, went into the dining room and grabbed a tissue from the box on the hutch.

"Mrs. Williams, when I played outside, at her age, mom NEVER let me leave the yard. I just don't get it."

"Maybe she went inside to put your brother down for a nap. I just don't know what happened, Alex. I was inside. Unfortunately, accidents happen." They sat quietly for a minute.

"This day sure started out great," he frowned. "I didn't even want to go to summer school. Maybe if I'd been here . . ." He stood up and looked outside, tears forming. A large cloud covered the bright sun. "Can I go down with the little kids and watch cartoons? I need to be distracted."

"Of course you can. Want more juice or another cookie?"

"Sure. These really are good. Thanks a lot Mrs. Williams." He took another cookie and walked slowly out of the kitchen, his head down.

As soon as he left, Sally opened the fridge to see what she could scrounge up for dinner. There was enough for a salad so she decided to get comfort food and ordered a pizza from Lou Malnati's. She looked at the clock nervously. It was now 4:30 p.m. She reached into a cabinet for a wine glass, poured some Merlot thinking: *Alex is right; this day sure started out better than now.*

When the phone rang, she took a deep breath and grabbed it quickly, before the second ring. "Hi, Lisa, dinner together? Great idea; I already ordered a pizza, to be delivered by 5:30." She hung up and went out to the stairs and called down "Brett and his mom are coming over for pizza in about forty minutes. Want to go outside and play until then?"

Alex carried his brother into the kitchen. "He needs to get changed so I'm going over to get a diaper."

Sally told him she'd already brought some over.

When the pizza arrived, Lisa called everyone inside. After they washed up and sat down, Alex gave the blessing. Dinner went about as smoothly as possible considering the unspoken tension. There were no leftovers. They went back outside to swing and Alex volunteered to watch his brother.

Lisa said, "I'm really getting worried. Over six hours have passed and not a word, even from the police. What could be keeping Alicia from calling?" She put the glasses in the dishwasher and looked outside. Eventually they went into the living room to wait, each with a glass full of Merlot.

Fifteen minutes later, the doorbell rang and Sally went downstairs, wondering if the police finally had their questions for her. When she opened the door, she saw Barry Butchikas. He looked very upset, his black hair stood straight up on his head, tears streaming down his face. His red and blue plaid tie was loose and his blue oxford rumbled. Instead of standing up straight and showing off his 6'3" frame, he bent over and held onto the door handle as he walked ever so slowly inside.

Sally felt extreme panic; her heart starting beating rapidly and her hands felt sweaty. His demeanor told her bad news would be coming.

CHAPTER 7
REALITY

"Where are the kids?" he asked quietly as he moved into the foyer and put his shaking hand on the bottom of the black wrought iron railing, his body hunched over. His face showed a strain of sadness, his forehead creased with wrinkles. "I have some very bad news."

Sally took his arm to steady his balance and said, "Sit on the stairs a minute Barry. Can I get you something?" She felt a knot in her stomach while she looked at his pained expression.

Lisa stood at the top of the stairs, concerned with his demeanor. "They are outside playing; should I call them?"

"She didn't make it." He burst into tears. Sally sat down on the stairs too, stunned with this news and leaned over to give him a hug as her tears flowed freely.

Lisa gasped and grabbed the railing. She looked at Sally as if to ask: what should we do? "Lisa, bring him a glass of wine." She touched his shaking shoulder. "I'm so very sorry Barry. Where's Alicia?"

"She's at home trying to get some sort of composure so she can tell the kids." He looked up at Lisa and took the glass from her, downing the wine in one large gulp.

"What can we do to help?" Lisa asked, tears welling up in her brown eyes. She too felt helpless and wanted to ease his burden, knowing this to be an impossible task right now. They were in shock and a few minutes of stoic silence seemed to give each a minute to shed more tears.

He spoke first. "Give me about ten minutes and then just tell them to come on home." He wiped the tears from his face with the back of his hand. Lisa took out a tissue from her jeans pocket, passed it to him and took another to wipe her eyes. Sally reached over and took the wine glass as he stood up slowly and walked out, bent over like a very old man. She motioned Lisa to go into the kitchen. They sat down in the chairs mechanically, both in a stupor by the reality of this morning's accident which now seemed a long time ago

"They'll know something is wrong by our faces," Lisa whispered, looking outside. "Did the police ever call you? Did you recognize any of those girls?"

"No. I think I have seen two of the girls before. I'm pretty sure they live here. I don't know about the driver." She turned toward the back door. "I'll just stand here by the door for a few minutes, and then call out to them. From where they are, they won't be able to see my face clearly. They can leave by the side gate and not have to come inside," Sally said slowly, pushing a strand of auburn hair behind her ear. She worked to get her voice in control.

"Do you want to tell Brett by yourself?"

Lisa sighed, looked outside again and then up at Sally, who had filled up the teapot with cold water and put it on the stove.

"No, together, 'cause I'll never make it home without crying." She tapped her fingers on the table. "I just can't believe this. At least Nate will be home later. She put her hand on Sally's arm; "Will you be alright here by yourself? You can stay with us if you need the company."

"No thanks. Seth will be calling later and I'll unload on him. Do you think enough time has passed?"

She squeezed Lisa's other hand and stood up to open the door. Mustering all her courage to keep her voice calm, she called the boys and Brett to come inside and told Alex his parents were home. She turned away quickly, leaving the sliding door open and then took out some tea bags.

A loud anxious voice called up to her; "Any news Mrs. Williams?" He carried his brother and held his sister's hand while they walked toward the stairs.

Sally stood in the doorway with her very best calm face and said, "Yes, Alex. They will tell you; you use the side gate, please? Good night now." She closed the door as the boys came inside.

"We need something to drink, mom," Grant said looking from one concerned adult face to another. He opened the 'fridge and took out the juice. Lisa took down the plastic cups and motioned everyone into the living room. Sally fixed the tea and followed them, walking ever so slowly, her knees shaking every so slightly.

Strong emotional words came slowly to her overwrought mind. Sally felt unsure of how to say what needed to be said. A tough situation ensued for all. Everyone cried and sat in stunned silence for a few minutes. Lisa and Brett left for home as soon as she could walk without crying and the boys eventually went to bed without a bath, prayers or a story.

Later when Seth called, he too took the news badly and told her "Maybe this vacation will help."

They only talked for a short while as Sally continued to sniffle. She could not even venture thoughts of a vacation at this time. She wondered to herself how they'd survive this crisis. For once, she took an extra long, hotter than usual shower and then fell asleep on a wet pillowcase, no mystery novel to ease her mind tonight.

CHAPTER 8
DOOM

Loud thunder and drizzling rain tapping against the bedroom window woke Sally the next morning. She had forgotten to put down the blinds and close the curtains. As one eye opened, then the other, she forced herself to awaken as she stared outside at a dark grey overcast sky. The day had started out as she felt, gloomy. Then she remembered: The Accident. Thinking of her six-year-old neighbor, now dead, made her shutter. Grant had looked forward to starting first grade with a friend, and now *She's gone*, she thought. She felt overwhelmed and sad again, tears forming in her already swollen eyes.

The clock flashed 6:30 a.m. and this meant the electricity had gone off some time during the night. Flipping back the covers, walking over to her dresser and grabbing her watch she looked at the time, 7:30 a.m. She glanced back outside and thought she saw a glimmer of sunshine peeking out from one of the large grey clouds.

"Boys, time to get up," she called out from her bedroom door. "We need to find out how we can help Alicia and Barry this morning." She walked into the bathroom to brush her teeth. Puffed eyelids greeted her freckled face and disheveled auburn streaked hair. Putting toothpaste on her brush caused her to pause briefly and she whispered: "Thank you Lord for my children and help me to be a beacon of peaceful light to my neighbors today."

Hearing crying, she walked out into the hallway and looked into the bedrooms, across from each other. Grant, sitting up in his bed, said "Mom, I had a really bad dream last night." His face looked so sad, his eyebrows crunched together and his forehead creased with worry. She walked into his room, put her arms around him and gave him a comforting hug.

"What did you dream?"

"Andromeda died 'cause some dumb girl drove too fast." He wiped his eyes. His mouth dropped open at the same time and his eyes stared at her. "No, no. Not a dream, right?" He closed his eyes, shed a few more tears and put his head in her lap.

She shook her head and after a few minutes stood up, going back into the bathroom to get a tissue. "No dream, Grant. There was a terrible accident and you're right, a girl did hit Andromeda with a car and she died at the hospital." Tears formed in her eyes and she hugged him again.

Three year old Garrett stood at the doorway and whispered, "I saw what happened, Mommy. The car hit her and she didn't get up." He walked over to her and sat in her lap, tears flowing down his freckled cheeks. She gave him a hug.

"Oh Mom, I dreamed over and over about the car hitting her." Grant put his back on the pillow and curled up in a ball.

"Let's say a prayer, o.k.? Then we can have breakfast and go over to see how we can help."

Just as they finished their cereal, juice and toast, the phone rang and they both jumped.

"Hello." She didn't recognize this voice.

"Is this Sally?"

"Yes, who is this?' She sat down in her chair.

"Hi. You don't know me, Sally. I'm Alicia's sister, Carolyn Gibson. She asked me to call you. Do you have a minute to talk?" Her voiced sounded strained.

"Hi, Carolyn. Hold on a minute, please." She put her hand over the mouthpiece and said, "Boys, this is Alicia's sister. Please put your dishes in the dishwasher, get dressed and play quietly until I finish talking to her."

"Sure Mom," Grant said. They walked out ever so slowly.

"Thanks for holding, Carolyn. We've had a rough night as I'm sure you know from talking to your sister; how's she doing this morning?" Sally put her head down onto her hand, supported by an elbow on the table and breathed out slowly.

"Alicia asked me to call you with some instructions. They left early this morning, driving back home to Pennsylvania for Andromeda's funeral. Most of our family lives out here." Her voice seemed calm and collected, probably saying these things over and over, having called others in their family, Sally thought.

"Sure. We were just on our way over to see. . ."

Carolyn interrupted. "She hoped you could pick up the mail, feed the dog and let him out twice a day. She left the side garage door unlocked and a key on the work bench under a large bag of dog food."

"How long will they be gone?" Sally asked.

"They weren't sure, but at least a week." Suddenly her voice sounded tired and anxious, ready to end this call.

"Can I get your phone number? We are going on vacation in about 3 days so I can put a stop on the mail and ask another neighbor to feed Ralphie."

"Sounds great, Sally. I'll leave you to take care of the details. I know Alicia will be very grateful as this has really been tough on all of us. Here's my number. I still have more calls to make."

Sally could tell now she was really ready to hang up. "If anything changes, I'll be sure and let you know, Carolyn. Do you have a name and number for the funeral home so we can send flowers?"

There seemed to be a hesitation. "No, not yet. Actually, they are quite sure they don't want anyone to waste money on flowers and have considered financial donations to an organ transplants organization. Thanks anyway. Really need to go now. Bye."

She hung up quickly leaving Sally in a state of uncertainty and questions unanswered: *organ transplants? What could this mean?*

CHAPTER 9
CHANGE

Sally hung up the phone questioning what she just heard. She took a deep breath and went over to the stove to put on water for a cup of tea. She decided a call to Lisa should be next, since her services were offered without her permission.

After getting an agreement from her and hanging up the phone, Sally said out loud: "Thank you, Lord for great neighbors." She fixed Constant Comment tea, for a change this morning, and decided next on her list would be getting the boys clothes ready to pack for their vacation.

The phone rang again, disrupting her plans for packing. She put down her cup of tea and answered the phone.

"Oh hi, Seth. So good to talk to you. Alicia's sister just called and asked if we could help out by feeding Ralphie and get their mail. They left early this morning to drive back to Pennsylvania."

He answered quickly. "How's the body getting there? Sure seems like an added expense to me."

"I didn't even ask about the body. She said something weird about donations to an organ transplant organization in lieu of flowers." Sally looked into the quiet backyard.

"Look, just take one step at a time here. Maybe they have a reason for this; don't worry about it now. I'll be home in two days and we'll get everything sorted out and get away. Gotta go. Love you."

Somehow the next two days passed quickly. Taking Ralphie out twice a day, feeding him and getting everything ready to be packed into their truck kept them busy. They boys were unusually quiet most of the time and helped by picking out their clothes. They ate their meals with little conversation and went to bed early both nights after prayers, no story.

By the third day, everything was lined up in the garage, ready to be packed into the truck. Seth came home just before dinner and yet another tearful rendition came from each of the boys. Together they talked over their concerns while sharing another favorite dinner for Seth: meat loaf, mashed potatoes, green beans with onion and bacon bits, Sally's sourdough rolls and sour cream chocolate chip cake and vanilla ice cream.

"I asked Lisa if she and Brett would take care of Ralphie and I stopped their mail." She told all this to Seth as they cleared off the table and filled the dishwasher. "Oh, I almost forgot some good news. Our paint color has been approved."

"Great. I decided to paint the house myself after we get back to save some money. No reason to pay someone else when we can do this, right?" He grinned at her, knowing this would not go over well.

"What do you mean we?"

"You can easily paint the lower half without needing a ladder and I will do all the rest. Besides this will be a chance to have some more time together." He kissed her neck, put the towel on the rack and turned to leave.

"I'll give the boys their bath tonight and read them their story. You heat up the water for tea and we can go over your plans for the drive out to Flagstaff."

She put down the dish towel and filled her favorite copper tea kettle with cold water, turned on the gas flame, took out two cups and one tea bag. Laughter from the bathroom caused her to look down the hall, getting a direct view into the bathroom.

"Look dad." Garrett giggled as he stood up and covered himself with a handful of bubbles making a Superman pose.

She sat down on a kitchen chair and looked out the sliding glass door to the wooden deck. *Only a few days ago they were playing outside having fun, not imagining what terrible tragedy would come with the accident,* she remembered. Fresh tears formed just as the water started boiling. She put the tea bag into her cup and added the boiling water to steep for one minute. Then she put the same tea bag into Seth's cup, knowing he liked his tea much stronger. She took their tea and a plate of homemade peanut butter cookies with a chocolate kiss into the living room and put them on the coffee table. She walked into each bedroom giving each of them a strong hug and gentle kiss after their finished their prayers.

As soon as she sat down and before she could grab a cookie and her tea, Seth started changing all her plans for the trip after only glancing quickly at her papers.

"South Dakota is really out of the way. Could you just pick out two forts for them to see and be done?" He seemed exasperated with her list of places to visit.

"I have only fourteen days and I wanted to get there quickly so we can enjoy our time there. I'd like your help to decide where to put the cabin, step off the measurements, and then help me put in the stakes."

"Seth, this is our vacation too. The boys are interested in seeing all the old forts they helped pick out. How many days did you want to take to drive out and back?" She tried to keep her voice calm. She had already figured out four days each way, leaving five days in Flagstaff, knowing he liked to drive no more than eight hours a day.

He took a large gulp of tea and looked at her with concern on his face. "Can we make another trip for forts or even better, just pick out the two best ones, one on the trip down and one on the trip back?" He put his cup down on the table, grabbed a cookie and leaned back into the couch cushion, taking off his belt and pulling out his denim shirt.

Sally felt uncomfortable with his decision. All the trips to the library to look up and plan neat places for the boys to see had now been wasted. Considering the last few days of sadness and trauma with Andromeda, she had no fight left. She put on a good face and said, "Fine, I'll pick only two. Just figure out how many miles a day you want to drive so I can call the KOA campgrounds and make our reservations." She gave him the list of campgrounds.

As he perused the list, he looked up and asked "Do you have enough play stuff for the boys to keep them busy each day of the drive?"

"Yes. I have new puzzles, coloring books, a few games and some of the books we checked out of the library about the forts they wanted to see." She had worked hard to coordinate some of the books and maps based on the places she thought they'd be visiting. Taking another deep breath, she decided not to bring up anything else.

"Could we leave as soon as you finish your calls in the morning? I'll get up a little earlier and pack everything." Suddenly he seemed anxious to wrap this up. He yawned, picked up his cup and put it back on the tray. "Look, I'm really beat. With five landings, this was a long day."

As she looked at this face, she realized tired seemed like an understatement.

"I'm going to take my shower and hit the sack unless you have something else. Don't forget now, no nightgown tonight." He grinned and gave her a peck on the cheek.

She closed her eyes for a few seconds during the kiss and kept her composure. Picking up the tray, she said, "I should be ready to leave by nine a.m." She knew there would be time to continue this discussion during their trip. To get a good night's sleep, she'd have to let this one go. She went into the kitchen and set out the cereal, silverware and bowls for breakfast. She made a note to remind herself to make the sandwiches as soon as they finished eating so they'd be fresh. She picked up her list of forts and went into the bedroom to get ready to take her shower.

CHAPTER 10
FUN

Staking out the location of their future house on their two and a half acre property filled with ponderosa pine trees didn't take as long as Seth expected and there was time for a day trip to the Grand Canyon. In the bright sunlight, the colors of the rocks in the canyon seemed so dramatically bright in yellow, rust, tan and brown. The distance from top to bottom where the Colorado River could be viewed gave the boys many new things to talk about besides losing their friend.

The two forts Sally had picked out to see turned out to be just the right number to visit and somehow they really enjoyed their time away from home. Yet, the pending return and the boys' reaction to one less playmate continued to bother Sally. Many nights the discussions before, during and after dinner revolved around cars going too fast, playing in the front yard instead of a backyard and explanations of life and death.

Seth finally heard about the reason for the unusual names for Alicia's children.

"Barry's last name (Butchikas) is Greek, and he always wanted to pick names with this background. Andromeda had been his sister's name. When she died in a car accident at sixteen, he always said this would be his daughter's name. He felt overwhelmed with guilt since the same thing happened to his daughter."

"You are right about unusual names, Sally. When I had to look something up in the phone book I really was surprised to see all the Polish and German names," Seth added.

Both boys seemed a little anxious during the last hour of the trip home, as they came closer to their home and their neighbors. When Seth turned the corner onto their street, Grant exclaimed "Why is there such a big sign in the girl's yard?"

Sally looked surprised too as Seth answered, "It's a real estate sign;

looks like their house is up for sale." He shot Sally a look as he whispered "What now?"

Both boys answered at once, "No."

"Boys, we'll find out when we get home. Try not to worry just yet." Sally had no idea their neighbors had planned to move and wondered what happened while they were gone for two weeks to get their house on the market so quickly.

Sally looked past this sign to their freshly painted house of desert tan and cocoa brown trim. Her mouth dropped as she asked, "Seth who painted our house? I thought you said we couldn't afford to have this done."

"Surprise." He grinned broadly, hoping this treat would make her day. "Before we left, I made some phone calls too. The price to get the house painted came in much lower than I had planned and the college boys who were recommended had the time off before returning to school. I knew I had overtime pay because of the assigned trip, so I decided to get it done while we were gone." His grin changed into a large smile, now seeing this surprise went over better than he imagined.

"Really looks new, Mom," Grant said. "I like the color too." Sally wondered how many conversations he remembered about all the different choices for his dad's favorite color, beige, and all the shades of tan and brown they had on the approved list to choose their first and second choices.

"Can we go next door?" Garrett asked.

"Just a minute fellows. We need to unpack the truck first, then you need to empty your suitcases and put your dirty clothes into the hamper." Sally felt another feeling of surprise overcome her with Seth taking charge here instead of her having to tell the boys what to do as she always did in the past. They actually ran up the stairs and into their bedroom, unpacking with haste.

After the boys left, Sally asked, "How about Lou Malnati's pizza tonight? I'll ask for delivery and this way we won't have to unpack as quickly as the boys did." Seth nodded as he lifted the table saw up and pushed it carefully down the ramp he made.

The next two weeks flew by with preparation for the school year taking precedence: doctor appointments, getting shots, buying supplies and new clothes.

Grant seemed genuinely disappointed Andromeda wouldn't be sitting next to him on the school bus, and he'd be stuck with his bossy next door neighbor, Alan. His younger brother Garrett worried about his choice of preschool for a few days after he found out Brett would be attending the one at the clubhouse. Seth had four day trips for the rest of the month and Sally had to deal with the police and their questions. They wanted Grant to testify and even volunteered the name of a counselor who specialized in trauma situations. On their trip, they had talked about this at length. Both Seth and Sally were worried about the outcome of having to go to court. Both boys seemed adamant about testifying to help Andromeda rest more securely, knowing they had helped give the driver her justice. Finally, they agreed the boys could talk to a counselor. Sally set up the appointments quickly, knowing once school started their free time would be limited.

Grant said regularly, "Even though I don't want to remember what I saw Mom, I really need to do this for her." Sally suddenly looked at her son in a different light, a little boy changed forever and starting to grow up.

She continued to call Alicia regularly, and finally they made a date for lunch during the first week of school. Lisa suggested she and Sally walk around the subdivision while the little guys were in preschool until the weekly social activities started. They would bowl, learn ceramics and join the women's discussion group. Three meals a day, weekly washing, cleaning the house and getting the final preparations for school kept Sally very busy. Seth had four days on and three days off for the September schedule. And so, a pattern established itself.

CHAPTER 11
ALICIA

On a bright sunny day the last week of August, Aldebranne and Garrett played quietly in his room on Friday morning, the first week of school for their brothers Alexander and Grant. Another neighbor had made plans with Lisa to do her two favorite activities, shopping and lunch. Sally volunteered to watch Brett for the day.

Alicia sat down at the kitchen table after Sally had taken the children's lunch downstairs to the family room so they could eat while they watched cartoons. Alicia's first bite into a buttered sourdough roll made her mouth pucker a little and she quickly washed it down with a sip of sun tea. She looked up at Sally with hesitation and took a deep breath before she dropped her bundle of breathtaking news. Her younger brother had a kidney transplant several years ago and this operation sparked their interest in organ donation.

"At the hospital, the doctor told us a little girl needed a kidney and a little boy needed a liver. We didn't hesitate one minute." Tears flowed from her sad brown eyes as she buttered another bite of roll and took a slow sip of tea. "My brother had three more pretty good years thanks to someone else's selflessness. She is still living, even though only as an organ donor."

Sally gasped, looked at her intently and asked, "Is this why your sister said we should have people consider a donation of money to this transplant group?"

"Yes. We support them and wanted to return the help given to us." She sighed and looked out the window. "As soon as we found out our precious daughter wasn't going to survive, we knew we had to help someone else. We wanted to give her heart and anything else, but the doctors said right now, only liver and a very few kidney transplants were successful in little children." She wiped tears from her cheek with her napkin and took another long sip of tea.

Sally felt overwhelmed with this news. Her heart pounded as she responded. "She is in heaven now, Alicia. For you to make such an unselfish choice at a time of unbearable grief is just overwhelming, even for me. I don't know if Seth and I could have made such a decision." She put her hand over Alicia's and gave a little squeeze.

"Are you religious?" Sally asked, tears streaming down her cheeks.

"We were raised Catholic, and always believed in God. We have asked Him some serious questions lately. We believe she is whole again in Heaven and because she helped others, her death wasn't in vain." Slowly she buttered another piece of roll. "We haven't told the children about the transplants because they had such a hard time with the funeral while we were in Pennsylvania. Now the police are filing charges against the driver and want us to testify because someone decided her death should be listed as involuntary manslaughter even though they were speeding only 5 miles over the limit. This is really too much." She sighed and put her head in her hands, resting her elbows on the table's edge.

Sally put down her fork and said, "I was wondering what we could do here in the subdivision to help. I plan to go to the next board meeting to see what can be done about lowering the speed limit and getting more signs posted. I don't think our police force is big enough to patrol regularly, so our board must do something." Her heart pounded as she thought about those girls and what their future could be if convicted. "I wonder if they will all go to jail, or just the driver."

"Lowering the speed limits is a very good idea, Sally." Alicia actually smiled just a little. "I keep remembering how the kids were playing ball and have asked myself a hundred times why I didn't insist they play in the backyard." She looked despondent as she pushed a piece of dangling reddish streaked hair behind her ears.

"Yes, I've thought of this too. We can't change the past, but we sure can change the future by getting these speed limits enforced or changed to a lower limit. There is still no reason for someone to drive over the speed limit knowing there are so many children who play outside." Sally looked out the large kitchen window wondering how long before the fall colors and cold windy weather would arrive.

"Hopefully we can get this all settled before we move. I just can't take the pressure anymore." She tapped her fingers on the table and took another sip of tea.

"I know those girls are at fault, yet going to a juvenile detention center or prison sounds almost as bad as death to me. Some times you have to wonder about how things turn out." She pushed her chair back. "Barry's boss had talked to him about a job transfer several months ago, but he didn't want to leave just as the new school year started." She looked out to the backyard and sighed. "I think moving might be the best thing now."

Sally had a difficult task; she wanted to be supportive yet felt an overwhelming sense of shock at this news of organ donation. She became lost momentarily in these thoughts. She tried to figure out where to proceed next in their conversation when three little children came into the kitchen with empty plates and asked if they could go outside and play.

Alicia stood up and agreed to them playing outside, but only in the back yard. She hugged her daughter and then walked toward the dining room. "Thanks so much for lunch and letting the kids play this morning. I need to get back home because Andrew should be waking up from his nap any minute now."

As she walked out of the kitchen, Alicia turned around and asked, "Can she stay another hour? I really need to make some phone calls."

"Sure. They'll be fine." Sally felt uncomfortable knowing Alicia left Andrew alone in the house once in a while when he napped, even though she was as close as next door. She decided to go out into the back yard and kick the soccer ball around with the little ones to let off some nervous energy. She decided not to share the information of organ transplants with her boys now because she wasn't ready to talk about this most sensitive information any time soon.

CHAPTER 12
BOARD

Sally and Lisa decided to go to the next board meeting together. Seth agreed talking to them about a lower speed limit would get things going in the right direction. They decided to walk over to the clubhouse on a balmy September night.

"Lisa, you sure look different with makeup on. Wait, you have a new hair cut and color too. Isn't this called a shag?" Normally they always dressed in sweats or jeans and a t-shirt.

"Glad you like it. My hair appointment had already been scheduled, so I decided I should put on a good face for this meeting. I thought you'd like to see me as I used to look, before motherhood dominated my life. When I worked, I put on makeup and a matching outfit everyday. Do you like my new black shorts, yellow and black plaid shirt and black sandals?"

"Yes I do. I didn't even think about dressing up, so I just put on clean jeans and a blouse. You look much nicer."

"Don't be silly. You look fine."

As soon as they entered the clubhouse, they were asked to sign in. They picked up an agenda which named all the board members and included their phone numbers. They took their seats, noticing how many other people were there.

"Welcome. I'm glad to see such a good turnout for tonight's regular board meeting. My name is Steve Smith and I am the president of our homeowner association. Since all board members and block captains are here, let's get started. Oh, here comes our association lawyer." Everyone turned to look at a distinguished looking man in a pinstripe suit entering through the clubhouse front door.

"After roll call, would our guests please introduce themselves and state their reason for coming?" He sat down and completely overpowered his chair. He could have been 6'5" or more, Sally thought. His jet black hair, thinning on top and sideburns down to the bottom of his ear lobes presented quite a sight. His shoulders were quite broad and a slightly plump middle hung over his belted slacks. He wore thick wire-rimmed glasses and a thin black moustache covered one end of his mouth to the other. He spoke with authority.

A short pencil thin woman with fiery red hair stood up and introduced herself as the secretary. Suzanne called each name and put a check mark on her paper when they responded. There were ten board members and twelve block captains. The preschool had a mother volunteer and the ceramics and painting teachers were there too.

As the guests introduced themselves and stated their reason for coming, Sally seemed surprised at the variety of problems to be covered at this meeting. The majority of complaints had to do with monthly dues, lawn upkeep, messy yards, problems with stray dogs and cats and overflowing driveways with extra cars, motorcycles, and boats.

One homeowner, Hank Balliteria, seemed particularly concerned about some of the rules. "We are new here. Even though we had a block captain person come over to explain most of this stuff to my wife Lonnie, I just can't understand how you can force some of these issues."

The association lawyer, stood up quickly. "Hank, my name is Daniel. I have represented this particular group for over five years. Weren't you told about this before you closed on your house? Have you read any of these rules?" He adjusted his red and yellow striped tie and sat down.

The meeting went strictly by *Robert's Rules of Order* and each person had only a specific number of minutes to voice their opinion. The president kept control. Time to speak was marked by the secretary who appeared to enjoy calling "Time." Only thirty minutes had been allowed for speaking, yet after Hank's questions and Daniel's answers, Sally's concern brought up a lot more discussion. The board decided to table the discussion on speeding until the next month's meeting. Hank would not be put off and told the lawyer someone must be sure the Realtors tell prospective homeowners what they are buying. Steve asked for a board member to chair a committee to investigate these two problems. Ingrid, who happened to be a full time realtor volunteered as well as Paul, the vice president. Steve then asked Hank to be a member. Listening to some of the whispering going on in the crowd, Sally learned the driver who killed Andromeda turned out to be a daughter of one of the board members, Brian Murphy. He was the same man who called them about their paint color choices. His position was grounds and property maintenance.

Dues problems were assigned to the treasurer, Connor, who said he needed to get more specific information from the homeowners involved and would report back at the next meeting. He looked to be the youngest of the members, with a blond crew cut, clean shaved face and no sideburns. Like almost everyone else, he wore jeans.

The president then reminded the other homeowners who complained about the monthly dues to read their copy of the association bylaws since they covered most of these questions. Steve said Daniel would be invited to the next meeting if the treasurer could not resolve the concerns brought up tonight.

Lisa and Sally decided to stay a little longer and find out what each board member had to report. They were interested in the ceramics and painting classes.

The treasurer told of some contractors raising their fees and should the board consider finding others. He had also been told the electric and water rates might go up next year and wondered if there would be enough to cover this increase. He asked if, at the annual meeting, they should consider raising the monthly dues. After the allotted time to talk ended, the president tabled the discussion until next month

As each board member gave their report, Sally took a few notes and confided to Lisa there seemed to be a few problems with finances. She thought her feelings about Brian, the property director were right when he stood up to report about those who needed to have their houses painted. He weighed well over 250 pounds, she guessed, and wore a short beard speckled with grey. His black-framed glasses were the latest style. He spoke as abruptly to the board members as he had to her on the phone before they went on vacation.

When the social director talked about the list of activities planned, the bowling league sparked Sally's interest even more. Lisa noted the ceramics class and bowling had been scheduled for the same morning. She raised her hand. "Ingrid, who plans the dates for these activities? I heard a conflict of days for the bowling league and ceramics class."

The ceramics teacher, Babs, a very large heavy woman with short black hair stood up and asked what could be done since so many women who bowled also expressed an interest in her ceramics class. Ingrid seemed surprised and asked if they could meet to reschedule.

The block captain chair, Andrea, reported five houses sold and four new families had moved in since the last meeting. One of the few not in jeans, she wore black slacks and a red pin striped blouse with a red and black scarf wrapped around her shoulders; her white blond hair had been tied into a pony-tail with a red ribbon. One of the block captains, Jessica, raised her hand. "I'm pleased to introduce one of the new people on my block who moved in a few months ago." She turned to Sally and said to the board members, "Isn't this great? She is already getting involved." Then Hank's block captain, probably feeling as though she should have done the same thing, introduced Hank.

About nine p.m., Daniel, the board lawyer, told the visitors the board needed to go into a closed session to discuss a legal matter and terminated the meeting. As they walked home, both speculated as to what happened and who might be suing.

Lisa said, "I've heard via the grapevine those homeowners who sued over things like paying the monthly dues and what color their house must be painted have lost in court. We never read the rules before we moved in, did you?"

Sally sighed out loud. "I have one better; we didn't find out until closing we were moving into a homeowner's association. Our sellers were delinquent in paying their dues and our lawyer really gave them a piece of his mind at closing. Neither realtor seemed to know what had to be presented in order to close." She looked at Lisa.

Lisa's eyes widened. "Our block captain gave the rules to us about two weeks after we moved in. No one mentioned anything about monthly dues at our closing. Guess we were lucky our sellers paid."

"What do you think will happen when we meet with Paul to talk about getting the speed limits lowered?" Her question showed genuine concern.

"Don't have a clue. I only met him once at a tennis potluck just before you moved in. He seemed nice enough. You should see him serve, what a powerhouse."

She looked at Sally, "I sure hope they change the days for the bowling and ceramics. We really have a lot of fun. Have you ever bowled or made ceramic pieces?"

"Yes, I used to be on a bowling league in Flagstaff, and had a decent average. Never did any ceramics; what does this entail? I'm not very crafty unless someone shows me exactly what and how to make something."

Lisa answered with a smile. "Babs is a fantastic teacher and she shows by example before anyone starts a project. What's your average? Maybe you should be on my team."

"When we lived in Arizona it was 165." She looked up at the sky filled with shining stars, reminding her of the clear skies when they lived above 7,000 ft. in northern Arizona. "I hope it's not Monday, my day to wash and clean."

"Well, that's solved; you are going to be on my team. Will you consider joining our league, please?" Her voice asked positively yet in a non-demanding way.

"Everything will depend on Garrett's school schedule and if Seth bids to be home during the week. I can't remember if I signed him up for morning or afternoon classes. Which days does Brett go?"

"He's signed up for five mornings a week. This way I can be involved in all the social activities. Our current newsletter should have everything listed. The women's discussion/study group is great, too." As they turned the corner onto their street, Lisa waved good-bye and walked up her sidewalk.

"O.K. I'll read what's involved and decide which ones I can do. The women's group sounds like something I'd like. When do they meet?" She stopped at Lisa's driveway waiting for an answer.

"I'll tell you everything tomorrow. Maybe I can find last month's newsletter. Haven't you received a couple of them?"

"No, I haven't received any. Guess I can call Jessica and ask her. Maybe this is the position I could get on the board if I decide to run. Thanks again for coming with me. See ya tomorrow."

She crossed the street and walked down to the fourth house and went inside, wondering if meeting new people in any of these groups would open up better possibilities for getting support to change the speed limits.

CHAPTER 13
RESIGNATION

Fall brought weekly soccer games. Garrett and Brett felt quite unhappy when they learned three year olds couldn't play, and they would have to wait two more years. When Seth had weekends off the Williams family spent Saturday mornings at the soccer fields. Sally enjoyed meeting other moms and pushed hard for support to get the speed limits lowered, even though, to her surprise, she met some resistance.

She and Lisa attended the October board meeting and Sally commented on a new look for Lisa. "Did you put in some more streaks? Your color looks different again"

"Yes. I really do like these different shades of blond. She trimmed off a little more too. I just love going to see my beautician. She always wants to try something new and I'm always a willing guinea pig."

Although she and Lisa were about the same height, 5'6", Lisa had always worn her hair long, straight and brown. Normally when they walked, neither had on make-up and tonight Lisa had again 'put on her face' and looked quite chic.

"Glad you like it, Sally. Nate really doesn't like this shag cut 'cause he's always seen me with long straight brown hair. This is so easy to take care of and I really like this style."

Inside the clubhouse, they were the only two homeowners. They observed the conflicts between some who could have or should have spent money allotted to their budget. Many seemed to agree a budget should be followed, yet there were others who said all money allotted needed to be spent. Some argued frivolous findings hidden in monthly reports should be dumped or at least voted on by a majority. The rest felt this needed to be resolved before the annual meeting, always held in November.

"Who would have thought ten volunteers could disagree so much when they live here too," Lisa said. "You'd really think they didn't have a vested interest in what happens to their property and this neighborhood."

"Seems as though we need a new point of view and I'm going to ask about the procedure for getting elected." Sally responded. She and Lisa had talked about running for the board, but Lisa wanted no part of the conflicts. She had only been to two meetings and felt a strong dislike for a couple of the men and their whiny attitudes.

"Are we still in open mike for questions and answers, Mr. Smith?"

"Yes we are and please call me Steve. Who are you?"

"I'm Sally Williams, a new homeowner; last month I came to the meeting to talk about getting the speed limit lowered and you volunteered me to be on a committee. How does someone get elected?" She pushed her hands into her jeans pockets and sat down.

"Thanks for the reminder; yes, I do remember your proposal. I'll give your question to the membership director, Ellie Dobrowski."

A tall thin woman with flaming red hair, grey-green eyes sporting a purple knit pants suit, bright enough to knock out anyone's eyes, stood up. She picked up a pile of papers and flipped through them until she found what she needed to continue.

"In our CCRs, (Codes, Covenants and Restrictions) one needs at least thirty signatures from neighbors whose dues are current. Then, they must place their name in nomination before the annual meeting. Are you interested in running for a position on this board? Terms are two years."

Sally stood up, "Yes I am."

Ellie looked at Steve, then back to Sally. She swallowed, folded her arms and said, "I had planned to make an announcement tonight anyway, so I might as well do this now because you have given me an opportunity, Sally." She looked back to Steve and announced, "Please accept my resignation immediately and take my proposal in the form of a motion to replace me with Sally, tonight."

Steve stood up to comments and mumblings from many of the other board members.

--- "Can we do that?"

--- "Why are you resigning?"

--- "Do we want someone no one knows?

--- "Isn't she the one who wants to lower the speed limits? Ellie, no."

"Order, please. Ellie you must state a reason for resigning before your term has ended." He spoke matter-of-factly, wondering what the rules said about this specific situation.

"I'm resigning due to my husband's job transfer. We'll be leaving within the month, going to Phoenix." She smoothed her white blouse and took off her green and purple plaid scarf, twisting the ends to ease her nerves. She smiled and waved her hand across her face, as though using a fan, indicating heat from the desert.

"Are there any comments or questions from others?"

Sally and Lisa looked around, quite surprised, knowing they were the only non board members in attendance at this meeting.

"Seeing none, I'd like to ask you two to please step outside for a minute while we discuss this proposal."

Lisa stood up first and looked at the board. "I'd like to say something before we leave. You'll be doing a great service to our community if you appoint her. In the few months I've known this woman, I'd sign her petition in a minute. Thanks."

They both went outside and sat on the porch bench, waiting.

Sally spoke first, "Sure didn't expect this tonight. Don't know if I'm ready to start now since I'm still doing research on speed limits. Did you know this place used to be a garbage dump?"

"Yes, I've heard rumors of the sort, but never anything specific." Lisa's curiosity seemed piqued. "How did you find out this information?"

"Really amazing what you can find out at the library, especially talking to the research librarian. She's quite talkative and really helped me find some good information on how to get laws changed. This will be more of a challenge than I had first imagined, but luckily for us, the accident is our proof. Just doesn't seem right a six-year-old had to die before a necessary change can be implemented." She leaned her back against the building and sighed. A lot of homeowners were still upset knowing nothing had happened yet with those teenagers.

"Didn't you feel a little creeped out, knowing we live on piles of garbage?" Lisa's eyes closed as she held her nose.

"Actually I did, because I had no idea how many dumps were around this area, Lake Calumet being the largest and closest to us. Did you know a lot of stuff dumped into these places takes over thirty years to decompose? Years ago in Chicago, corporations dumped waste from glue factories. Those steel mills had no regulations for their waste when they unloaded their crap into poorly-designed landfills which really weren't regulated until the 1970s."

Lisa smiled and patted her on the shoulder. "Well, if you aren't an encyclopedia of information. I'm really impressed, Sally. You have done your homework on landfills. What does this have to do with speed limits?"

Just then, the door opened and a hand motioned for them to come back inside.

"How 'bout we continue this another day?"

Lisa nodded as they went back inside to learn of Sally's fate or fortune.

CHAPTER 14
MEMBER

The board of directors voted and decided overwhelmingly to allow Sally to take Ellie's place on the board. The position started immediately and Lisa whispered to Sally, "I'd like to stay."

Sally moved up to the table and accepted her new position. "Because Ellie and her family will be moving out of state, she will meet with you at your earliest convenience to go over her job description." Steve said. After the rest of the board gave their reports, Steve reminded everyone of the annual meeting. They would have their regular meeting on the second Tuesday to go over everyone's report and prepare for the annual meeting.

Sally asked, "What about those items from last month's meeting tabled until tonight and those special committee reports?"

Steve mentioned they were all tabled until the next meeting. "I know the speed limits proposal is important to you, Sally. Now you have another month to get your information while you find out what your position entails." His voice sounded so matter-of-fact, she wondered if there were potential problems.

Afterward, Ellie came over to Sally with a small calendar in hand. "What date will be best for you?" Her voice sounded relieved.

Knowing Lisa remembered which days the social activities occurred, Sally asked, "When is bowling and the women's group?"

Like a waiter reciting a menu, she said, "Bowling is Thursday morning, the women's group is the second and fourth Wednesday morning and the ceramics class is the first and third Tuesday morning." She stood up and showed Sally her calendar with each activity already listed on the correct day. "Remember, we walk every afternoon between four and five."

Sally knew she had decided against the ceramics class for fall, so she told Ellie Tuesday morning would be perfect.

As they walked home against a chilly wind, Sally asked, "Do you think this will be a time-consuming job? Even though soccer will finish in another week, Grant brought home a flier from school and wants to learn how to ice skate. I hope I didn't make a mistake here." She looked over at Lisa and asked, 'Will you help me if I need some?'

"Sally, I don't have a clue what this will take, but you know I'll help whenever I can and certainly will volunteer to be on your committee. You'll have to meet with the block captains right away to give them your take on information for the monthly newsletter." A breeze blew toward them more forcefully and she zipped up her lightweight red jacket.

"Oh gosh, you're right." Suddenly her voice sounded a little worried. "I forgot about writing a monthly update. I know the social activities director Ingrid will do all the social stuff for planning parties. I'll call her tomorrow and see if she has already met with the block captains so I can get the right update for next month's news." As she looked at her walking buddy, her worried face showed a tightly closed mouth and pensive eyes.

Lisa looked away and then down the block at the houses across the street. "Really Sally, this is kinda neat. You'll have a pulse on everything which goes on here. Maybe your first page could be about changing the speed limits."

Sally looked at her and smiled. "Good idea. I'll see if I can get some writing done tomorrow. If you promise to proofread everything first, I'll try to summarize on one page about the speed limits."

Lisa nodded. "I wasn't an English major for nothing you know. We'll see how much I remember about writing."

The next morning, after the boys left for school, Sally decided to make another favorite dinner for Seth tonight before she scrambled their lives with her new volunteer job. She took out a container of frozen spaghetti sauce from the freezer and put the lasagna noodles on to boil. She put on water for tea while she grated the mozzarella cheese. The phone rang and she put down the grater to grab it before it rang again.

"I'll meet you in front of your house in ten minutes."

Greenebriar's Garbage

She quickly looked at the wall calendar and said, "Oh Lisa, I forgot, can you give me fifteen?"

"Sure. Did you remember to invite your new neighbor? See you in a few."

As quickly as possible she grated the cheese and put the beautifully shaved strips into a Tupperware container. Then, she turned off the tea water and drained the noodles putting them and the sauce in the 'fridge. She hurried to her bedroom to take off her slippers, get her loafers, run a comb through her hair, put on mascara and change from her sweats into jeans and a pink sweater.

She locked the front door and walked out to the sidewalk to wait for Lisa who crossed the street and smiled. "Did you forget about the women's group today?"

"Yes I did 'cause I wanted to have a great dinner for Seth so I could set the mood before I tell him what happened last night at the board meeting." She zipped up her jacket and shoved her hands into warmer pockets. "Cynthia isn't home, so I wrote a short message and left it on her front door in case she gets back soon. I still have some difficulty seeing someone different living next door."

"Have you heard anything about the lawsuit?"

"No. Alicia just mailed a postcard saying they had arrived in Wilkinsburg and would be staying with family until they closed on their house."

As they walked down two long blocks to Pamela Czarnecki's house for the meeting, Lisa continued, "Where is this town? I can't remember where. . ."

"They are near Pittsburgh, in a suburb called Swissvale, which is a town or two away from their family in Wilkinsburg."

They arrived at Pamela's house and followed several women inside to the large family room where coffee and tea were set up. At the table, Mary Jane Trumps, one of the board members, put down a plate of different fruit breads.

"So glad you are a board member, Sally. Maybe we can get some things done now." She pointed to the plate of breads. "I made some new breakfast breads for us to try today: strawberry, apricot, apple, and of course our favorite banana." She smiled broadly and smoothed her sweater over ample hips as she waited to hear how the bread tasted.

Pamela welcomed everyone. "Please get your food and drinks before we start because we have a guest speaker today. I really think you'll be interested in what she has to say. All of us could probably use some help in cooking better for our families."

Just then Cynthia walked in and looked for a familiar face; when she saw Sally she walked over to her at the food table. "Thanks so much for leaving the message. I had a couple of errands to finish this morning." She tightened her blond streaked red pony-tail and grabbed a plate as she put her car keys into her jeans pocket.

"Before we start, I see there is a new face so I'd like the person who invited our guest to introduce her." She pointed to Cynthia.

Sally stood up and introduced her new neighbor. "Everyone, please welcome Cynthia Cincilina who moved into Alicia and Barry's house, next door to me. They have one son, James. She is at home, like the rest of us, and her husband, Clark works in sales for Marshall Fields."

Sally then started around the circle with introductions: "Pamela Czarnecki is our host, then Ingrid, Andrea, Suzanne and Mary Jane are board members, Betsey Schmitz, Maria Palmer, Babs Sanchez, our ceramics teacher. You know Lisa, and finally Anna Murray whose husband is a board member."

"Hi. Thanks for the warm welcome. We are glad to be here. Since I probably won't remember all of your names, don't hesitate to remind me when I see you around."

Pamela stood up saying, "We are having a different format today. I'd like to start by reading from Colossians 2:5: *For though I am absent from you in body, I am present with you in spirit and delight to see how orderly you are and how firm your faith in Christ is.*" She looked up at everyone and said, "Let's start with a prayer. Lord please help us today as we talk about a way to be more orderly in our ideas about food consumption, shopping, and hearing about a new way which nourishes us without using drugs as a supplement. Keep our hearts and minds open to different ideas. Thank you to those who made our snacks, Amen."

She raised her head of black curls and looked at their speaker with a broad smile. "I'd like you to meet Glenda Galloway, a representative from The Feingold P.A.T.H. of Illinois, who is our guest speaker today. Anyone here familiar with this organization?"

A majority of heads shaking no answered her question quickly.

Since no one raised their hand, Glenda, a short petite woman who wore her hair in a bright red shade and dressed professionally in a wool jacket, crisp white blouse and tailored black slacks stood up to face her audience. She started telling everyone about Dr. Benjamin Feingold and his struggle in over 20 years research with patients who were considered too fidgety and busy for regular classroom activities. She held up his books, Why your Child is Hyperactive, and, The Feingold Cookbook for Hyperactive Children, co-authored with his wife, Helen.

Her first question piqued everyone's attention. "How would you know if your child is just overactive versus acting like a regular child?" No one answered, so she continued. "Some symptoms Dr. Feingold found are: being aggressive, abusive, and destructive. Sleeplessness and activity considered to be 'hyper', over and above normal exuberance of children are two more. This behavior includes inability to concentrate in school, short attention spans, and an over abundance of rowdiness." She then quoted from page three of their cookbook.

"No longer are all letters plaintive cries filled with desperation from concerned parents. There are now a growing number of success stories (from over 14 countries) in response to dietary management. Instead of disruptive households,. . . thousands of children's scholastic performances have improved dramatically without the crutch of medication which masks an underlying problem and cures nothing." She looked around the attentive group and said, "There are only four major changes for your shopping: no BHA or BHT preservatives and no artificial food colorings or flavorings in the food you buy. For many of you, this will mean cooking from scratch and using a specific list of food brands which don't have these items listed under ingredients."

Glenda closed her book and looked around her attractive audience, all with perfectly applied makeup and current hairdos in the latest shades. "Does this sound familiar to anyone? The good news for us is there is no risk with this type of food management. When your child's behavior improves, you'll know if this will work for you and your family." Her eyes widened as she raised her eyebrows. "I'm here to tell you we tried this for a few weeks and noticed such a dramatic difference in our son's behavior, we are convinced of this idea: proper nutrition versus medication for our child. This is why I have volunteered to be a spokesperson."

Pamela stood up and thanked Glenda, asking for questions. The next hour a lively debate ensued with the closing remarks directing everyone to the monthly meeting, held at the library next week.

On the walk home, Sally told Lisa she would definitely attend the meeting. "Should I plan to pick you up?"

"Right now I don't think so. Brett is so laid back and quiet like his dad, he's the opposite from Garrett. You should go. Didn't you say his pre-school teacher made a few negative statements to you about his behavior in school?"

"Yes, she did, at our first parent meeting. She told Seth he should consider medication and he responded quite angrily, because he thinks of him as a regular little guy." Sally scrunched her eyebrows and looked straight ahead. "This is why I think we should investigate this group a little more in-depth. Neither of my brothers were active, busy little guys. Grant is more like his dad, quiet and reserved.

"I'll be anxious to hear what you find out Sally. No one said parenting would be easy. You know some days are quite a struggle for me, and I only have one."

Sally started to cross the street, then stopped, looked back at Lisa and said, "You'll be the first I tell."

She walked up the stairs onto her porch, unlocked the door and went back to finishing dinner. She made phone calls to the block captains for their next meeting. She hoped Seth would have a good flight and landing today, and come home in a better mood. She had just enough time to finish making the dinner before she'd have to pick up Garrett from preschool; today was her turn to drive. She put on the tea kettle as she layered the lasagna noodles remembering all the key points of Glenda's presentation and wondering if maybe this would be the answer to Garrett's restlessness.

As a surprise, Seth planned to take the boys to see a new movie, one which had been touted as something completely out-of-the ordinary. They came home in great spirits, both boys still in a state of euphoria over space ships, great new monsters and music to keep anyone awake.

"Star Wars is something so different, I think you'd really like it, Sally." Seth shared some interesting ideas about their son's behavior and commented on one of the most surprising parts of this different movie: three-year-old Garrett sat still for the entire time, never once wanting to get up, go to the bathroom or even get more snacks.

Grant seemed as taken with this movie as his brother. "Mom, you should go see this one. The fighter planes are not like anything I've seen on T.V., and all the characters were so different from regular people."

"There were two robots, Mom. They had weird names, and I remember them, R2-D2 and C-3P0. They talked funny and walked funny too. I hope you will go see this movie and take us again. I really liked it." Garrett looked at her with such a positive attitude; he grinned from ear to ear.

For the next few weeks, this movie kept them entertained when they remembered specific scenes. They played some of the fighting sequences with pretend light saber swords.

During an afternoon walk, she posed a question to Lisa.

"Guess what we'll be looking for during the Christmas holiday shopping? After bowling this might be another fun afternoon to try and find these toys."

Lisa answered, "Maybe we should go to this movie."

CHAPTER 15
BLOCK CAPTAINS

In early November, fall continued to bring a change in the daily weather as the last leaves fell and a continuing chill christened each morning. Seth had been able to have some weekends off and now took Grant to his ice skating lessons, giving Sally extra time with Garrett to practice his colors, letters and numbers.

Sally held a meeting with the block captains to pass along her ideas on how to better the communication with their block of homeowners. She also needed to get some necessary information to write a newsletter article. All twelve came to the meeting at her house along with the social activities director, Ingrid Fielding.

She fixed hot water for tea and her hot chocolate mix, along with several different breads she enjoyed at the women's discussion group made by Mary Jane. Seth drove the carpool today and with his errands, he'd be gone most of the morning.

Block captain chairman and board member, Andrea Czolowski started the meeting by introducing the captains to their new membership board member. Each stood up, and told their block and something about themselves.

Nancy VandeVenter, married, 3 children, Daly Dr.
Helen Franks, m., 4 children, Forbes St
Christi Thomas, no children, Patterson Place.
Jessica Jankowski, m., 4 children, Dakota Dr.
Dawn Egbert, widow, Carriage Ct. & Great Falls St. East
Louise Domenici, m., 5 children, Cushing Ct. & Great Falls St.W.
Carole Anne Dalton, m, 3 children, Carver Ct. & Sycamore St.
Sherryn Wright, m. 2 children, Columbus Ct. & South St.
Vicki Stafford, m., 3 children, Carolina Ct. & Delaware Dr.
Alice Larsen, divorced, 2 children, Perdue Place

Kathy Rinaldi, widow, Lake Michigan Dr.

Dorothy Howe, divorced, (lives with her parents) Penn Place

The first thing Sally asked them to do was a group activity to get their ideas on what worked for them and what didn't. She randomly selected three groups of four and gave them a list of questions to discuss. She walked around each group and listened to the problems they shared.

- --- "Some of my neighbors don't want others to know their business."
- --- "Both parents are working and I have difficulty getting in touch with them."
- --- "I leave messages and no one ever calls back."
- --- "Some people on my block don't agree with our covenants and don't want to get permission to paint their house."
- --- "A lot of neighbors don't keep their pets leashed and when I remind them of the town law, which takes precedence, they become angry."
- --- "Many don't think they should have to pay extra money to rent the clubhouse."
- --- "Some want longer hours at the pool."
- --- "Tennis tournaments need to be scheduled for spring and fall, not just summer."
- --- "Most of the people on my block want to take away the monthly dues."
- --- "My neighbors think there are too many activities for wives during the day when others work and can't come."
- --- "Scouts should have meetings at a more convenient time."

After they discussed their ideas and some of the problems, Sally walked over to her chart of suggestions and welcomed everyone. She took a sip of her hot chocolate and started her presentation about her concern on lowering the speed limits and how this led her to becoming a board member.

Andrea asked the first question. "What can we do to help you with getting the speed limits lowered, Sally?

"I'm really concerned about this too," Louise added. "I have one of the longer streets, the inside circle around the entire subdivision. Many afternoons I've stood on the curb, yelling for drivers to slow down."

Andrea stood up and looked at her group of mothers. Suddenly she saw a potential political problem getting solved. "I think we should get organized and start contacting our elected city, county and state representatives. This could be a great way to get candidates on our side if they want our support for the next election. There are a lot of neighborhoods in South Chicago and I can really see this going somewhere."

Louise took off her thick brown eyeglasses and spoke with conviction. "I'm willing to be in charge of such a group if I can get at least five of you to help me. My children play outside a lot and I don't always watch them every minute when they are across the street at the park. You know how it is... the phone always seems to ring at the wrong time." She reminded everyone how many children would be walking to the new elementary school next fall and wondered if they could find more support from the principal and school board.

"Sounds like you have a great plan, Louise." Sally felt relief to hear such support and gave her folder of research to Louise who decided when her group would meet.

Frances raised her hand and asked if she could share a problem. "I have one of the larger courts, with five families. The way things are going, a lawsuit might be filed so this would become public anyway. I just wanted to give you a heads up." She took a long sip of coffee to gather her thoughts. She had a lot to say.

The five families on Carriage Court started off innocently enough, having once a month dinners together. They all hit it off and started sharing progressive dinners every other weekend. "I really don't know all the particulars, but one night, after too much beer and wine, one of the husbands suggested they throw their keys into a pile and go home with someone different."

A sound of silence overtook the room and then, gasps and short sentences uttered by a few of the women.

"They started to get organized because some of the wives were uncomfortable with the possibility of a child walking into a bedroom at night and finding another man in their mother's bed. On Friday nights, they would have happy hour only. Then five pieces of paper would be placed in some sort of container. Four would be blank and one had babysitter written down. On Saturday night, the family who had picked this paper had all the children over to their house for pizza and a slumber party. The other four wives would fix a dinner for their 'date', who would spend the night." She looked around the group. Sounds of surprise continued to come from nearly everyone's mouth.

"To make a long story short, one of the wives, Darlene, is now pregnant and doesn't know who the father is. The reason this is a problem is she had been told she couldn't have children. Her two little boys are adopted." Frances took a long sip and continued her story.

"One morning over coffee, she felt so overjoyed to know she could have her own child, Darlene casually mentioned this concern to another wife who told her to get an abortion. This wife told another who told her husband who told the other husbands. Since one of these men is a lawyer, they all banded together for this lawsuit. Each says he's willing to take responsibility to raise the baby if it is his." She sat down, feeling a huge load fall off her shoulders.

For the next half hour, everyone voiced their opinion, many agreeing she should not kill part of herself, but have and keep her baby.

"How can you have a baby if you don't let the growing process finish?" Christi looked at everyone with concern. "If she didn't want to get pregnant, she should have used some kind of birth control."

"But she thought she couldn't get pregnant."

"Ladies, let's not have an argument about this now."

Most agreed this woman needed their support. Several volunteered to visit her.

To get back on task from the previous discussion over the speed limits, Sally asked if they'd be willing to meet after the annual meeting to discuss their results.

"With Thanksgiving coming, I'd rather wait until early December," Dorothy said. We'll all be at the annual meeting, Sally and you can just announce what we're going to do. I really don't see how we will be able to do much until after the holidays."

Everyone agreed and Sally set the date for their next meeting, a Christmas party cookie exchange.

Seth decided not to go to the annual meeting, so Sally and Lisa went with Nate. Brett came over to stay with the boys as Seth volunteered to babysit. The meeting had been scheduled for 7:00 p.m. in the gym of a neighboring school. Since this was not only her first meeting, but her first one as a board member, Sally felt a little more nervous when she saw the number of people sitting on the bleachers.

"Nate, how many do you think are here? This is quite a turnout."

"Didn't you look on the sign-in sheet? We were number 252."

Sally looked at him in disbelief. She had been distracted by another board member and didn't sign in. There had been a group of tables set in front of the bleachers, and she had been told to go there first and sit behind a sign with her name. As she sat down, she continued to show surprise at the number of people walking inside. She took a long sip of a Coke placed at her nameplate. Many of the other board members came up to this table to take their place

Steve Smith started the meeting, welcoming everyone and introducing the board members. After the secretary and treasurer gave their reports, there would be an open mike where people could come up and ask general questions before each board member gave their report.

There were about ten people in line when the questions started. Even though they had gone over the procedures at the last meeting, Sally felt a little nervous looking at all the homeowners who would decide if she stayed on the board or not.

"Hi. My name is Alice Dratch. I've lived here five years and my question concerns the newest member who did not get voted in by any of us last November. Is her position legal?"

The board lawyer Daniel signaled to Steve as he stood up to answer.

"This is a great question to start our meeting tonight, Alice. Ellie resigned due to a move out of state; her husband has a new job. The rules were checked to make sure someone could be nominated at the meeting. There were no others vying for this position, and because of her interest in getting the speed limits lowered, the board members thought she'd be a great temporary replacement and voted for her to take Ellie's place. Tonight, she will be voted in by the homeowners at another part of the meeting."

"Hi, My name is Jack Smith. We are new here and wonder about the legality of forcing people to paint their houses a specific color."

Once again, Daniel answered this question using the Codes and Covenants of Regulations (CCRs) set up by the original owner of the land, based on Illinois law for homeowners associations.

"My name is Peter Rinaldi. We are new here too. We were never informed about this association when we moved here. Why not?"

Steve answered this one. "We have had many complaints about this Josh. Like the other associations here in Eden, we are working with realtors and the state licensing program to make sure everyone knows this information must be presented to potential homeowners. Maybe you could help us with this project. Interested?"

Peter turned around and looked at his wife who nodded her head yes. He responded to Steve immediately. "Yes, I would like to get involved and would like to get other volunteers tonight who had the same experience." He turned around to face those in the bleachers. "I'll be at the door to get your name if you'd volunteer to help me."

"My name is Mark Swiderski. My wife and I are interested in the pre-school. We just moved in two weeks ago and found out from our next door neighbor some person should have come to our house and given us this necessary information everyone keeps talking about. Our realtor said nothing about having to pay monthly dues."

The preschool representative stood up immediately and introduced herself, saying they'd talk as soon as the meeting ended.

"My name is Amanda McCowen. We are new here too and still don't understand the legal aspect of the rules held over us. Can we get out of our sale since we weren't told anything about this association, rules or dues?"

Daniel stood up quickly. "Amanda, there is not enough time here to answer your question in detail. Please call my office tomorrow and we'll set up an appointment to talk abut your specific situation." He walked over to her and gave her his business card.

The rest of the questions went smoothly. After each member gave their report, Steve opened the floor for nominations for Ellie's position, Membership Director, and showed his surprise when no one came forward. He asked again.

Turning to the lawyer, he asked him to make the nomination for Sally.

Looking at the audience, Daniel stood up, looking at the audience and said loudly. "Since there are no nominations from the floor, I want to put Sally Williams name up to be the director for Membership/Newsletter."

Lisa stood up and said, "I second this nomination."

Since there seemed to be no discussion, the question was asked and all who were in favor voted with a raise of hands. Sally was elected with a majority of over 200 hands. The meeting ended shortly after this vote. Lisa and Nate came up to the head table immediately to congratulate her. She had been surrounded by the board and everyone gave their congratulations.

On the drive home, Nate said, "I really thought you'd have someone who'd give you some opposition Sally, especially after the first open mike question."

"Well, the good news is now you are official, Sally." Lisa turned around and continued. "Do you think Seth is hoping you didn't get elected? What do you think he'll say about this new commitment you've made?"

"When I get home, I'll see what kind of reaction I get. Thanks for the ride."

CHAPTER 16
THE JUDGE

Alicia and Barry clearly made their point to the police involved in investigating their daughter's death. Six months had passed and they were settled into their new home, job and school. They refused to come back to Chicago for a trial and told the judge they felt prison would solve nothing for the driver or her passengers. "They must learn something here."

The first week in December, the driver, Gail Murray, came with her parents, Brian and Anna, to the courthouse. Judge Thomas Tarkanian presided over their formal hearing. Gail's friends, her passengers, Becky Ingalls and Jenny Erthner, were scheduled to arrive thirty-five minutes later.

Behind closed doors, the judge said, "I have thought long and hard about the decision I must make for you with an agreement from the Butchikas family. Luckily for you, there isn't much law precedence on this type of specific situation. They are adamant about no prison time for you, or going to some type of juvenile detention, Gail. Although I see their point, you did commit a crime and I must charge you with involuntary manslaughter." He shuffled some papers, took out a long yellow sheet and placed it on top of the others. His silver rimmed glasses sat perched on top of his perfectly shaped nose and he stroked a small white goatee as he looked over at her parents, who appeared as nervous as Gail.

"This is a very serious offense for a new driver who recently turned 16. My ruling is: 1) you will be on probation for five years and may not get so much as a single ticket; 2) you must drive with an adult for the next three months; 3) you will attend a defensive driving class for four Saturdays in a row; 4) you must write a paper for presentation to every area high school you can reach before you graduate." He looked up from his yellow legal sheet, a stern look on his face. "I will read your account of what happened, what you've learned and how you could have changed the outcome so as to severely scare every teenager who listens to your speech." He looked over to her parents, then back to Gail, knitting his graying eyebrows tightly. "Driving is not a right Gail, but a privilege, and one which you can lose forever if you don't take these choices of your punishment seriously."

Gail blinked rapidly with each additional sentence and tears spilled down her flushed cheeks. She looked from parent to parent and then back to the judge. First, she felt overjoyed to hear there would be no detention place for her, but then she felt over-whelmed with the second part of her sentence, writing a paper he needed to review first. What seemed to be the hardest part of the sentencing for her would be writing her version of what happened. She had to stand up in front of unknown peers and read what she wrote so sincerely as to scare each one enough to make them think twice every time they get into a car.

"Because of the holidays, I will give you one month to write this paper, a minimum of thirty minutes speaking time. I would prefer one hour in length." His voice sounded stern yet not as severe as one might imagine. He passed her some papers and told her to sign each one with a clear signature.

Her father shifted his large frame and asked, "Do we need to have legal representation for this, Judge?"

"Not at all, Mr. Murray. Your daughter is just saying she drove the car, her two passengers were there and she hit Andromeda because she drove at a speed which exceeded the posted limits." He passed a black fountain pen to Gail whose slim fingers continued to shake as she picked up the pen.

Brian and Anna looked at each other showing worry and concern. Brian, now with his glasses off, wiped his creased, sweating forehead with a handkerchief. He looked at his wife whose scrunched eyebrows, wide eyes and pursed pink lips painted a picture of her fear and frustration. She wanted to talk, yet felt so relieved. She seemed overwhelmed there would be no time served. She watched in irony as though a window had opened for her emotional release to now fly out into a chilled December air.

She grabbed Brian's pudgy fingers and looked at the judge, forcing a weak smile. "We are so thankful to the Butchikas family and to you, Judge, for taking away the possibility of her going away. Gail is a wonderful daughter, caring sister and honor roll student. She knows what she did can never bring back this darling little girl and having to speak in front of her peers just might save someone else's child."

Brian decided he'd better say something significant too, yet the words just rolled around his overloaded mind. He remembered the newest board member, Sally somebody, who lived next door to the victim's family, and who had come to the board to find out how to get the speed limits lowered. He tried to speak slowly to ease his nerves.

"Judge, I am a board member of our homeowner's association. Maybe Gail's speech could be made into a much shorter version to be presented to our members who have already talked about working politically to get the speed limits lowered." He breathed out a large breath of air in relief.

"A fantastic idea, Mr. Murray." A small smile changed his facial expression. "You are right. Gail should speak to all the area neighborhood associations. Getting the speed limits lowered is another positive solution to those who drive without paying attention to the children in these areas." He took out his yellow legal paper and wrote this down.

"Gail, I'm adding this one additional task for you to do. You can work with your fellow passengers on this and take turns going to other homeowner neighborhoods. At least two of you must go together. I'll leave the details to you." He passed another sheet of paper for her to sign.

The phone rang and his secretary reminded him of the time. "This is all for today Gail. I'll expect you back in one month. Please make an appointment with my secretary before you leave, and if your friends are here, send them in." He stood up, towering over Gail's dad who at 6.2" now seemed short.

"Thank you so much Judge. I really didn't want to go to a detention place." Gail pushed her strawberry blond streaked curls off her still flushed face, smoothed her blue knit print jacket and shook his hand which didn't feel as sweaty as hers.

They walked into the waiting room and his secretary took out a large calendar for 1979 and asked her when she could come back again. Jenny Erthner and Becky Ingalls, along with their parents, were sitting on the overstuffed couches looking quite nervous and worried. Jenny continued to twist a single strand of long black hair around one finger while Becky clasped and unclasped her hands. Before they could speak to Gail, Judge Tarkanian called them inside. Both stood up and walked slowly toward his office. They looked at their parents, forcing small smiles, worried about what would happen when the door closed.

CHAPTER 17
PASSENGERS

Both sets of parents stood up immediately as Judge Tarkanian motioned for the girls to come inside his plush office. As she went inside, Jenny noticed four overstuffed black leather chairs and a huge black desk covered with piles of manila folders. The parents, still standing, looked over at his secretary, LaRaye Littlefield, who said, "Just the passengers, please." They looked at each other, surprised by this and sat down quietly.

Then his secretary stood up. A petite woman, she took off her red framed glasses to offer them something to drink along with ". . . my favorite made from scratch fruit breads." She wore her white hair very short and moved efficiently to fill four coffee cups quickly.

When the wood paneled door closed, Jenny's dad asked the secretary, "Why can't we go in too?" His forehead wrinkled with deep creases as he brushed his hand through his graying black hair.

"Since your daughters were only passengers, the judge just wants to hear their version before passing sentence." She stood up, took everyone's order and gave out four cups of black coffee, then passed a plate of her homemade fruit breads and Christmas napkins.

Inside the masculine office, dark paneled walls and rows of leather bound law books filled five long shelves of a beautifully carved bookcase. Becky tightened the band holding her red curls in a ponytail, continuing to take in the office décor. Black ink prints of the old water tower, the Tribune building over-looking the river and other Chicago landmarks covered one wall. Two large black framed diplomas showing his undergraduate degree from Loyola and his law degree from Northwestern hung on the wall behind his huge desk.

Jenny sat nervously looking only at the judge's stern face and his sharply pointed goatee. She continued to push strands of her long black hair behind her ears, first one strand then another as her left foot tapped up and down on the richly colored carpet of red, gold and black.

Thirty long minutes later each girl had tearfully told what they remembered, over five long months ago. They both admitted distracting Gail with conversation and loud music, which 'might have' prevented her from zeroing in on driving down a street more slowly.

Getting them to admit to these distractions took some firm questioning from the judge. When satisfied with their versions, he gave out his sentences.

"Even though neither of you drives yet, Becky you are the closest to sixteen. You're already taking Driver's Ed, right? You will have a little more to do than Jenny. Both of you will write the same paper as Gail." He took off his glasses, looking directly at Becky. He spoke quietly, yet forcefully. "You will speak to all of the Driver's Ed classes in your school before spring. You both will take a defensive driving class, different from the one Gail is taking, and yes, you will speak to those taking this class about the responsibilities of being a perfect passenger."

He looked back down at his yellow legal pad, then up again, his face still serious as he reminded them how lucky they were because Andromeda's parents wanted no detention of any kind.

"But sir," Jenny said hesitantly, with a little quiver in her soft voice. "I just sat in the back seat. Why should I have the same punishment?" She felt so guilty asking this question because she knew the accident had been her fault.

He scowled at her, his mouth turned down as if in a frown. "Young lady, the law doesn't care where you sat. I'm making the decisions here and you have no say in this outcome. You were in the car and you admitted to distracting the driver, no matter how little." He closed the yellow pad by folding over the two pages where he had his notes and put it inside a large manila folder.

"Both of you will have a six month probation when you start driving and each of you WILL write this paper and make this presentation." He stood up and pointed to the door, "Good day ladies."

They stood up, dazed by the sentence and went outside into the waiting room where the secretary gave them some papers to sign. The Erthners and Ingalls stood up, looking at their daughter's faces and wondered what happened. When they finished signing the required forms, everyone left in silence. Only outside in the hallway did the worried parents hear what happened.

Mr. Ingalls spoke with an emotional tone, "Don't you think we should get a lawyer?"

Mrs. Erthner answered immediately. "I've worked as a paralegal, and we are so very lucky they didn't receive anything worse, like going to jail or one of those juvenile detention centers. We should be thankful, learn and go on." They walked down the large stone staircase in silence. Before leaving the building, each daughter thanked their parents for coming and offering so much support. Jenny and Becky agreed to let well enough alone.

The second Monday in December dawned with a chilly dampness and cloudy sky. Sally hurriedly fixed the boys breakfast, as they rose a little later than usual. Grant ran out to catch the bus and Garrett stood by the dining room window to wait for his car pool. Seth would be home later tonight and Sally had another full day. The phone rang as Garrett opened the door and said to his mom, "Bye."

"Let's go finish our Christmas shopping and have lunch, my treat." Lisa's voice sounded so bubbly and cheery. Sally, never a morning person, looked out the kitchen window already knowing her answer.

"Sorry Lisa. Don't you remember? Monday is my day to stay home, do the wash, change the sheets, vacuum, dust and plan the week's menu. Seth will be home tonight and I have a delicious dinner to cook. Maybe tomorrow."

Lisa's tone changed immediately. "What do you mean you stay home on Monday? I can't believe you plan your food for a whole week. Have you finished your Christmas shopping?"

"Look, Lisa, we've known each other over five months now and this is what I always do on Monday. Sorry you forgot, but this never changes. I can't believe you don't plan. How do you know if you have all the right ingredients if you don't have everything written down?" She took out her grocery list and Betty Crocker cookbook while she waited for an answer.

"Look, some of us just decide what we want each day. Around noon I pick out what I want for dinner and if I don't have it, I use whatever I have. Come on, just one morning. Please. . .I said I'd treat for lunch."

"I can go any other day this week. Sorry. Can't you call someone else? I will still be able to take our walk." She sat back down on one of the kitchen chairs and opened the cookbook to the main dish section.

"O.K. I know when to accept defeat. If I can't find anyone to go, I'll call you back and we can pick another day."

Sally settled down to plan five dinners as she leafed through her cookbook. She put water in the tea kettle to boil and then looked through her stock of canned goods and frozen food to plan her grocery list for Thursday morning, when most stores started their week-end specials. When she finished this task, she vacuumed all the bedrooms, living room and dining room.

Downstairs, she took a load out of the washer and started folding a load of clothes when the phone rang. She ran upstairs instead of answering the phone in the family room. Taking out a piece of leftover quiche and putting it in the microwave, she answered the phone by the fourth ring. Shouldering the phone to her ear, she heard, "Hey. Just a quick minute to say I should be home tonight. What's for dinner?"

Seth sounded relaxed and Sally guessed the eastern snow storm must have skipped through the skies, not causing any delay. She set her table with a pretty red and green Christmas holly and mistletoe placemat and then put on fresh water in her copper tea kettle for her second cup of tea. She turned the flame on low as she reused her bag of Constant Comment tea.

"Hi Seth. What good news. I'm planning another of your favorites, fried chicken, mashed potatoes, brown sugar-glazed carrots, and sour cream chocolate chip cake." The microwave beeped, so she slipped the quiche out quickly and then fixed her tea.

"Yum . . . I'm hungry already. Three days of eating out just isn't what it's cracked up to be and I just can't wait. Thanks in advance for giving my starvin' stomach something scrumptious to eat on my first night back. I'll call you when we land. Love you, bye."

Sally looked out the window to the now clouded grey sky. "Just be careful Seth; a snow storm is predicted to hit about five p.m." She hung up and ate lunch, listening to Paul Harvey's version of the news at noon. Two loads of laundry later, Sally had folded and put away most of the clothes. She changed sheets on all three beds and went outside the garage back door to bring in a couple of loads of wood for a fire tonight.

She looked at the clock and realized the boys would be home soon, so she changed quickly from her comfy Monday workday pj's and robe to clean sweats and sneakers. She ran a comb through her disheveled hair, penciled in eyebrows, added mascara and blush and went downstairs to put the last load of wash into the dryer. She glanced at her watch again and went upstairs to open the front door as Garrett closed Glenda's car door. She waved good-bye to her and the other children as he bound up the stairs, smiling.

"Guess what we did today, Mom?" He took a paper out of his jacket pocket and handed it to her as they went inside. "We made a present for you for our Christmas tree."

He hung his hat and jacket on his hook on the inside of the closet door, went upstairs and sat down on a kitchen chair, then blurted out, "It's a surprise but I can tell you if you really want to know." He picked up the glass of milk and held it up to her. "Can I have hot chocolate instead, please?"

She nodded, put the water on to boil as she stared at the paper, taking out her homemade hot chocolate mix from the Feingold recipe book. His class would be having a party and each child needed to bring a wrapped, five dollar toy and a snack to share for fifteen. Parents were invited to the sing along program. After about fifteen minutes of sharing his day, he left to play in his room. Sally mixed up the flour mixture for the chicken, peeled the potatoes and left them to soak in cold water. She took out the butter, eggs and sour cream to make the cake as Grant came in the front door. When he finished sharing his day, she mixed the cake batter and then put the pans in the oven. With last minute instructions to the boys, she looked out the window to see Lisa crossing the street for their walk. After putting her house keys in her pocket and turning the lock, she stepped outside to a cold afternoon.

Their walk passed in a rapid blur as Lisa shared her shopping solutions for mall madness two weeks before Christmas. "I really looked for Star Wars toys, Sally, but no store had anything." Together, they planned the cookie exchange for the block captains and the Christmas dinner they'd be sharing.

After Seth arrived home, everyone raved about the melt-in-your mouth chicken as well as the no bumps in the mashed potatoes, carrots and cake. After the nightly routine of bath and stories, Seth and Sally settled in front of a roaring fire with a glass of port.

"I don't mind letting you know this trip, with two near misses, a belligerent first class passenger and an almost birth from another passenger is one I'm glad is over. I am so ready to rest for four days." He took a long sip of port while Sally tried to compose her thoughts, not able to get past the 'near miss' and 'birth'.

"Do I really want to hear about this trip now, Seth? I'd like to have a good night's sleep with you without a picture of your plane plummeting to the ground."

Seth looked intently into the warming fire, orange and blue flames shooting up. He chose his words carefully. "You're right; I shouldn't scare you. Leave it at this: those of us in the cockpit were more poised with professional behavior then a junior controller who almost made a fatal mistake when his supervisor looked away to help someone else." He continued to tell the good news; they averted a daunting drastic disaster and the pregnant passenger didn't deliver on board.

Sally put down her glass and leaned over to give him a reassuring hug. They both stared into a burst of blazing flames as his favorite composer, Beethoven played on an eight track tape.

The next morning, Sally rose a little earlier to make sourdough pancakes. Seth drove the carpool and she prepared for the regular board meeting, anxious to hear Brian's account of what happened with the judge and the sentencing. She had to bring a snack to share as the board voted against having a Christmas party with spouses.

Greenebriar's Garbage

Lisa called to talk and ask for a ride to the meeting while Sally prepared her snack of almonds stuffed inside dates and wrapped in bacon. Seth finished his errands and came home for lunch, as she cooked the snacks and prepared another standby favorite of tomato soup and grilled bacon and cheese sandwiches. They agreed, once again, to take down the artificial tree from the attic to decorate instead of going out and buying a real one. He grumbled, "I went to Toy r Us and they didn't have any toys from Star Wars, much less an X-Wing fighter. No one could even verify if any toys were made for this holiday season, so we'll have to come up with something else."

The weather changed drastically between three and four, so the afternoon walk had to be canceled. Dinner went smoothly enough and Seth cleaned up after dinner, promising stories while Sally left for the board meeting. After roll call and minutes of the previous meeting, and a quick review of last month's annual meeting, everyone helped themselves to a plate of goodies.

The treasurer, Connor Pawlowich, brought up his usual list of delinquent homeowners. "We settled the last two out of court, yet one man insists on his day in front of a judge. If anyone wants to attend, we have a date set for the last Monday in January. I am still hopeful our lawyer will prevail with his famous tersely-worded letter. My main concern tonight has to do with our continually rising heating bill. Something needs to be done because parties here have the heat so high, this place is too hot for the preschoolers who come in on Monday morning."

Lisa, the only homeowner present in the peanut gallery raised her hand. "At our house, we have an attachment which automatically turns down our heat at 11 p.m. and then kicks back in to 70 by 6:30 a.m., so we are comfortable when we get up, an hour later. The timer doesn't cost very much and Nate installed it himself." She looked at each board member. "Maybe you could get someone to put in this type of device with a lock and explain to those having parties why we have to do this."

Two other board members voiced their agreement, saying they used the same device. Steve called for the question after the motion had been made and it passed, 8-2.

Brian then asked for the floor to relate his story about meeting the judge and the sentence Gail received. He asked for a month when she could come present her speech.

Andrea Czolowski, the block captain chair, told how they had been working to get petitions signed for lowering the speed limits. Everyone agreed her group of block captains would work together with Gail using the ideas from this judge to contact the city and area legislative reps to have a new law enforced for lower speed limits in the neighboring subdivisions. Suzanne told Brian they could have Gail speak at the February meeting.

Many talked about how helpful this speech would be, to remind everyone to slow down. Several also voiced their approval with the block captains trying to get the speed limits lowered. Wishing everyone a "Merry Christmas" the meeting closed in a record two hours.

As the boys understood more and more about the calendar, dates and seasons, this year proved to be another tough one to celebrate Christmas. In the past, whenever Seth came home was the day they chose to celebrate. This year, Seth would be gone on Christmas. They talked it over and just decided to say Santa knew of this problem, and for them alone, he'd bring presents a couple of days early. This would be the Williams family secret. No one else could know because then they would want to get their gifts early too.

"Another disaster solved," Seth said. "I wonder how much longer we'll be able to get away with this?"

CHAPTER 18
LOST LOVE

After the hectic holidays and New Year's party at the clubhouse, the Thursday bowling league finished at 11:30 a.m. the second week of the New Year, 1978. Sally and Lisa went to lunch with their team partners, Lonnie Balliteria and her block captain, Dorothy Howe, and Joanne, one of their neighbors. Lonnie and her husband Hank had moved in last fall and Hank had attended a board meeting to find out about the rules required for living here.

As soon as they ordered, Lonnie asked Dorothy some questions about remodeling. Even though this house had been their first one to own, both she and Hank didn't like the decorating styles in the bathroom or kitchen, much less the color scheme.

Sally jumped in right away. "We found five layers of linoleum in our kitchen when we put down a new floor. The job took longer than my husband planned just because each family before us put down a new floor over the old one. What a mess."

Before Dorothy could answer, Lisa and Joanne told their stories about repeated renovations. By then lunch arrived and everyone talked in-between bites of vegetable soup and hot pastrami sandwiches.

Dorothy finally answered Lonnie's question. "We used Better Baths and Kitchens."

Joanne asked if this had been the original name of the store because one had been suggested to them when they moved and she remembered a different name.

"Yes Joanne. This store did have a different name many years ago." She pushed a lock of black hair behind her ears, looked back to Lonnie and continued. "One of the original ideas for block captains came from a lady who used to work for Welcome Wagon. By incorporating helpful hints to each new family as well as companies to use, we would save a lot of money by not having to pay fees to this advertising company,"

"I didn't know Welcome Wagon charged fees." Lonnie looked questioningly at Dorothy. "How did this work?"

"Rather than go into that Lonnie, you just need to know many of the new neighbors have given us feedback from the businesses we recommended and a few were dropped."

She sipped her soup slowly, pushing her red framed eyeglasses up onto her forehead. "For me, another reason is one of our board members works there and really goes out of his way to get us the best deals. He's a local guy, from Joliet, I think." She looked at each of them with this question, "Did you use this store?"

Sally and Lisa said their husbands did the work themselves, but Joanne said, "Yes we did. He's our clubhouse and pool board member, Doug Pulchowski. He did a great job for us." She tightened her dark brown ponytail and rushed her fingers across a freckled face, wiping off some bread crumbs in the process.

Lonnie froze in her seat, not able to move anything. She quickly looked at her soup and sandwich, taking a bite while trying to remain calm and not show shock at hearing this name from her long forgotten past. *Can't be the same Doug*, she thought immediately. There wouldn't be two Doug Pulchowski's from Joliet, or could there? Her heart pounded so loudly she just knew everyone hears this sonorous sound.

"Sally and I saw him in action at the first board meeting we attended last fall. She wanted to get some help on getting the speed limits lowered after her neighbor's child died. She was struck by a car driven by one of the board members daughters."

"Oh I remember reading your take on this in the monthly newsletter, Sally. I'm so glad you were elected at the general meeting. We sure needed some new blood on the board," Dorothy added. She brushed her pink fingernails through her black hair, streaked with auburn highlights. "Your newsletter pieces are helpful for us block captains because you give us information we can use to help those on our street who are sick or having problems. Where do you . . .?"

Joanne interrupted. "He'll get our vote to do the job, Lonnie. The prices at his store are really competitive and if you find a lower price somewhere else, he'll match it." She looked at her soup and took a small sip, then said, "You really should call now. I've heard January is a slow season for remodeling."

By now Lonnie had regained her composure. "Thanks a lot. I really appreciate knowing someone had a good experience there. This homeownership is turning out to be a lot more work than I ever imagined. As a single person, I never could afford to buy a house on a teacher's salary and then along came Hank."

She smiled so broadly, Lisa said, "Must be a newlywed, right?"

Blushing slightly, Lonnie said, "Yes, this is almost the end of our first year. Because I'm only teaching part-time, I must confess I'm getting spoiled with all these activities to keep me busy. Best of all, is getting to meet such great neighbors."

She took another sip of tea as slowly as possible. "I'll get on this right away 'cause I'd sure like to have a new bathroom before school starts this fall. We'll celebrate our first anniversary in August with a party for both sides of our family."

They paid their bills and left the restaurant. Since Lonnie drove by herself, she said good-bye and walked over to her car quickly and sat down, resting her head back on the seat and closing her grey-green eyes. Her legs continued to shake as her thoughts rambled from today's conversation to one many years ago. She realized she now had a new problem to handle, one which involved information she never shared with anyone, not even her mom or best friend. *Do I have something to share with you Doug . . . probably not going to be your best news of this New Year.*

CHAPTER 19
LONNIE

Lonnie came home from lunch, shaken with this news about the possibility of meeting her former boyfriend. She walked into the kitchen, and looked at the calendar, tears forming. Then, she remembered a birthday: another one she would miss. She sat down to a jumbled mix of emotions, sadness and fear as she remembered what happened.

FOURTEEN YEARS EARLIER

She pushed open the half closed door of the phone booth and put down her purse after taking out ten cents. A shaky finger dropped the dime into the slot and then fit into each of the black round holes to dial the phone number she had copied down last week. She twisted her fingers inside her pants pocket nervously while she waited for the ringing phone to be answered.

"Doctor Jones office, this is Laura speaking. How may I direct your call?"

"Hi. I'm calling to get test results," Lonnie spoke with a shaky voice.

"Hold on, I'll connect you."

She tapped her fingers on top of the pay phone trying to keep calm, even though her insides were rumbling with concern. She waited patiently.

"This is Stephanie Kaufman. I need your name and which test results you want." She spoke in a manner which sounded pleasant and reassuring.

"I'm calling to find out pregnancy results, number 621, Nancy Smith." Her voice shook as she said the number.

"Please hold while I locate your file."

Silence, waiting . . . more feelings of nervousness and then her inside voice saying take a deep breath in; now, blow out slowly. She pushed her auburn bangs off her forehead which held beads of perspiration.

"Thanks for holding." Her voice sounded a little more up-beat now. "Great news; the results are positive. Can the doctor see you next Thursday about 2:30 p.m.?"

Lonnie's knees started to shake un-controllably as she grasped the entire pay phone with her left hand, barely whispering, "Can you change the appointment to after 4:00 p.m.?"

"Yes, we have an opening at 4:15. We'll see you then. Bye now."

Lonnie took another deep breath and said, "Thank you."

She hung up the receiver and pressed her back into the wall of the phone booth while her shaking body sunk slowly to the dirty floor. Her head fell onto her knees and she felt her heart hit against her chest with loud thumps, again and again. Tears formed quickly and she said out loud: "No, no, no; this just can't be happening."

What seemed like an eternity later, she heard a knock on the door and a voice called out, "Are you alright?" She waved her hand, shook her head yes and tried to regain some sort of composure. With her feet anchored firmly to the floor, wobbly legs pushed her body up. Lonnie leaned her back against the plastic wall and inched her way up, ever so slowly, hands grasping side walls for support. She took her purse, looked away from the door, wiped her tears and without looking up at the person standing outside, pushed the door open and walked out and away. For a minute, she didn't remember where she had parked her car. She walked on unsteady legs, still shaking. Thoughts of disbelief and fear overpowered her thoughts.

When she found her car, she took out her keys and with fingers still shaking, forced her car key into the lock. Then she jerked open the door, slid onto the blue vinyl seat of her beloved '67 Mustang and slumped down. Her head leaned back and tears flowed down her flushed cheeks. Her heart pounded while her insides twisted up like a tight cord of rope. She forced her body to regain some form of composure before she drove away and back to the school where she needed to finish her afternoon of student teaching.

Lonnie looked at her watch and realized her lunch break would end in ten minutes. She knew she needed to get herself together before walking back into the elementary school. Wondering out loud, she asked herself, "How will I get through this afternoon, Lord? What have I done?"

A handkerchief soaked up the tears on her wet cheeks. Getting through this afternoon would be the easy part. Now she'd have to write a letter she never dreamed would have to be written and felt sad as she tried to imagine Doug's reaction. Then, she'd have to tell her predicament to a doctor she didn't even know. What other crisis would she have to endure over the next few weeks, trying to hide a pregnancy until school ended?

"Well Doug, you are on your way to Vietnam and I'm pregnant." she whispered out loud. She opened her watery eyes, looked at the ceiling and mumbled out loud, "What am I going to do now?"

CHAPTER 20
WINTER

Excessive snowfall and unprecedented cold temperatures continued into February and the Greenebriar subdivision settled in for another month of winter. There were only two parties scheduled at the clubhouse and the weekly bowling league now encouraged carpools to get to the bowling alley. Ceramics classes had been canceled for the entire month and the women's study group decided to meet only the last week of the month.

Sally had settled into her board position as membership director and newsletter contributor. Then she added Grant's Saturday learn-to-skate in nearby Orland Park to her schedule. Seth had a schedule of four days on and three days off for this messy month. Every now and then the boys would ask about their former neighbors. When she received a letter, she'd share. The new neighbors, Cynthia and Clark weren't quite as sociable, even though her son James went to school with Grant at the new neighborhood elementary.

Lonnie made the difficult choice to go to Better Baths and Kitchens and meet Doug, nervous yet concerned he could be the same person from her past. She and Hank had not been in town for the annual meeting in November and they spent her entire two weeks off from school during the Christmas break in Cancun, Mexico. She often told herself not to put off the inevitable, yet she became more and more afraid, thinking about seeing Doug again, alone.

Sally stopped working on the March newsletter to answer the phone on a Tuesday morning.

"Hi, Sally." When she recognized Seth's voice, her heart fluttered with worry, knowing he rarely called when the boys weren't home. She looked out the kitchen window at the snow filled yard and grey clouds, remembering another severe storm had been forecast for early tonight.

"'Fraid I have some bad news. I won't be home tonight." She braced herself against the kitchen wall as she heard a sigh, thinking: *This is his job and he's not in charge of schedule changes.*

"Oh no, Seth. Are you all right; did you get sick?" She tried to make her voice sound calm and not harsh.

"I'm fine. We had a passenger who passed out. Due to severe medical problems, we were forced to return to the terminal. Because of this delay, crew scheduling said I'd be over the limit to fly home after all the paperwork and the process the medical people needed to follow to remove her from the plane."

Sally reacted with sheer panic as her voice rose in pitch. "Did she die?"

Now he sounded more like himself. "No, sorry I gave you the wrong impression there. The person sitting next to her called a flight attendant for help because she had a seizure and lost consciousness. He didn't know what to do." His voice seemed to slow down now as if he were telling a story to the boys. "The flight attendant asked if a doctor was on board and since no one responded, she came up to the cockpit to tell us the passenger remained unconscious."

Sally relaxed a little and took a long sip of her lukewarm tea.

"I called air traffic control and the supervisor said we had to turn back since there were no medical people on board to stabilize her. We were almost an hour out, so after we received clearance to turn around and come back, I had a feeling we'd be out of luck for me getting to come home." Suddenly, Sally heard 'tired' in his voice. She decided she should be supportive and positive.

"Don't worry Seth. I'll save tonight's dinner for tomorrow. The good news is she is getting the treatment she needs and didn't die on your watch. The boys will be disappointed, of course, but we can wait another day. Maybe next month you could bid for three days on and four off."

She looked out the window again and realized she'd have to get up a little earlier in the morning if the storm hit tonight since it would be her turn to drive for the preschool

"O.K. Gotta go. Thanks so much for understanding and not getting mad. Love you. See you mañana."

Sally felt relieved and proud of her behavior when Seth mentioned not getting mad. She did remember other times she'd not been so pleasant when he called with a schedule change. Since there would be a board meeting tonight, she'd have to get a babysitter. Looking in the 'fridge and then the cupboard, Sally decided to go ahead and fix macaroni and cheese with ham chunks and green beans with bacon and onions since the boys were looking forward to one of their dad's favorite dinners after a long trip. She took out a pork roast to start a slow thaw for tomorrow night's dinner.

The phone rang again and Lisa asked, "Are we on for our walk this afternoon?"

"Well, if the storm doesn't hit. Can I call you back? I need to finish the newsletter before tonight's meeting." Quickly eating a peanut butter and jelly sandwich, the tea kettle performed its regular routine of boiling water, and Sally settled in with another cup of blackberry tea with lemon honey.

She went back to finish her writing and after an hour of nonstop concentration, she realized the boys would be home soon. The carpool really worked out well for her. On those days when she didn't have a nonstop schedule of errands or activities, she did so enjoy her 'alone time', Lisa's name for peace and quiet. Usually she listened to her golden oldies radio program while she cleaned or cooked. She finished the final page, put two bananas and two glasses of milk on the kitchen table, then put on her coat to go outside and wait for the boys to come home. She walked down the porch stairs as the bus came around the corner. Grant came up the driveway with a broad grin on his freckled face just as a tan and green station wagon pulled into the driveway. Garrett bound out of the car, waved good-by and hugged her legs.

"Thanks Ingrid." She waved and went inside to share her news. Grant looked at his mom with concern. "Mom, don't you have your meeting tonight?"

"Yes, I do. If the storm hits first, I might stay home if I can't find someone to sit with you guys." She quickly ran through her list of names wondering who could come at such short notice.

"We can stay by ourselves. I'm six now and I know what to do in case of emergencies." He seemed to stand a little taller and showed determination on his face.

"Yes, you do know what to do. I just can't consider your first night alone when such a large snow storm is predicted because the power could go out." They put their peels in the garbage and looked out the window at the darkening sky.

"Brett's mom and I are going for our walk soon, so let's try you staying alone for one hour and see how you do. We can decide about tonight later." She called Lisa and told her to come over.

Taking out her hat, gloves and scarf, Sally reached for her heavier coat. The boys settled in to watch their favorite afternoon cartoons as she called out, "I'm locking the door so don't open for anyone, o.k.?"

"We'll be alright, Mom. Don't worry."

"Hi Sally, boys all settled in with Seth?" Lisa adjusted her hat and scarf.

"Not today. He had an emergency medical mess this morning on the west coast and called to say he'd be home tomorrow." She tied a long scarf around her neck and shoved her gloved hands deep into her pants pockets. Just as they started walking, a very cold breeze blew behind them.

"What about the board meeting tonight?"

"When we finish, I'm going to start calling around since the few high school kids I know all take the late bus home." She put her head down as the breeze changed directions and blew into her face. "Any suggestion besides Anna, Jonathan, or Beth?"

Lisa kept her head down too. "None right now." She turned her head sideways to look over at Sally and not get a gust of chilling wind in her face. "Hey, I have an idea. I want to come to tonight's meeting and since Nate is home, Brett would love the company."

"Gosh Lisa, you are wonderful to make such an offer. Thanks."

They increased their speed just a little and continued to walk, heads down with no more conversation until they completed the inside circle on Great Falls, ending at Lisa's house.

"I'll be over about 6:50." She crossed the street quickly, hurried to her house and went inside, calling down to the boys, "Dinner in about fifteen minutes; don't forget to wash up."

Garrett came into the kitchen, walked over to the stove and stood on his tiptoes to look at the dinner. "Sure smells good, mommy. I'm glad this is something I can still eat." She bent down to give him a hug.

She knew he meant them eating using the ideas from the Feingold plan. She really felt proud of their efforts to eat right and help Garrett adjust. The Feingold group met monthly and the speakers always seemed to have a new approved brand of food to buy. He smiled and took his place at the kitchen table.

She served each and asked Grant to say the blessing.

After they talked about their day at school, Sally said. "I have a surprise for you tonight, boys. Lisa invited you over to her house while we go to the board meeting. After dinner, please pack your pjs and toothbrush in your overnight cases."

After they cleared the table, rinsed their dishes and put them in the dishwasher, Garrett left to pack and Grant stayed to practice his five minutes of Spanish.

He spoke hesitantly. "Buenos días. Estoy bien, y usted? Me llamo Grant. Hoy es miércoles.

"Muy bien, Grant. Hasta luego."

Sally gathered her pages for the newsletter and the boys took their tiny suitcases into the garage as the phone rang. Seth called to see about the storm and Sally told him their plan. The boys hurried back inside to say hello on the downstairs phone.

"Just drive carefully after your meeting ends, if there is snow. Love you guys." Sally noted the concern in his voice and responded.

"Lisa will be with me, and so far, no snow. You be careful too and fly home safely. We love you too." She hung up quickly and they drove to Lisa's.

They walked up to the clubhouse, noting the colder chill in the wind. Steve started promptly and even though there were empty seats, the secretary, Suzanne, spoke each person's name as stragglers stepped in out of the cold. Committee reports were given out of order and Sally read her newsletter page of info, informed by her block captains: five houses for sale, one new baby. The treasurer, Connor, announced with regret another lawsuit against two homeowners who continued to refuse to pay monthly dues.

"I know the question on your minds, so rest assured, the answer is yes. Our lawyer and I made numerous attempts not to go to court. These people refuse to believe our rules will take precedence. The date for their case is March 2, in Orland Park at the courthouse, if any of you are interested in coming." Heated discussion followed for and against going to court, as Daniel their lawyer settled the debate

Brian asked for a few extra minutes for his report on the grounds contract. As he stood up, he wiped his wet forehead and took some papers out of a manila folder. "After spending weeks calling previous contractors as well as new prospects, I found no one to offer the same rate as last year. Each contractor wanted to raise their fee, some by as much as several hundred dollars. I must recommend we agree to a contract with LLS, (Larry's Lawn Service). He did a good job last year and did not raise his rate for the coming year."

He took off his glasses and looked forcefully at each board member, as if to say 'I've done my job, now you do yours and vote for this contract.' He sat down, wiped his wet forehead again and put his glasses back on. "Wait, I forgot something important." He said his daughter couldn't come to this month's meeting and would like to get on their agenda as soon as possible to make her presentation on the accident involving the death of a neighborhood little girl.

Doug asked, "Before I comment on your daughter's accident, let's finish the discussion about the lawn upkeep. Why would he not have a hike in his rate if everyone else did?"

Brian did not stand up again and tapped his pencil on the table a few times before answering. "Most of the contractors wouldn't commit to such a large amount of area to be mowed without hiring additional staff. Last year, Larry learned on the job." He pushed his papers away from him, looking down at them for a minute before he continued. "He figured out a way to minimize costs with the same number of mowers."

"Look guys, we have to go with him or risk another dues increase." There, he said the dreaded words, Dues Increase.

Another lively debate ensued with Steve limiting each person to only two and a half minutes. Even though Doug seemed to be the most vocal against the hiring, the vote passed to hire LLS.

As Mary Jane stood up for her presentation on the clubhouse rentals, Steve interrupted to ask the secretary to call Brian's daughter to schedule her appearance at the next meeting. Mary Jane had a long list of grievances from the holiday parties, continuing into January reservations. "I know you don't want to hear about increases in dues so I've come up with a very simple solution." She took out a list of names from reservations for parties on a long yellow sheet of paper and passed it around the table.

"As you can see from this list, we've had over 14 parties since Thanksgiving and the majority of homeowners paid their $25.00 deposit and had it returned." She looked at each member and took a deep breath before continuing. "I want to up the price for the deposit and only give back a portion. To support my idea, I called four other homeowner associations in neighboring towns and found most charge double."

She sat down, a relaxed look of relief on her face and said to Steve, "Doug can tell you how many nights he's been called over here for noise complaints." She nodded her head at Doug, waiting for him to give more information. Doug added his two cents loudly, yet more positively than usual. The results of the vote were to increase the deposit to fifty dollars and on inspection the next day, if the place is absolutely spotless, half would be returned.

As Suzanne verified the vote, the lights went out. Everyone sat in stunned silence, waiting for them to come back on. After five minutes, Steve went over to the pay phone and called the electric company to report the outage. He heard a recording saying: "due to the snow storm hitting the area many main lines are down. An estimate of when returning power could be restored is unknown." They walked out of the room as carefully as possible; Steve opened the front door. Swirling snow and a whistling wind met them as they walked slowly out to the parking lot.

Sally and Lisa drove home carefully; both were thankful they had only four short blocks to cover

"The boys are sleeping soundly and I'd be worried for you to carry them inside alone and with no electricity," Nate said as they came into the kitchen through the garage.

Lisa nodded her head. "You can sleep on the couch in front of the fire Sally, and we'll be sure and wake you up early enough to get back home and drive your carpool. I'll even make you guys breakfast."

Sally sat down on a kitchen bench and took the cup of tea Nate had made after lighting the gas stove with a match. Lisa took hers as well and said, "Please consider this, Sally. With Seth gone, you'd get really cold and we can keep the fire going."

Sipping the warm tea, Sally realized she'd never been alone in their house with no electricity, and knew their replacement load of wood hadn't been delivered yet. "Guess, we'll be better off here. Thanks so much." She let out a sigh of relief.

"You can use one of my nightgowns and I'll help you make up the couch." Lisa went upstairs to get everything needed for her guest. As the wind howled outside, Sally settled in for another new experience and hoped Seth would get home safely with no closed runways or another diverted flight.

CHAPTER 21
REALITY

On a cold overcast day, Lonnie sat in her car and twisted her purse handle nervously, looking across the street at the Better Baths and Kitchens storefront window. Now almost the third week in February, she had called to make her appointment with Doug. In the back of her mind, she just knew he would be the same person. Joliet, their home town, was so close to Greenebriar, she just couldn't imagine someone else had the same name. She had gone over her conversation with Doug in her mind many times. She locked her car and walked across the street, breathing as calmly as possible. The front door looked ominous, as though guarding a secret inside. She pulled down on her black wool jacket and walked inside, telling herself to remain calm.

"May I help you?" An older man with thinning brown hair approached her. He held out his right hand. "My name is Keith Jones. Welcome to our store. Are you browsing or looking for something specific?"

"Hi Keith. I have an appointment with Mr. Pulchowski. Is he here?" She glanced around the store waiting for his answer.

"Yes he is. I'll go back and tell him you're here while you continue to browse." Lonnie felt nervous and worried at the same time. She walked back to look at the counter filled with brochures and stopped suddenly as she looked at the wall with all the employee pictures hanging in alphabetical order. Doug looked just like himself, only a few more wrinkles across his forehead, a fuller face and no handlebar moustache or shoulder length black curly hair.

She braced herself against the counter. She knew what she dreaded to tell him, for over fourteen years, became a reality when she walked in this door and saw his picture. *Doug is really here.* She tried to get some sort of composure, knowing this would be more difficult than she had imagined in her discouraging dreams.

About the same time of morning, the women's study group met and talked about all the positive feedback from those who went to the regular meeting of the Feingold Association of Northern Illinois. Even though the location had been over an hour drive away, several went to this meeting.

Pamela opened the meeting with prayer and Bible verses for February's agenda of accepting our emotional feelings, as she said "Because Valentine's Day is difficult for many." She read from Psalm 55:1-2, *"Listen to my prayer, O God, do not ignore my plea; hear me and answer me. My thoughts trouble me and I am distraught . ., Oh, that I had the wings of a dove! I would fly away and be at rest. . ."*

"Lord, we lift up those who are distraught and need soothing during this emotional holiday as we learn to become better wives and mothers through Your Word. Bless those who are here and nourish our bodies with this food so lovingly prepared. Amen."

She reminded everyone to get something to eat and drink. The women were divided into groups of three with each group receiving a list of questions and Bible verses to support these questions. They had thirty minutes to read, discuss and prepare a summary for presentation to the others.

For another hour, each group talked about their ideas for using emotional ups and downs more positively. Most of them agreed the job of mother turned out to be a lot harder than they imagined when they dreamed of marriage, many years ago. A great suggestion from the first group encouraged them to phone someone when they were having an emotional problems or breakdowns with their children. Everyone agreed to pick at least one woman from the group as their helper/supporter for the next month and to work hard to use this support to work through emotional upheavals with prayer and positive discussions.

Cynthia, Sally, and Lisa walked home in a chilling wind, agreeing this meeting turned out to be a big help for those who were alone or having problems.

"See you tomorrow for bowling Cynthia." Lisa waved good-bye as they crossed the street and hurried into the warmth of their homes.

Lonnie waited at the main counter staring at Doug's picture on the wall. She felt her stomach churn and gurgle. Then she heard a long sigh announce her name and turned to see Doug, the one and only love of her life. She grasped the counter as her knees shook. Her mind seemed to float up into space as she looked down at him, older and a little heavier, the same man.

"Lonnie, I just can't believe my eyes. I didn't even connect your name since you obviously are now married. Lonnie Favero, Balliteria." He looked down at his message paper with her married name. He extended his hand and grasped hers, shaking fingers and all. He leaned back against the counter and looked deeply into her startled eyes, wide with surprise.

"I had your name from some neighbors and wondered immediately if you were the same person, Doug. I've taken over a month to get up the courage to come in because we do need work done in our bath and kitchen." She stuffed her hands into her jacket pocket and looked around the area to see if anyone stood close enough to hear their conversation.

"Come on back to my desk and let me look at my afternoon appointments. Can you come to lunch?"

She looked at her watch then nodded yes.

Doug looked to the desk behind him and said, "Keith, I'm taking my client out to look at the two rooms they'd like us to remodel. Should be gone at least an hour." Keith checked his office chart and nodded yes as Doug took his jacket off his chair and motioned her out the back door. "Hope you don't mind driving with me?"

Her mind racing, Lonnie decided to suggest some out of the way place to eat, then thought this might not be best if someone saw them. *It's just a business lunch until I say differently, so don't make a big deal out of this,* she thought.

They settled into a booth at a local diner. Doug spoke first after looking at his menu for a little longer than normal.

"I just can't tell you how glad I am to see you. When I came back from Vietnam, your mom said you had transferred to a college out of state. She wouldn't give me your address or phone number because you were engaged." He unfolded his napkin and looked at her with concern. "I was crushed, to say the least. Why didn't you write to me?"

Lonnie had no words to describe how she felt toward her mom, who obviously lied to Doug. She certainly never told Lonnie about his phone call. Her knees shook under the table and her stomach churned, trying to imagine in just a few seconds how differently things might have turned out if she had received his phone call. Her mom died just last year, after her marriage to Hank. There could be no confrontation. She took a sip of her steaming coffee to give herself a minute to compose a somewhat sane sentence.

"I can only say now, how sorry I am to hear what my mom did. I had no idea. There is a very rational reason I didn't write." She paused, looked at him and took another sip of coffee. "This is going to be the hardest thing I've ever had to say." She knew it was now or never, so she took a deep breath to speak the words she'd waited so long to share. The waitress delivered their food just as her mouth opened. She took in another long deep breath, waiting for her to leave.

Doug, unsuspecting, grabbed the mustard and ketchup and then added the onions along with the extra lettuce and tomato slice. "What do you mean? Weren't you engaged?"

He took a big bite of his hamburger, and dipped a large fry into the glob of ketchup in the corner of his plate.

Once again, Lonnie waited. She knew he had to chew this bite before she ruined the rest of his lunch.

"Doug, this is difficult for me to tell you. I've never told another soul what I'm going to share with you. First, I wasn't engaged." She bent her head a little lower as she leaned across the table to whisper.

"Second, I just couldn't write to you because I was so scared. I didn't know what to do with my news, so I told no one and did nothing, but survive, one day at a time."

"What are you talking about?" He really looked at her face now, trying to figure out what she meant. He saw concern and dread in her face, a frown on her mouth. There were tears in her eyes.

She interrupted his sentence by whispering, "Pregnancy. I had our baby and she was adopted." Her hands shook as she grabbed his one hand while his other hand covered his opened mouth. The wide eyes and raised eyebrows showed his sincere shock at this news.

There were a few minutes of absolute silence as Doug digested the sentences he heard, shaking his head back and forth, whispering, "No, no. Why didn't you tell me?" He put his head in both hands, elbows propped on the table and sat there, saying nothing.

"You're telling me I have a daughter out there somewhere?" He lifted his head up and she saw tears form and spill down his cheeks.

"I just can't believe you've kept this secret all these years. How could you do this to me? Didn't you think I had a right to know?"

Lonnie just looked at him, feeling the knot in her stomach tighten, knowing she had probably made another big mistake by not sharing this news with him at the time.

CHAPTER 22
SURPRISE AND SECRETS

Seth secured a schedule everyone liked for the month of March, four days off and three days on. He had finished all his 'fixing-up-the-house' chores during the last two months and realized he would finally be able to work on his model plane. A new project had to be considered when he found two rotting support beams under their back deck. He knew they would have to be replaced. *Guess being a homeowner means the repairs are never finished,* he lamented quietly to himself. He found some graph paper to figure out the correct size of the beams he needed to replace when the phone rang after dinner.

"This is Jeff Crawford. May I speak to Seth Williams?" He ran his fingers through his premature graying black hair. Jeff volunteered to help with one of the major goals in AYSO soccer for this season: to get as many dads involved in coaching as possible. At the organizational meeting, he said, "Sure, I can make some phone calls."

"This is," Seth answered, not recognizing the voice on the other end.

"Seth, I'm helping recruit coaches for this spring session and I know your son Grant played soccer last year. His coach is getting transferred to another state and we need someone to take charge of this team. Will you be available for training and weekly practices?" He kept his voice low key and positive, not demanding.

Overcome with surprise, Seth sat in the kitchen chair looking out at the park across the street. "With my schedule at work changing every single month, there is no way I could be a main coach, Jeff. I'm more than willing to take training, since I know nothing about this game." He took down the calendar beside the phone and flipped to April.

Jeff, not at all prepared for this response, answered with a question, "Where do you work?"

"I work out at the airport and my schedule involves traveling each week where I'm gone for several days, then home. My schedule changes every single month, and I almost never get the same days off." He decided right then maybe he could be some sort of assistant or other type of helper.

Jeff thought a minute before answering. "I'm sure the other parents on the team would be willing to have practice on a different day each week as long as they know which day you'll be here. If you don't mind my asking, what do you do at the airport to have a different schedule each week?"

Seth looked at the calendar, trying to guess the amount of hours he'd need to plan, teach and then attend the weekly games.

"I am a pilot. This sounds like a big time commitment and I'll have to talk this over with my family but I can tell you now, I will be an assistant coach for this first year and then see how this works for me."

Noting a positive determination from this dad, the third he had called tonight, Jeff decided he should take what he could get with this phone call and go on. "All right, Seth. I've put you down for assistant coach. Someone will call you back and tell you about the training. What days are you available this month?"

After Seth hung up, he walked into the bathroom to help get the boys ready for bed.

"Guess what I just signed up to do?"

Two weeks after their initial meeting, Doug came over to Hank and Lonnie's house to take measurements for remodeling their main bathroom. They both had been nervous wrecks at their first get together, and now, even though she felt more comfortable in her home, Lonnie sensed a new set of uncontrollable nervousness take over her thoughts.

"Today is my part-time teaching day Doug, so I only have two and a half hours to give you this morning. You'll have to measure fast." She walked down the narrow hallway pointing to their outdated bathroom of gold and green flowered wallpaper, green tub, toilet and double sinks.

"Wow, you are right; what a designer's nightmare." As Doug took his pad and measuring tape to the bathtub, he looked back at her with a pained expression, creased forehead and tightly knit eyebrows. "I've thought of nothing else but my daughter out there somewhere."

Lonnie started to cry and reached for a tissue. "Please try hard not to make this any more challenging for us."

He interrupted. "Challenging? You have known for over fourteen years and I've had only two weeks to deal with this absolutely brain numbing news. I've really been shell shocked while trying to maintain some sort of composure at my house. I must tell you this has been next to impossible with two rambunctious boys running around all day long." He wrote down measurements on his pad with a shaking hand.

Lonnie noticed this and for a split second remembered when she first found out; *maybe I'm not supportive enough. I never thought how he'd take this news.* "Look Doug, I can't apologize enough for what's happened. I can only control how we work through this now. I have no knowledge of who adopted her, where she is now or when this took place. Maybe we can call the adoption agency and see what kind of information they can give us."

A week later during the Thursday morning bowling league, Lisa talked about Gail's speech about the accident to the team they were bowling against. The members of this team had not known a presentation would be given at the board meeting. One of the bowlers, Margie, an oversized woman, to say the least, stated her thoughts loud enough for all to hear.

"We should have known about this so we could have attended this board meeting. Maybe she could do this again, what do you think, Sally?" She looked at her partners, who were shaking their heads in approval.

"Thanks for your input Margie, I'll bring this up at the next board meeting." Since Seth would be driving the car pool today, Sally and Lisa decided to go out for lunch. No one else could go, so they settled on the neighborhood diner closest to the mall.

"Guess what I received in the mail yesterday?" She grinned while rummaging through her purse to pass an invitation to Lisa.

"Wow, I can't believe you've been out of high school for fifteen years. Are you going?" She looked at the engraved invitation in red and white bold faced letters "I've never been to any of mine since we live so far away, but you could go since you don't have to buy a ticket."

Sally looked up from her menu. "I didn't even think of not having to buy a ticket. Guess I'll tell Seth I want to go and make sure this won't interfere with our vacation to Arizona. The main reason I'm sharing this with you is I need to lose some weight. I wanted to step up our exercise plan besides our daily walks." She held up one arm and shook it, pointing to the jiggle of dangling skin.

"I don't see where you'd lose any weight, Sally. You look fine to me. Everyone has jiggling skin under their arms." She put down her menu, waiting for the waitress to take their order.

"Then I'll go back looking like I did then, at 125. I'm going to let my hair grow out too. Where can we find some exercise classes?"

"I'll check around, but I know some of my neighbors take an aerobic class at the Y, so I can check there first." She looked around for their waitress.

"There is a new program called Stepping, I think. I'd love to shed a few too. Let's just plan on going together. We'll just have to find a day which fits for both of us."

They ordered the soup of the day, split pea with ham and a large salad to share.

"What do you think of Margie's idea to have Gail speak again? You could put the info in next month's newsletter so there would be a good turn-out."

The waitress brought their food and they sipped their soup silently. After Sally took a bite of her salad, she agreed. "You are right Lisa. I'll bring this up at the block captain meeting next week and see what response I get. Maybe April would be better to encourage everyone to think about slowing down with the kids coming back outside to play and soccer practice starting."

"I just can't wait for winter to end and the snow to melt." Lisa said.

We're just not used to this much cold since both of us were raised in southern Missouri."

"I forgot to tell you, Seth volunteered to help with Grant's soccer practices. I think the head coach is Mark Beals. His son Richard is a little older, maybe eight. He's a novice like Grant, so he's staying with the 6-7-8 year old group. Do you know them by any chance?"

"Yes, I do. His wife Hannah is in my ceramics class; you'd really like her, Sally. She's a very busy lady and always comes up with fun stuff to do after our classes. I think she is going to school too, getting a Master's degree." She took another bite of salad and a sip of tea. "Brett still talks about playing soccer and doesn't understand why he must wait until he's five. How's hockey coming along?"

"He likes it so far. I can see this could become another time consuming sport. I really thought skating lessons would be the end. But once a hockey stick had been introduced, Grant couldn't wait to play in a game where he could score goals."

"Do you think Seth would mind if Brett starts learning to play soccer this spring by going to a practice or two with Grant's team?" Sally nodded as she took another bite of her salad wondering if she should have asked Seth first before agreeing with Lisa.

CHAPTER 23
DOUG

Marlene and Doug decided on building an in-ground pool instead of a family room. Although she seemed positive the CCRs did not allow for such construction, Doug assured her he could get approval from the board since he, as an active member, donated so much time to the maintenance and upkeep of the clubhouse and pool.

In early April, Doug had earned a three day week-end from working so much over-time, and decided he'd rent a backhoe to dig up most of their backyard. Marlene and the boys would go visit her parents in Joliet and when they returned Monday night, the yard would be ready for the pool installation.

When the big day arrived, Doug rented a flatbed trailer to haul the backhoe to his property. He drove carefully, turning the corner slowly, into the subdivision. He actually felt relieved he arrived at his backyard with no problems.

His very nosey neighbor from across the street, Thomas Tullis came over first and peered over Doug's fence. Then he walked around the back to an open gate. His tall thin body leaned against the fence, hands on his hips and aggravation showing on his perfectly shaved face.

"What are you doing so early on a Saturday morning, Doug?" His voice, clearly agitated, rose in pitch as he finished his question.

"Good morning to you too, Thomas." Looking at his watch, he reminded Thomas lunch would be in less than two hours.

"Some of us enjoy a quiet day now and then on Saturday mornings, Doug. You haven't answered my question. I don't see any permits displayed." He took off his glasses, cleaned them with a handkerchief and tried to remain calm.

"Look Thomas, I don't have to answer to you. I have only so many hours rental here and I need to keep digging." He felt angry and also worried, knowing he had no permits, much less board approval.

Thomas took a hand off his hip and pointed a shaking finger at Doug. "You do have to answer to me because, like you, I'm a dues paying homeowner here. I know the rules you profess to follow as an elected board member." His voice level continued to rise in what he considered to be justified anger.

Doug turned away and did not answer. He started digging and did not see Thomas leave. He continued to ignore most of the people who came to the gate and peeked inside. If he saw neighbors he recognized, they received a wave. All others were ignored. He worked until six p.m., closed the gate and went inside for a beer and Marlene's lasagna. He knew he'd have to figure out how to get a permit fast and thought he'd call Paul, the board vice president who had been a member of his clubhouse/pool committee.

He slept soundly and awakened to the ringing of his phone.

"Morning, Doug. The boys and I wondered how much dirt you dug up yesterday." Her voice sounded cheerful and awake. He glanced at the clock and his eyes widened quickly. The time showed nine a.m.

"Hi Marlene. Thanks for not calling any earlier. Guess I really needed the extra sleep. You just woke me up." He no longer felt groggy.

"Did you finish digging down to the ten foot limit you decided we'd need?"

"Almost there. You are right about the board's approval. I'm going to call Paul after he comes home from church."

Marlene showed her agreement as she answered, "Great job, Doug. I know how much you want a pool, yet I have a nagging feeling which won't . . ."

"I know dear," he interrupted. "I'll find out and let you know tonight. Tell the boys hi for me. I really need to get started." He said good-bye, hung up, put on his robe and went out front to get the Sunday Chicago Tribune.

As he looked up to a sunny sky, he noticed dark clouds in the northwest. Although he neglected to watch the weather report on the late night news, he realized today might be a shorter work day if this storm arrived before he finished. He hurried through his cereal, juice and coffee while glancing at the sports page to see how the Blackhawks did in the play-off game.

Gulping down his last sip of coffee, he dressed quickly and went outside to start this chore thankful most of his neighbors were in church. After about forty minutes, he saw the storm moving in fast. A huge flash of lightning streaked across the darkening sky. He decided he could make one more scoop. An aroma of gas drifted up to his nose from the latest pile of dark dirt. Doug looked down into the large empty space and froze to the backhoe's uncomfortable metal seat in shock at the sight in front of him.

CHAPTER 24
SHOCK

He looked away quickly and then he forced himself to stare at the unexpected sight before him. He shivered in the cold wind from the approaching storm. A piece of plastic had been uncovered and a bony hand protruded. He glared again, not believing his eyes. A loud clap of thunder rolled across the sky and Doug took this as a sign of bad news. He glanced up at the sky, wondering how long before the rain came. Then he scanned his closest neighbors to make sure no one looked out their window to see his scary find. He realized time would not be on his side if he didn't hurry and decide what to do next.

Rain drops started hitting the cab. Doug carefully moved one more pile of dirt, completely uncovering the plastic package. A faint smell of gas lingered for a little while and he waited until it blew away. He jumped down from the cab into the deep hole, and pulled a

short skeleton out from the grave of dirt. Carefully, he picked up this shocking surprise and struggled to carry it inside his garage through the open side door. He closed the door quickly, locked it and took a deep breath. With a pounding heart and shaking hands he pulled away the covering and found a complete skeleton. He slumped onto the floor, his heart beating so loudly he thought it would explode out of his chest.

"What is this?" he whispered out loud. He put his hands against the wall for support and stood up slowly. He walked over to the whitened bones and noticed, right away, a gold wedding band. Beads of sweat trickled down his face and his heartbeat increased as he put on a pair of work gloves, picked up the bony hand and removed the ring. The inscription read FMD, 6-28-59, Love Always, SMD. He pulled the plastic back over and went back inside the house as quickly as his shaking legs could carry him. He grabbed a beer from the 'fridge, took a large gulp, then another, sat down at the kitchen table and grabbed the phone off the counter. He stood up immediately and walked nervously around the table, cradling the receiver on his shoulder, the extra long cord swinging. Then he put the phone back down on the kitchen table and took a deep breath. Dialing the phone number of the Eden police station with a quivering finger gave him a minute to breathe and figure out what to say. In a quiet voice, he asked to speak with the officer on duty. He explained what happened, stood up again and walked around the table to calm his nerves.

"Please send an unmarked car, no siren, and wait until dark." His voice actually trembled as he spoke in a pleading request. He gave his address, went back to the kitchen table, sat down and took another large gulp of beer. Then he waited, holding his head in his hands as his temples throbbed.

He started talking to himself, out loud. "No pool. Cover up as fast as possible. Tell Marlene the board didn't give approval." He prayed quickly for the body and this person's family, who probably never knew what happened. Most of all, he hoped no one saw him drag the plastic into his garage. He hadn't seen a dead body since Vietnam, although none of them were skeletons. He tried to decide what to say when the police arrived. His hands continued to shake as his legs quivered.

Twenty long minutes later the doorbell rang. He walked over as slowly as possible, trying to regain some sort of composure.

"Good morning, sir. Are you Doug Pulchowski? I'm Officer Sam Gregorczyk. May I come in?"

"Yes, yes I am. Of course, come inside. Thanks so much for not using a siren and coming in an unmarked car; you know how nosy neighbors can be." He spoke slowly. Still shaking from his unexpected find, he looked up into a young, smooth face with blue eyes. He still couldn't believe what happened in his backyard on a quiet Sunday.

"I wish you could have waited until dark." He walked back into his safe kitchen, pointed to the garage door and asked, "Mind if I stay here while you look?"

Officer Sam shook his head and opened the door slowly. He only stayed there about five minutes and returned. His face showed concern, his expression taut and his brown brows scrunched up.

"Now, tell me again what happened, and don't leave anything out." His voice sounded authoritative, yet compassionate.

Doug swallowed, fingering the wedding ring in his pocket. He explained what he did. He still felt unnerved. His voiced sounded shaky and unsure.

"We'll get a forensics team out to scour the area since you moved the body, without authority." His voice tone sounded angry.

"You don't understand sir. The body, I mean skeleton, has obviously been there a very long time; I saw nothing but dirt and the plastic. I have neighbors and . . . I'm on the board . . . and I didn't get any permits, and . . ." He stopped rambling, and took another large gulp of beer. Then he took a deep breath trying to figure out how he'd have to explain himself to his neighbors.

"Take your time, Doug. Probably many of your neighbors know this area used to be a dump site for Chicago's garbage back in the '50's and '60's. No one can fault you for digging up something no one could have imagined . . ."

Doug interrupted. "As I tried to tell you, I have no permits or permission to do what I did. I don't want anyone to see . . . I need to get this covered up quickly so I don't have to explain anything other than I changed my mind and decided on a family room instead of a pool." He felt his point didn't seem to be getting across and tapped his fingers nervously on the table.

Officer Sam tried to show empathy as he looked straight into Doug's fearful face.

"The law is the law. I'll ask if this can be done low key, but unfortunately there are no guarantees in a possible murder case." He walked over to Doug and put a reassuring hand on his shaking shoulder.

"You must get some control here because this is now out of your hands." He put on his hat and turned to leave. "Look Doug, I'll do everything possible, but you have to know this is big news. The reporters who cover the police beat will find out sooner or later."

Doug put his head in his hands, trying to find some solace in this new bit of inconvenient information, knowing there might not be much peace and quiet in his life for a while, something he just couldn't handle right now. He didn't want to deal with what could come from anyone here, much less a bunch of reporters

"Thanks Officer Gregorczyk. I know you're right. At least I'll have tonight to figure something out." He looked out the kitchen window. The storm had passed and a streak of sunshine peeked through a grey cloud.

"Afraid not, Doug. The forensic team will be here tonight."

He walked down the hall and put his hand on the front door handle. "Try to remain calm. Don't anticipate anything just yet."

"I'm sure the rain didn't help, but my concern is getting this very large hole filled up and the backhoe I rented returned by five tomorrow evening." The crease in his forehead tightened as he nervously brushed his fingers through his black hair.

"Please remember to have them come in an unmarked car and no uniforms, alright?"

"Doug, I can't promise anything right now. Since we are such a small area police force, I'll have to call Joliet and find out procedure. Someone will call soon. Good night."

Doug stood up and walked around in a circle, stopping at the stereo, where he popped in an eight track of Beethoven's 5th symphony. He couldn't believe his fate. He walked over to the 'fridge and took out another beer. *What will I tell Marlene?*

CHAPTER 25
FORENSICS

When the phone rang about ten minutes later, Doug actually jumped.

"Hi Doug, this is Ingrid. Can you come over for dinner tonight? Robert thought you could use some company after your long weekend of digging."

She always sounded so upbeat and willing to help any of the ten families who lived on their block. Doug sighed and took a sip of beer.

He put on his best voice and said, "Ingrid, you guys are so thoughtful. You know how much we appreciate all your help. I'm just beat tonight and I won't be good company. Thanks so much for your generous offer. I'll just heat up Marlene's lasagna from last night."

Ingrid, ever persistent, who never gave up on anyone when it came to a meal, replied with a calm voice. "Doug you have to eat, right? I'll just send Jason over with a plate and you can return it tomorrow. Since you know me so well, I'm only taking one answer."

Doug smiled, knowing he'd met his match. The way he felt right now, he'd just as soon have ordered pizza delivery from Lou Malnati. "O.K., you have a deal. I do appreciate your concern. Really I'm fine, just beat." He sat down at the kitchen table and took a deep breath. He realized this horrific night had just begun because he knew who'd be coming over next, a forensic team.

"Tell Jason to ring the doorbell twice and leave the plate. I'm going to take a shower right now. Thanks so much Ingrid. Bye." He hung up and started thinking how he would go about telling Marlene there would be no pool. *Maybe this won't be a problem since I'm really the only one who wanted one.*

Standing under the soothing hot water, steam rising all around, Doug tried to relax. The running heat poured over his tense body. He washed, dried off quickly and put on clean sweats, just as the doorbell rang. Instead of Jason and dinner, two strangers stood in front of him.

The men, in dark pants and white shirts, stood before him solemn as could be. The taller of the two wore a red, white and blue Cubs baseball hat, and dark rimmed glasses. The lower part of his face showed a red beard and moustache.

"May we come in?"

Doug closed the door as quickly as he could, feeling a little nervous knowing Jason could have walked into this mess, a*nd what would I have said to cover?*

"I'm still a little rattled, guys. Come in."

The taller of the two said, "My name is Jeff Martin and my partner is Jon Bednar. We left our car down the block so as not to arouse suspicion, as ordered." Both gave a strong indication they did not like a block long walk. Each carried a small rectangular black bag.

"Look sir, we need to get started. The sooner the better, then we can leave and get this behind you." He spoke rapidly using his hands, while gesturing for the location of the garage.

Doug stuck up his thumb in a jerking motion toward the garage as the doorbell rang twice. He took another deep breath and whispered to himself, "Stay calm and show Jason your good face."

No one stood on his porch, and Doug breathed a sigh of relief as he bent down to pick up a large plate covered with silver foil. He sat down at the kitchen table and savored the smell of Sloppy Joes as he took off the foil. The sandwich filled only one part of the plate. Macaroni salad, chips and carrot sticks covered the rest. He concentrated on eating and pushed tedious thoughts out of his head. Ingrid's delicious dessert finished the meal, sour cream chocolate chip cake. How many times had he devoured this at block parties? Comfort food might just get him through this night. He faced a perilous path of unanswered questions and had no idea how many roadblocks would be in his way. He changed the eight track tape from a symphony to a Bee Gees eight track. He grabbed his beer and sat down to finish the Sunday paper.

About thirty-five minutes later the two men emerged, pulling off their plastic gloves and looking a little worn out. "Since it is dark now," Jeff said, "I'm going down the block to get our car and pull up to your back gate. We'll carry out the skeleton as quickly as possible." He actually looked at Doug with some concern, putting one hand on his shoulder.

"Sorry you've had such a tough time, sir. Officer Gregorczyk told us to remind you to go down to the Eden police station tomorrow and sign some papers pertaining to this investigation." He started out the back door then turned around, looking intently at Doug with genuine concern.

"Sometimes we forget what it's like for a greenhorn to see their first dead body, much less a skeleton." He sounded sincere and worried a little about Doug's attitude.

Doug looked surprised. His eyebrows rose up on his creased forehead. "Thanks so much for your patience with me. I do appreciate your efforts here tonight. I'm just beat. You can imagine I sure didn't expect today to be like this."

After they took the skeleton and left, Doug took out a bottle of Johnny Walker Black and poured himself a tall shot. He downed the liquor in one large gulp and went over to his recliner, to finish reading the newspaper.

About twenty minutes later, the ringing telephone woke him from a sound sleep. "Hi Doug. We are so anxious to hear about your day," Marlene started.

He interrupted her. "Before you go any further, Marlene, you were right. We can't build our pool, so tomorrow I'm putting all the dirt back into the hole. After it settles, we'll put on the family room." He felt so relieved to pass along this little white lie

"Shall I expect you guys for dinner? I'd really like to take you and the boys out for your favorite pizza, Lou Malnati's."

"O.K., Doug. I'm really glad you checked on the pool before we put in the cement. I think a family room will be perfect." Her voice sounded so upbeat and not at all upset about the lost pool. Doug felt another burden lift off his weary shoulders.

"We are planning to leave just after lunch, so we'll be home in plenty of time to go out to dinner."

"Great. See you then. Bye." He hung up with a smile on his face

Greenebriar's Garbage

while his fingers turned the ring in his pocket around and around. *How can I turn this error into my favor? Bet someone would pay a lot for this information.*

He slept soundly. After breakfast he attacked the hole with the backhoe using speed and finesse to replace all the dirt. He finished just after lunch and decided a quick bowl of soup would suffice. He loaded the backhoe onto the trailer and called the police station to say he'd stop by after he returned the machinery.

Fingering the ring as he walked into the police station, he felt nervous.

"I need to speak to Officer Gregorczyk; is he here?"

The receptionist, a young teen with long black hair and dark red streaks, pointed behind her, then jerked her hand left and put up two fingers. Doug walked down the hallway, turned left and knocked on the second door.

He heard, "Door's open, come on in."

"Thanks for taking care of this, Doug." Sam stood up and offered his right hand which Doug shook.

"I appreciate you handling this so quickly and quietly. I have to tell you I sure slept better last night." He smiled just a little.

Sam, however, did not appear to be the least bit jovial. He picked up a #2 yellow pencil and a pen and passed them to Doug along with a pile of papers. His thinning brows knitted together as he spoke firmly.

"You must fill out each page now. I pressed hard on your behalf to let you fill in that hole without further investigation. You had a good point about the skeleton having nothing forensics could really check. Since it had been wrapped up in plastic, whatever might have been around it is certainly long gone." He grimaced.

Surprised by his gravity, Doug replied quickly, "Thanks so much, Officer. I really appreciate your efforts here. Where can I go to write?"

"You can stay here. I need to make some calls to the forensics office in Joliet and see what they found out about the skeleton. I'll be gone about fifteen minutes. Need any coffee? Since we'll probably be speaking a lot more, just call me Sam." His voice sounded efficient and just loud enough to get his message across.

After about twenty minutes of writing, checking boxes and answering pages of questions, Doug put down his pen just as Sam returned.

"About done?" He seemed to be in a hurry as his words flew out of his mouth.

"Yes I am. If you can't read my writing, or have any questions, just call me at work or home and identify yourself only as Sam, no more."

"Sure thing." He took the packet, walked to his desk and sat down, shaking his head as though he too couldn't believe what happened to Doug. He did not expect to get approval from his Captain for the hole to get covered up without a more thorough investigation of the site. He knew how difficult a job the forensic team had. Trying to identify a skeleton buried many years in plastic would probably have to be sent to Chicago or maybe even another state. He immediately wondered about a mob connection.

Doug walked outside to a bright sunny day, fingering the ring in his pocket which he neglected to mention in his long report.

CHAPTER 26
UNRESOLVED

Doug managed to get through the rest of the week and the next one while May marched in with the first spring flowers, bringing color to his front yard. Marlene spent her free time calling contractors to get references and prices to put on their family room addition. She also wrote the proposal to the board of directors for their permit.

He had a busy work schedule because his fellow employees needed to display all the new bath and kitchen fixtures they bought in March at the spring trade show at the McCormick Center in downtown Chicago. This turned out to be a hectic month for the store as a lot of homeowners had waited patiently for these new purchases to be displayed so they could pick out their choices and get started on their remodeling projects before summer.

"Thanks for calling Better Baths and Kitchens. This is Doug Pulchowski. How may I help you today?"

"Hi Doug, this is Sam." He took a deep breath, knowing the information would not be what Doug had expected. "I've received the final report and wanted to let you know the findings are inconclusive. No one can make positive identification since there were no teeth in the mouth or hair follicles on the head. I'm going to give everything to the Joliet police. We are just a small force for the five subdivisions here in Eden."

"Thanks for calling, Sam. I'm disappointed, but maybe this can be my new project. I've really become interested in dumps and what rules they had for piling up trash in open spaces back then." He terminated the conversation and went back to unpacking boxes, trying to decide where his display would be located.

The chilly spring continued well into May. Tulips bloomed in many front yards, while a colorful addition of pansies poked out from scattered snow piles planted by brave gardeners who started their flower beds early. Grey skies and a daily whistling wind kept the cold hovering over the subdivision; many children wore coats, hats and gloves to soccer practices and when walking to school.

After seven months as a volunteer board member, Sally felt a little more comfortable with her job. Most of the block captains and some board members worked hard to use the necessary information from Gail's presentation to get the speed limits lowered in all the Briar neighborhoods. Yet there seemed to be some sort of subterfuge among some board members which she just couldn't figure out. At some meetings, she watched confusing behavior. Of course no one knew about the trauma Doug had experienced the last two months with finding a skeleton and dealing with the police. He sometimes seemed a little more high-strung at meetings. He continued questioning every voting decision as his tone of voice rose and his face contorted at each confrontation. All lawsuits against the HOA had been won in their favor and the heat problem with parties at the clubhouse worked more smoothly after the addition of the heating control device. The supplemental money coming from party cleanup deposits helped balance their finances more than anyone imagined. With a minimum of two parties a week, at $25.00 per party, the treasurer picked up at least two hundred extra dollars a month. The social committee had big plans for the summer schedule: two tennis tournaments, three barbecues and a Fourth of July dance, including a volunteer fireworks show. There were at least two private parties per week through August.

Soccer practices had been arranged with no conflict in Seth's schedule for May. He and Mark seemed to work well together as Mark did know something about the game and rules for playing. Both men took the AYSO training and passed the written tests for coaching and refereeing. Grant enjoyed learning how to play, and the days Garrett tagged along brought a new closeness to the three of them.

For his final test of the year in second grade Spanish, Grant practiced with his mom, adding the new sentences he needed to memorize.

"Hola, señora, ¿Qué tal? Me llamo Grant. ¿Cómo se llama? ¿Que día es hoy; sabes la fecha? Hoy es jueves, el veinte y cinco de mayo. Me gusta aprender español. Hasta luego."

Marlene volunteered to be in charge of both soccer teams for her boys and always seemed to have phone calls to make for bringing juice and fruit for snacks. Today, she decided to call in reverse order and dialed the Williams family first.

"Hi Sally, this is Marlene. I'm calling for May juice assignments. Do you have a particular week you would like to bring snacks?"

"No I don't, so I'll just take the first weekend. Don't you have your older son's team as well?" Before Marlene could answer, Sally said, "I'd like to volunteer to take care of this team since I have already talked to Hannah, Mark's wife, and she decided to help organize the parents for snacks and car pooling."

"Really? This would be great. Thanks so much."

"Grant is really enjoying having his dad help coach his team. He is looking forward to starting second grade at the new elementary school. You are so lucky since your boys will only have to walk half a block. Is Josh looking forward to second grade?"

Marlene wrapped the phone cord around her fingers nervously. "He's had a little more difficulty adjusting to first grade since he's one of the heaviest boys in class. We hoped he'd be able to loose weight with all the running soccer requires."

Sally sensed her frustration and remembered some of the snide comments made at the soccer field. "Maybe summer camp will help Josh gain more confidence. Did you get the advertisement brochure? It says players will receive one on one instruction."

She wrote down the date for snacks on the calendar and waited for Marlene's response.

"Parenting can be so hard." Her voice lowered in pitch, trailing to barely a whisper.

"Learning a new sport is always a challenge, Marlene. I bet you and Doug will get him on the right track during the summer. I've heard the head of our AYSO is really concerned with some of the snacks parents are bringing and is stressing only water and orange slices instead of cookies and soda."

Marlene sighed. "Paul and Patsy really came down on the Cub Scout leaders because when their boys came home from meetings, they were really wired after having soda and candy. I've heard Patsy is really involved with this Feingold group and has worked hard to change the leader's ideas of snacks."

Sally smiled, remembering her first meeting with this group and their constant support when they decided this might be the way to go for Garrett's restlessness. As she brushed her auburn bangs off her forehead, she decided to add some more positive thoughts about this group and invited Marlene to the next meeting.

The May Study Group continued their focus on women, with emphasis on the wife and mother role, because so many seemed to need help. The major concern they shared had to do with how much more difficult managing a household became as the children grew up and had different wants and needs, such as soccer practice or music and dance lessons. The majority concurred with the mentor idea from a previous meeting and shared how just calling one person helped them a lot when they felt stressed. The suggested book for everyone to read for encouragement had been well received by the group, Norman V. Peale, <u>The Power of Positive Thinking</u>. Several women had suggested this book was a phenomenal help to them on days when they just couldn't seem to function any better than a robot. "Laughter seems to have become something from the past, before children," said one of the invited guests.

Several of the specific bathroom items Lonnie and Hank had picked out for their remodel project were on back order. Doug had difficulty talking to her regularly with his family room construction project getting started. There had been a few arguments to obtain the board's approval at the May meeting. He decided to call Lonnie and set up a lunch date to continue a conversation he had never expected

"Mrs. Balliteria, this is Doug from Better Baths and Kitchens calling

Greenebriar's Garbage

to set up an appointment." He hung up and decided immediately to contact some of his other walk-ins to set up dates for their projects just in case his calls and appointments were monitored. He felt a little nervous thinking someone might wonder why he called her so frequently.

Lonnie finally called back a few days later. "With the end of the school year, I just haven't been able to return your calls. Hank surprised me for our anniversary with a month long cruise, leaving two days after school ends, so looks like I'll have to put the remodeling on hold 'til we get back."

He hung up the phone, disappointed, because he wanted Lonnie to contact the adoption agency in Joliet. He then decided immediately to finish his research on the owner of the former garbage dump and put into action his idea to get a little extra money each month. Almost every night, Doug would look at the wedding band he hid in a desk drawer and wondered if his research at the library would ever come up with any answers. He finally found a list of all marriages in Chicago for the date inscribed on the ring and so far, none of the names matched the initials inscribed inside the band. His meddling mind continued to have unrealistic ideas float around his overworked brain trying to figure out a way to have this work in his favor.

As another way to clear his mind, Doug really enjoyed the time he spent with his sons at soccer games on Saturday. The finale for the spring season would be a soccer tournament with two neighboring home owner associations on the Memorial Day holiday weekend. Because of the block captain's involvement with these groups about lowering the speed limits, someone decided this would be a great holiday get together. Doug wanted to get more involved with this game since his boys enjoyed playing so much. He had to work some Saturdays. Sometimes he felt so overloaded with what needed to be done at home, at work and with his children. The most overwhelming problem for him now involved what he wanted to do with the information Lonnie sprung on him: find a daughter he never knew existed. *Wouldn't my life be great if I could just run far away for a while?* He wanted to hide in a perfectly heated cave stocked with his favorite food and beverages where he didn't have to plan, talk to anyone or think about anything.

CHAPTER 27
QUITING

The June board meeting started a little late. Steve, the president, who always arrived early, showed up thirty minutes after Vice President Paul decided he'd better get started. Steve looked a little worse for the wear, as some would quote an old saying. The secretary and treasurer had already given their reports, so everyone turned to watch him walk in, slowly, head down.

"Thanks for starting the meeting, Paul. I heard some disturbing news from two phone calls I took as I headed out the door tonight. Seems some people on this board are receiving what I'd call 'kick-backs' for services rendered, and others outright bribes. We need to go into closed session right away." His face looked tense and he grimaced as he looked at each board member while he spoke.

A homeowner attending the meeting stood up and asked, "What about when we are supposed to be able to ask questions and get some things settled? Can't we say our piece first, and then leave? I don't want to wait until next month to get this cleared up." He remained standing, looking from one board member to another for support.

Paul, who stood in front of the board, had not yet yielded to Steve. He looked around the table at nodding heads and addressed the homeowner. "Please identify yourself and state your concern. Then we can decide." Steve looked at Paul and mouthed 'Thanks" as he took over the podium.

"My name is Dominic Domenici. My wife, Louise is a block captain and we've lived here almost three years. The reason I'm here is because Jack Czolowski and I had a conversation with Larry, of Larry's Lawn Service. Jack is the husband of block captain board member Andrea, for those of you who don't recognize the name." He shifted his weight on a tall, thin body, from one foot to another, uncomfortable to be put in this position of filing a complaint.

"Anyway, Larry told me the only reason he continued this job had to do with a deal made with your board member, Brian. Since you've just mentioned kick-backs, Steve, maybe my complaint falls under this. I'd like to voice my concern and then if I must, I'll leave." His voice sounded soft and he spoke slowly as he looked at each board member.

Steve's brows crunched up tightly and his jaw clenched shut immediately as he looked over at Brian, who looked down to the table while his face flushed a bright pink. Steve tapped his fingers nervously on the podium. "Do I hear a motion to listen to Dominic's complaint first before we go into closed session?"

The motion passed and everyone looked from Brian to Dominic as Brian shifted his heavy body in the too small chair. When Dominic finished his statement, almost everyone stared at Brian, mouths open and eyes wide.

"Thank you for giving us this important information Dominic. If we have any questions later, someone will get back to you. I would like to go into closed session now."

Another motion passed. Dominic picked up his jacket and left by the front door.

"Brian, a serious charge has been made. Please give us the courtesy of an explanation before you lose this volunteer position tonight."

Brian, uncomfortable in a situation he'd been placed in unexpectedly, wiped his brow with the back of his pudgy hand, took off his glasses, closed and then opened his eyes. He took a deep breath before speaking.

"Yes I did make a deal with Larry. He did a good job for us last year. I didn't like any of the other lawn services, even though two did come in under his price."

He looked around the table at the gasps from his last sentence. "It's really no big deal. I just asked him to mow the lawns of some of our board members and mine in exchange for a guarantee of his company getting our mowing contract."

"Wait a minute Brian," Paul said.

Mary Jane interrupted him. "Is this why Larry came to my house and said he'd mow our lawn free for the summer?" Paul and Ingrid looked over at her, surprised and then nodded in agreement with her question.

"Look guys, this is done often in business. I didn't ask you because I thought you'd support my getting you free lawn mowing." He spoke a little faster with each sentence.

The treasurer Connor shook his head and added, "Ruth said something about free lawn mowing last week. I didn't even pay attention because I didn't make the connection with Larry."

Paul punched the table. "Your wife is told you'd get free lawn mowing and you didn't make any connection? What's with you guys?" His face showed disgust, his mouth in a frown.

Steve held up his hand, "Quiet, everyone. Let's keep this as controlled as possible. The phone call I received verifies all this. Jack is the one who called, telling me Dominic had planned to come here and tell us this information. Knowing there were lower bids you didn't even consider Brian is a very serious charge."

Another call Steve took had to do with favoritism for clubhouse parties. He then told Mary Jane the charge leveled at her committee for conflicts in rental dates. There had been preference given to some on the board. There were also problems with the pool maintenance crew. Doug blew up immediately.

"I'd like to know specifically what they said because I have very good notes and I've saved all the receipts for everything bought for keeping the pool chlorine current. Who said I didn't do my job? I want some names now, Steve." His voice rose with each sentence

The bickering and questioning continued for quite a while. Sally finally asked a question to try and get everyone back on track. "What do the CCRs (association rules) say about this type of situation, Steve?" She looked at each board member. "Did anyone break any rule which says they must quit? These are volunteer jobs, right?"

The secretary, Suzanne, quickly took out her copy of the rules. They were kept in the notebook for monthly minutes. She motioned she'd look through them as quickly as possible to answer this question.

"Look Steve, all of us volunteer for this association, and frankly, I don't think getting a free lawn mowing for a few months is that big of a deal." Connor looked around the table at each board member. "Do you really think this is cause for dismissal?"

Andrea spoke next. "I was home and heard Jack's point of view after speaking to Larry. I don't think this is the right way to go. If Larry had volunteered to mow lawns for free, fine with me. To be coerced by Brian is another problem altogether."

Sally looked at Paul, Ingrid, Mary Jane and Connor then asked, "I'm trying to figure out if you didn't like the idea of free mowing or you just haven't decided whether to accept this or not. Can I have a decision from each of you now?"

Brian interrupted before they could answer. "Look, this is nothing new; remember we live in Chicago." He had put his glasses back on by now and his face color had returned to normal. "Larry really didn't put up much of a disagreement when this had been presented to him. He really wanted this job. Look guys, we're only talking about five lawns."

"I don't get this, Brian" Steve looked at him intently. "You're telling me this is a deal you made with him before you came to the board meeting? You argued so fiercely for him, never mentioning the two other lawn services gave you a lower bid."

He looked over at Suzanne, still flipping through the pages of the CCRs. "Suzanne, when you finish there, would you go to the January minutes and read back exactly what Brian said about the lawn services bids?"

Steve sat down to regain some composure. Everyone whispered to each other. About a minute later he stood up, talking to Mary Jane next. "Can you explain these charges about you giving preferential treatment for dates for parties?"

Put on the spot, Mary Jane shifted her ample frame in her chair and pushed her brown bangs off her creased forehead with a shaking hand of perfectly polished red fingernails. She unbuttoned the top button of her red pinstriped blouse and dotted her glistening neck with a handkerchief before she answered.

"Yes, I did give preferential treatment to some board members and close friends who needed specific dates. Everyone who wanted a party did get a date in the month they requested, just not on a specific date for some." Her entire body seemed to let out a large sigh of relief as she looked to those board members whom she knew had wanted specific dates when other parties had already been scheduled.

Suzanne quoted from the rules of the association which stated specifically:'board members could not receive any preferential treatment of any kind.' She asked Steve. "Should I call Daniel?"

Steve answered curtly. "No, he's supposed to be here."

Pandemonium passed around the table as each board member tried to get their point of view heard, either about getting preferential treatment for parties or accepting free lawn moving services. Some voices rose in pitch and became louder after Suzanne read the rules.
There seemed to be some sort of unspoken uniformity all of a sudden as each announced their resignation

Paul, trying to keep some order, asked each to reconsider after Steve offered his resignation first.

"This is a volunteer job and I sure don't want to spend any extra effort where I'm not appreciated," Andrea said.

"I don't care what the rules say. Having a party or two is the least amount of repayment I can get for the hours I spend on some of this stuff," said Mary Jane.

"Sure never thought I'd get busted for a free lawn mowing proposal," Brian muttered.

"If you don't like what I'm doing here, you can shove it. I quit too," Ingrid responded quickly.

"You know, I've put up with a lot of crap from this group and I'm in agreement here. You don't appreciate my efforts, I would sure rather be home with my family," Doug almost yelled at everyone.

Within less than ten minutes, everyone but Sally and Paul had walked out the door. As they sat there in stunned silence, Paul looked at her, unprepared for what just happened. He spoke first. "I sure didn't expect this, did you?"

"No I didn't. Yet, these past few months, there seemed to be an underlying current among some members which I just couldn't put my finger on. I'm just wondering how many really did know about some of this. Tonight everything seemed to fall in place with the party and lawn mowing stuff."

They stared at each other, trying to figure out what to do next. Sally took the secretary's notebook and stopped the tape recorder. About five minutes later the front door opened. Both looked to see if by chance, they were all coming back. Daniel Gibson, the board lawyer strolled in, looking confused to see only two people sitting at a table.

CHAPTER 28
TEMPORARY

Daniel looked at the silent scene before him, two homeowner board members sitting in a stunned stupor. After he found out what happened, he too sat down quietly in complete surprise.

When Sally returned home, about thirty minutes later, Seth asked why she came home so early, remembering most meetings lasted at least three hours.

"Well, you are now looking at the new temporary president. Everyone quit." She looked overwhelmed, her forehead deeply creased, and her eyes looking tired. "Paul and I are the only ones who didn't resign. I just can't believe it. We have so much stuff planned for the summer." She just stood there, looking at him for a positive response.

Seth, amazed by her attitude, said, "You can't be president. You have so much on your plate now. We already have vacation planned for August."

She knew he wouldn't approve when Paul and Daniel both agreed she should take over. "I'm going to make a cup of tea first. Then we can talk about you giving me a little more support and a vote of confidence." She walked into the kitchen and called back out, "I can too do this."

When she returned to the living room, she looked at her dear husband who sometimes behaved so belligerently when her spare time became an issue. She turned down the volume on the radio station playing calming classical music.

"The first thing I'm going to do is find a temporary board until the annual meeting in November. This is only going to continue for four months." She took a long slow sip of lemon tea to gather her thoughts and hoped Seth would change his attitude.

He looked at her intently, remembering how he fell in love with her free spirit attitude over ten years ago. He knew she'd just love this challenge. Soccer would not start until the last week in August. There

Greenebriar's Garbage

might be another mother or two who'd volunteer to do snacks and car pooling. Seth sucked in his breath, smiled lovingly at her and took a deep breath before saying something he had not planned.

"What can I do to help?"

Her eyes widened in complete surprise, never expecting this offer. She took another sip of tea before she replied.

"Really? You'd be a big help if you'd take care of the boys tomorrow for breakfast and lunch so I can concentrate on making all the phone calls I need to find eight replacements. Dinner is all planned, so I should have everything done before then." She leaned over and gave him a hug.

A bright sunny day awakened the Williams family as the phone rang before 8:30 a.m. Lisa launched into her list of questions.

"This really needs to wait until our afternoon walk because I have a lot of phone calls to make . . . ."

Her walking partner interrupted. "Sally, this is something I can do. I'll call everyone I know to help find replacements. Please, let me help."

They talked for about fifteen minutes, going over job descriptions and potential candidates for these positions. Lisa agreed with Paul and Daniel. A new board should be picked before anyone who resigned had second thoughts. For almost three hours, with only a break for lunch, which Seth made, Sally called over thirty people before she had her slots filled. About one p.m. Lisa called back, her task completed. Sally called Paul at work to tell him the results of her calls. They agreed to hold a short board meeting Thursday night. Then she called all those who resigned and told them who their replacements were, asking for all files to be delivered before 6:00 p.m. Thursday night.

The new members were: Leah Lansing, secretary, Chris Kolanos, treasurer, Alexandra Hyatt, block captains, Mike Smith, property maintenance, Patty Breslford, membership, Emil Galloway, pool, and Nancy VandeVenter, social activities. Even though Nancy already had volunteered to be a block captain for this year, she assured Sally she could do both. Karen Murray finally called back to say she'd do clubhouse rental.

For all the arguments started by some of these former board

volunteers, who had called Sally during the morning marathon of calls, there was only one answer: talk to the association lawyer Daniel Gibson.

When four o'clock arrived, they were both ready for their afternoon walk. Sally's jaw actually hurt from doing so much talking. She succumbed to Lisa controlling their conversation by asking all her questions first.

"Did you have any idea some board members were getting preferential treatment for booking parties or having their lawn mowed for free? What did you do when they quit? Did they leave together or resign together?"

Sally rolled her eyes and shook her head. "No and no. I'm still just a little overwhelmed and I sure hope this will be settled by Thursday night. I think Patty will do a good job with membership and we've already scheduled her first meeting with the block captains for Friday morning." She looked at Lisa with a broad grin. "I really appreciate your help with the calls this morning; thanks so much. What pleased me most and what I really didn't expect, was everyone's willingness to step up to the plate after I explained what happened."

Lisa asked; "Since next week is our final get together for the study group for the summer, don't you wonder if Ingrid, Mary Jane, Andrea and Brian's wife, Anna will show up? Maybe we could change the conversation to compassion and forgiveness."

The walk ended none too soon and Sally started dinner right away. She had planned another breakfast favorite, sourdough pancakes, sausage and cantaloupe. The boys shared their fun day of playing soccer with a quick game Seth organized after lunch. Grant told his mom how much he liked having breakfast for dinner when they could enjoy eating instead of gobbling down a quick bite on school days and then rushing out to catch the bus. Seth looked at his boys, knowing what a tough time his wife had with the board resigning. He clapped his hands and looked at his wife saying, "Good dinner, Mom." Grant and Garrett looked at him and smiled at her saying, "Good dinner, Mom, thanks."

"I'll be glad when we can walk to our new school," Grant said.

The boys helped Seth clean up when another phone call came in from a disgruntled former board member. Speaking in a frustrated tone, her voice level going up and down, Ingrid droned on and on about the social activities already planned. She just knew her real estate business would suffer. Right away, Sally decided she just wouldn't listen to another adult whine away over a past decision they now regretted.

"Look Ingrid, tomorrow you can just bring all your contact information for the summer activities along with your file. I'll give the information to Nancy before the meeting. She'll need to call these people immediately so they won't be bothering you for decisions you can't make anymore. Our lawyer said I am within the law for what association rules cover and don't cover on this mess you guys left."

She grabbed her notebook to go over the list of activities already scheduled so nothing would be forgotten "Nancy is also a block captain, and well organized. She's home all day with her children and wants everything wrapped up in a perfectly finished package to present at our next board meeting." She looked out the kitchen window at a beautiful red sunset of orange, pink, and blue clouds, knowing 'red sky at night' meant a good day tomorrow.

"Maybe you should have thought this through a little more, Ingrid. The decisions are already made and you can't change your mind now. In a few days, after you've had a little more time to calm down, would you help Nancy as a committee member?"

Trying to end this conversation as quickly as possible so there'd be time for their stories, Sally added, "I've been on the phone most of the day; we can talk more tomorrow if you remember something else. I have to get the boys ready for bed. Bye." Without waiting for a response, she hung up.

Walking down the hallway, she heard Seth reading to the boys and decided to wait 'til he finished before saying goodnight. Once again, she felt relieved when he took over today and she said a quick prayer, thanking God for having Seth home this week.

After their showers, Seth and Sally sat in bed, books in hand. Before he started reading, he stroked her arm gently. "I'm so proud of you.

Today could have really been a lot more difficult, from the conversations I overheard. You handled everyone with great finesse."

She put down her book, surprised to hear such a compliment, and smiled at him. "Thank you so much for taking care of the boys today. Sounds like they had fun." She put her book on the night stand and yawned. "Guess I'll read tomorrow; I'm so tired." She fluffed her pillow, snuggled up to him and fell asleep in seconds.

CHAPTER 29
MEETINGS

The next day passed quickly. Sally felt anxious about the board meeting. During the afternoon walk she picked Lisa's brain, hoping not to forget anything for the initial board meeting and the one with the new block captain chair, Alexandra, on Friday morning. Another concern had been getting the rest of the minutes from Suzanne, who told Sally about her family vacation; they were leaving tomorrow.

"I can go over and get it when I pick up Brett this afternoon, after our walk. He's playing at the house next door."

"Great. Lisa, you are a lifesaver this week. Can you also be sure to get the box of tapes from this year's meetings?" With the walk over, Sally went home in no hurry. Knowing about the board meeting, Seth had planned to barbecue burgers for dinner. This had been his way to help out during a very busy week.

The board meeting went better than Sally imagined. All former members but one had submitted their files to someone to give to their replacements. Each had read the information. She and Paul thanked these new members enough times as to make some uncomfortable, so Daniel stepped in to assure everyone no laws were broken.

The plans were set for the rest of the summer, and each confirmed what they were to do, agreeing to come to the regular meeting in July. The signatures were going to be changed tomorrow, so any bills wouldn't be left unpaid. In less than two hours, everyone seemed secure in understanding the information necessary to help the summer plans continue with no interruption.

Sally went home, confident in what they had done. She now worried about the block captains adjusting to a new person in charge, again sure of her choice with Patty. The boys were already in bed. Seth sat in the living room, book on his stomach, his eyes closed. She went into the kitchen to make her tea and reviewed everything for tomorrow's meeting. Later, after waking Seth, they took their showers and fell into bed, ending another exhausting, emotional day.

The next morning she noticed his suitcase in the corner, and felt badly she had not remembered he was leaving on a three-day trip. After breakfast, the boys tried to help him carry his flight bag and suitcase down to the truck. "I'm going to be in Bangor, shall I bring home some lobster?" He waved good-bye, reminding them he'd be home soon.

Lisa called to see if the boys wanted to come over and play with Brett during the block captain meeting. "I'll ask them and call you back. I completely forgot Seth had to leave today for his trip. I still need to make a coffee cake for the meeting."

Sally took out everything to make her snack as quickly as possible when the phone ran again. Grant grabbed the receiver.

"It's Mrs. Hansen, Mom."

"Sally, I'm coming to the meeting in place of Andrea who couldn't get off work this morning with such short notice. Can I bring the girls over since I haven't been able to get a sitter?"

She looked outside to a cloudy sky and put her hand over the mouth piece as she whispered to Grant, "Do you mind if Janey and Christy come over to play while we have our meeting?"

"No I don't, mom."

Sally answered, "Not a problem, Barbara."

After putting two cakes in the oven, she took out some grapes, rinsed them and sliced some cantaloupe to put on a serving plate. She made a pot of coffee and put the water on for tea, arranging different choices of tea bags in a basket. Then she called Lisa to tell her the Hansen girls were coming over since a babysitter couldn't be found.

"Thanks again for offering to watch the boys; we are set."

Patty came over fifteen minutes early to get her questions answered. She drank her cup of tea first before setting up her agenda on the poster board Sally provided. Then Alexandra came, meeting Patty for the first time. By ten, everyone had arrived and started filling their plates and cups. After introductions had been made, Louise gave her report on lowering the speed limits. Sally told them Gail would be presenting her speech about the accident at the August board meeting. There were homeowners who were interested in hearing her version of the judge ordered story.

Louise Domenici thanked Sally for responding so quickly to get the board back on the right track after her husband Domenic had made his allegations at the regular meeting Tuesday night. She asked if she could be first to give her report since she had a very sad story to share and needed everyone's help. "One of the women on my block, Lydia, had been visiting her elderly parents in California about three times a year. Her latest visit, last month, had been to show off her newest addition to their family, a little boy, about two months old. Her husband told her he'd stay home with their three-year-old son and take Friday off." Louise choked and tears formed in her eyes. "When she came home on Monday, imagine her shock when she found a red hairbrush with long blonde strands of hair in the bathroom."

Nearly everyone made some audible sound to show their surprise, some immediately whispering to each other what might be coming next.

By now, most knew to wait until the story finished before adding their two cents.

"After composing herself, she confronted her husband who freely admitted he invited his girlfriend over for the three day weekend. Then he told her they had been together about four months, seeing each other weekly."

In her new position as chair of the block captains, Patty, piqued by curiosity and genuine concern, asked, "What can we do to help her now, Louise?"

Helen Franks jumped right in by answering, "My husband, Darwin is an attorney. He and one of the partners in his firm specialize in problematic divorces. Do you think she'd consider meeting with him?"

Louise said she'd pass along the helpful information. There were no other traumatic troubles to report and after all gave their block information, the meeting closed just before noon.

CHAPTER 30
WOMEN'S GROUP

The following Wednesday, Lisa and Sally walked to the study group, pleased to see a bright, sunny day. Not one of the former board members showed up and Pamela seemed very happy to welcome the new board members: Leah, Alexandra, Patty, Karen and Nancy, as well as wives of the male volunteer members: Ruth Kolanos, Maxine Smith, and Glenda Galloway. Most of the block captains were there, too.

Since this would be their last meeting for two months, after the opening prayer, Pamela asked if anyone wanted to talk about the recent actions of the board. Seeing a lot of nodding heads, she read a Bible verse on friendship and forgiveness: "If anyone sins because they do not speak up when they hear a public charge to testify regarding something they have seen or learned about, they will be held responsible.: Leviticus 5:1 and, "...so in everything, do to others what you would have them do to you..." Matthew 7:12

"I spent a little time looking for these verses because I know some of you are still concerned after Jack opened a Pandora's box and Dominic backed him at the board meeting last week."

A lot of opinions were aired, both positive and negative. The ceramics teacher, Babs Sanchez, and Barbara Hansen seemed to be the only ones who didn't think there had been anything out-of-line with the preferential treatment given to board members planning parties.

"You guys work way too hard and give up a lot of your spare time," Babs said. "If having a party at the clubhouse is one of the benefits, why not get first choice of dates?"

"When we wanted a party last fall, Mary Jane told me right away a board member wanted the same night. We changed our date; no big deal. I just needed to make a few extra phone calls," Barbara added.

The conversation lasted a little longer than Pamela planned. Because they used <u>The Power of Positive Thinking</u> again, their format changed just a little. With some luck, she tried to focus everyone's thoughts on the chapter they were to discuss today before giving out the reading assignment for July and August. Most of them still wanted to talk about the former and new board members, so the meeting lasted a little longer.

"I'd like to close with a verse from Luke 6:37. 'Do not judge, and you will not be judged. Do not condemn, and you will not be condemned. Forgive, and you will be forgiven.' This has been a difficult situation with the board, but passing along gossip won't help anyone. Enjoy summer and we'll see you in September."

The rest of the day passed quickly, with the boys playing and waiting patiently for their dad to come home. For a break, after lunch, they walked the three blocks to see the new elementary school building. Grant proudly said he could certainly walk this short distance by himself. Sally had planned another favorite dinner: shrimp salad and coleslaw, homemade applesauce, sourdough biscuits and sun tea when she remembered about the lobsters Seth would be bringing home tonight. She decided they could eat the salad tomorrow and started to fill a huge pot with water.

Just before Seth arrived home, Grant answered the phone with "Hi Grand-mom. Yes, we can't wait. Hold on, she's right here."

Sally talked with her mother-in-law about their pending visit to watch the boys. She and Seth had decided to take a short three-day trip to celebrate their anniversary at the end of June. Her in-laws planned to drive over from western Colorado and stay a full week before driving back. Their anniversary was three days before Seth and Sally's and they were going to celebrate together.

Suddenly the garage door opened and then the door from the basement slammed shut. The boys raced down to welcome their dad. He looked so glad to be home, yet his face appeared to be exhausted with crease lines indented in his forehead. Sally gave him a beer and asked how much time he needed to relax before he wanted to eat. She knew the hour long drive home became quite a drag as traffic was so heavy at this time. He gave her the box of lobsters and sat down.

After he drained his beer, Seth told her this trip had been another stressful one. His patience with the air traffic controllers had reached a high frustration level again. He went to the 'fridge and took another beer, downing it too quickly to suit her.

"Let's have a quiet dinner and let the boys talk. You seem to need a distraction, and maybe they will provide one just for a little while." She gave him a comforting hug, and took the lid off the pot of boiling water. "I know you want to talk about these things, but maybe this can wait until they're in bed." Sally seemed to be learning how to spot his moods, knowing when to be quiet and when to let him just drown his thoughts with a beer or two.

The boys came into the kitchen as Seth pointed to the box of lobsters and put his fingers up to his lips as if to say Shh.

"Wow, are they alive?" Grant looked at his dad and brother.

"Yes they are son. They must be dropped into the boiling water to cook."

"I've never cooked lobster before boys, so I'm just a little hesitant to pick them up and drop them into the water." Sally washed her hands and went to the package. As she picked up the first one, she looked away as she dropped it into the pot.

"Ouch."

Everyone started laughing except Sally who looked surprised and startled at the sound. Her mouth dropped open and her eyes opened wide. She realized a little too late the sound came from Seth and not the lobster.

She looked at the boys who were still laughing and then to her dear husband, who obviously needed a laugh and said, "Be glad I didn't drop the other one in your lap from shock."

CHAPTER 31
CELEBRATIONS

The anniversaries were over too soon. Sally enjoyed their trip up to the Dells in Wisconsin, driving the few hours north to a beautiful wooded area. Seth seemed to settle down, away from the hustle and bustle of airports, passengers and air traffic controllers. He also enjoyed visiting with his parents. Even though he encouraged them to stay, they wanted to get home before the holiday.

Lisa's family grabbed a table at the Fourth of July celebration set up near the clubhouse for the big barbecue, tennis tournament and fireworks. Seth and Nate had planned to have a soccer game with the boys and dads from Grant's team at the park instead of trying to find some room at the overcrowded pool. Lisa and Sally had signed up to play doubles tennis and watch the sign-in-table after the new treasurer took the money to the bank before it closed at noon. They were pleased to hear over a thousand dollars had been collected for the tickets. The fee of ten dollars per family covered the cost of fireworks and a band. After all the tables were set up for the pot luck dishes, each family cooked their own meat on barbecues provided by the board. Many women commented on the broccoli salad, sour cream chocolate cake and best ever brownies as well as the several of the pasta salads.

"Will you get all these recipes and put them in the next newsletter, Sally?"

Lisa volunteered to help Patty get all the information to be printed in the August newsletter. Then, stomachs full, everyone enjoyed the rock music of a local band and a great fireworks display. Another celebration of a Fourth of July holiday reminded them of their freedom to celebrate. Most in attendance knew a temporary board had been picked and were glad to know business would continue with volunteers running their subdivision in a more positive way.

Two days before the first official board meeting with the new temporary members found Sally a little upset from a conversation with Paul. He called the morning of the meeting and asked if she could replace him for the rest of the summer. He recommended one of his neighbors, Volker Coltanger, who had already agreed to the position.

"Paul, I'm so disappointed to lose you too."

"Well, Sally, I have thought about this long and hard since the board resigned last month. I have vacation, and both sets of parents are coming to visit us. We are really busy at work. Patsy persuaded me to take a short break."

Sally knew he worked for a home building company in Chicago, but didn't know what he did there.

"I'll sure miss your constant support, Paul. Since you say this is for only two months and you've already found a replacement, I guess I'm set. Have a great summer and call me in September.

As she and Lisa walked up to the clubhouse the night of the meeting, Sally remembered the pool had been cleaned yesterday to get ready for the Fourth of July festivities.

"I sure hope they didn't leave a mess inside." Lisa, always the optimist, reminded her of the clubhouse living room which they never used for their meetings. She had made a double batch of brownies with dark chocolate icing to help these new members be more relaxed, knowing food, especially dessert, would be a key to a great evening.

"Everyone can just relax on the couches and recliners while I serve dessert and coffee."

Sally planned to have everyone talk about how their tasks were handled in this first month of office. Daniel Gibson sat on the bench outside the front door. He seemed preoccupied with reading his notes. They approached the single story brick building. He heard them walk up and put down his notes, unlocking the door and giving Sally a new key.

"I made a key for you just in case Steve didn't give you his. Then I decided to have the locks changed. Now you and I and the clubhouse rental person will be the only ones with the new keys. This might prevent any problems from disgruntled board members who might come up here some night and take out their frustrations inside."

Surprised by his insightfulness, she took the key. "Thanks Daniel; I didn't even have this on my list." She looked up to his towering 6'5" frame and smiled.

Each member had received all their files, thanks in part to Daniel who said, "I made sure my secretary contacted every former member to tell them they had to turn over all their files after they quit."

So far, each understood their job description. There were only a few legal questions for Daniel to answer. The majority of the meeting covered what still had to be done for the summer with follow-up on jobs already contracted. The signature cards for their checking and savings accounts had been changed. One question came up about Doug's addition of a family room. Daniel told the new members everything had been approved at the May meeting, before he quit. Doug asked to have construction start two weeks after the board approved his plans. The meeting ended promptly two hours later.

"You really did a terrific job of getting everyone comfortable with their new positions, Sally. You answered all questions calmly and didn't lose patience at all." They walked home slowly and Sally patted Lisa's shoulder. "Thanks so much for helping out tonight. Your brownies are just the best. Everyone did seem more relaxed on the couches instead of sitting around the rectangular table"

Lisa said, "One month down and three more to go."

With relief, Sally replied." I'm not so worried anymore. We can do this."

Lisa looked at her best walking buddy and said, "Yes we can."

Sally went home to type up the recipe for the cake to put in the newsletter.

S. M. Drake

Sour Cream Chocolate Chip Cake

6 T. soft unsalted butter	1 ½ c. unbleached white flour
¾ c. sugar	1 ½ t. baking powder
1 T. sugar	1 t. baking soda and cinnamon
2 eggs; 1 cup sour cream	½ pkg semi-sweet chocolate chips

Cream butter and sugar. Add beaten eggs, blending well.
Stir/sift together all dry ingredients.
Add to butter sugar mixture.
Add sour cream. Mix well.
Pour into greased and floured 9 x 13 pan.
Scatter chocolate chips evenly over cake. Sprinkle 1 T. sugar over top.
Bake 350 degrees about 40 min., or until done when toothpick inserted comes out clean.

CHAPTER 32
SUMMER

The rest of the month passed quickly. The boys spent most days at the pool, with swim lessons in the morning. They practiced soccer at the park when their dad was home. Sally spent as much time as possible checking with each new board member. She followed up on questions from the July board meeting. She hoped to find out if any of these brave souls would consider having their name put in nomination for a permanent position at the annual meeting. Every week Sally or Seth walked over to the new elementary school with the boys to check on the progress of the construction.

Since he quit the board, Doug had time on his hands with no daily pool upkeep. His room addition would be finished by the end of the month. Emil, the temporary board member called him several times with questions. Luckily Doug had been able to answer them. He spent most of his spare time finding out about the former owner of the garbage dump now called Greenebriar by making an easy friendship with the college intern at the library. She helped him find out the owner's name, plus additional information of what had been allowed in dumps before government regulations started

Using this backyard discovery, Doug worked out his strategy carefully. He then made the initial important phone call as casual as possible before dropping an ace-in-the-hole:blackmail. Stephen Balliteria, former owner of the property, a garbage dump, did not take kindly to Doug's threats. Unfortunately he'd have to go along with this blackmail attempt until something better could be worked out. Stephen had been able to switch some accounts from one real estate property to another to have access to the thousand dollars Doug requested each month as hush money. One of his most loyal men, his brother's son, Hank, who lived in the subdivision, had requested a month's leave to take his wife on a special anniversary cruise, so this man couldn't be used right now. At a monthly dinner with fellow cronies, Stephen mentioned what had occurred with Doug's find. The decision making process had now been left to others who had to find out just who this skeleton could have been. Those in charge knew of other bodies and needed to check their records before any plans could be made. This would take more than a few weeks, and they decided to allow Stephen to pay this money for now.

Seth worked diligently to take down the rotten planks from the deck and the more he took out, the more he found. Since he had originally planned to just replace these planks, he had not filled out any papers for board approval for deck improvement. One Saturday, the other next door neighbors, Clara and Clark were out on their patio. Their son Alan kicked around a soccer ball. Clark called over to Seth.

"Looks like you have uncovered quite a mess there, Seth. Are you going to need any help? My brother-in-law works for a deck building company." He pushed his White Sox cap back onto his creased forehead and took a sip of lemonade.

"Thanks, Clark. Right now, I'm set. Guess I'll have to see how much needs to be replaced. If I need help, I'll be sure to get his name from you."

He picked up his hammer to continue when Clark asked. "I don't see a permit hanging anywhere. Did you get approval before you started this project?" He looked back at his wife who seemed to be telling him to ask this question.

Trying to restrain his response, Seth answered. "None is needed, thanks. I'm just repairing an existing structure."

"Just because your wife is the temporary president doesn't mean you don't follow the CCRs." By now, Clark had walked over to the fence and poked his head over the boards. Clara stood beside him, looking intently at Seth.

"Look, Clark, this doesn't concern you. When, and if I need a permit, you can be rest assured I'll get one" He put down his hammer and walked up the existing stairs. "See you later." He went inside and pulled a beer out of the 'fridge, continuing downstairs where he found Sally ironing.

He told her about the conversation with Clark. She assured him there wouldn't be any problem getting a permit from the board.

"I might have to replace the entire deck. Every board I take off shows me another one rotted, up to and inside the slots connecting to the house. I really wanted this project to be finished before we go on vacation so I won't have to use any of those days from our trip to Arizona."

"I'll call Mark, the new grounds board member and we can write up something today. Will you need to change any of the original design?" She put away the ironing board and iron in the laundry room.

"Depending on if I have to replace all the boards or just a few more, I might need to move the stairs over a bit. I really can't say until I check each plank. Based on what I've found so far, maybe I should just make it easy and take off the entire deck."

"Only you can decide how long this will take, Seth. You could certainly leave it until we get back. Then just work on it a couple of days a week until it's finished. I'm sure Nate would help you on the weekends if you really need him. We haven't planned to have anyone over for dinner before we go. Don't you think we could do without a deck for a month or two?"

He walked into the office and pulled out a notebook with his temporary plans and wrote out what he might need if he put on an entire deck.

Nate and Lisa had invited them over to grill burgers, and Sally had to make the coleslaw and potato salad.

"I'll be in the kitchen if you need me. We are to be there by 5:30 p.m." She walked upstairs and called to the boys who were playing a board game. "Anyone want to help peel potatoes for dinner tonight?"

CHAPTER 33
VACATION

The last week in July, Sally called Daniel to ask him if he would be able to chair the August board meeting.

"We already planned our vacation before the board resigned and Seth can't change his days off. I can go over the agenda with you and suggest you invite Lisa to come, since she's about as knowledgeable as anyone." They talked for about twenty more minutes. She felt comfortable leaving everything in his hands.

The rest of the week had to be spent going over what clothes to pack, how many hours a day they'd drive, and picking out the campgrounds where they would spend the night.

She canceled the milk delivery and called the lady from the Feingold food co-op to tell her they wouldn't be taking any food for August. Lisa volunteered to pick up their mail and water the plants.

The morning they left, a rainstorm let loose a torrent of water, so they had to finish packing the last minute items inside the garage. The boys helped make sandwiches and after a quick breakfast of cereal, bananas and juice, they left about seven am, heading south west for Flagstaff.

Seth told her this would be the time to clear her mind and relax during these two weeks away from her daily grind.

"I know you have a lot on your mind, but Daniel is quite capable of handling one meeting. You really need to rest. Everything has been so hectic since the board quit, and I must tell you how proud I am of how well you handled everything."

Sally felt relieved the worst had passed. She told him again how much she appreciated his help and support, then passed out the first snack. Later she took a nap while he drove the first two hour shift, heading down the interstate toward Missouri.

They enjoyed the peace and quiet of driving, listening to eight- track tapes of their favorite music and sleeping under the stars, even though they were in the truck under a camper cover. Sally and Seth took turns cooking dinner over an open fire on a grill provided by each campground.

As soon as they arrived in Flagstaff, they drove straight to their property. The boys helped set up two tents. Seth made a large campfire in the fire pit which had been made of large volcanic rocks. After he started cooking the burgers, he looked at his list of who needed to be called to get their house started. Their neighbor, across the road, had volunteered bathroom facilities. The boys ran over to use the toilet before they ate. After dinner, the Fullers came over to say hi and see what they could do to help. Sally gave them a coat hanger and a marshmallow to make s'mores for dessert. Gerry and Sarah lived in Tucson and came up just for the summer to escape the desert heat. They had been retired for only a couple of years and didn't want to give up their home. Both of them enjoyed driving up to Flagstaff, at an elevation of over 7,000 ft., for a few week-ends during winter where they could ski regularly.

The time passed too quickly, and before they knew it, their vacation ended. With Gerry's help, Seth secured a builder, electrician and plumber. After many phone calls, he finally found a person to put in the septic field the next week.

They were able to stop at two forts Sally had on her list from last year. Now Grant could use this information for sharing his summer vacation when he started second grade.

Rested and relaxed from this time away from the turmoil at home, they continued their drive back, talking about what they had seen at the forts. The boys speculated on what it must have been like to be in the cavalry, riding horses as the only means of transportation and living out in the real 'wild' west.

Meanwhile 'back at the ranch' . . .

The August newsletter reminded all homeowners about Gail's presentation. Just to make sure there were enough chairs, those who planned to come were to call Leah, the secretary.

Lonnie did not know about the board resignation until she read the temporary members names in the July newsletter. She had already decided to go to the August meeting, now knowing Doug wouldn't be there. Her husband, Hank, had a business meeting, so she called her neighbor to see if they could go together. After a quick salad, she walked over to Joanne's house and they went up to the clubhouse together, both surprised to see the parking lot full.

Each replacement board member gave their report in record time. Daniel then introduced Gail, who stood up and looked at the large crowd, surprised at the turnout. She felt a little more nervous because these were her neighbors and friends of her parents.

She took her notes and started slowly, speaking in a quiet voice, breaking into tears when she spoke of hitting the little girl who ran out into the street so quickly. Her two friends had come, too. Each took their turn to speak.

Becky had a tale to tell too, from the passenger's point of view. She spoke quietly at first and tied in her emotions as a non driver who also had a responsibility. She felt many teens didn't quite understand what role a passenger could play. Conversation and loud music played a part in distracting Gail as she drove down the street.

When she finished, Jenny spoke next. She had a story to share as well. In a weak voice she started off very slowly. Her guilt about the conversation she started, which had distracted Gail in the first place, bothered her. Of course, only Gail and Becky knew about this secret.

As she stood to face the audience, Lonnie froze to her seat, staring at this young lady who seemed to be her spitting image as a young teen. She recognized Doug's black hair, nose and jaw line. She couldn't help but notice the grey-green eyes, the same as hers. The more she stared, Lonnie felt certain she and Doug were the parents of Jenny Erthner.

CHAPTER 34
ANSWER

Sally helped the boys prepare for school. Garrett decided to go to the preschool at the clubhouse to be with Brett. This year, the four year old classes were every morning. Seth finished his last trip for August, relieved he'd finally get some time at home to finish the deck. Planning soccer practices would take up the rest of his spare afternoon hours this month. Everyone planned to walk Grant to school on his first day, taking the obligatory picture for second grade.

Sally and Lisa continued their afternoon walks and set up their schedule for the fall. They added an extra aerobics class to their list so Sally could continue to lose weight in preparation for her fifteenth high school reunion over the Labor Day holiday. They would go to this class two mornings a week, bowl, take the ceramics class and continue with the women's study group. Sally had applied to NIU to take one education class to get ready for part-time teaching when Garrett would start first grade in another year.

Just two weeks before school started, Lonnie left the samples she'd picked for the bathroom floor tile on the dining room table. She knew Hank would want to decide on the vanity, so she had several blocks of wood choices and colors. To prepare for this presentation, she made one of his favorite meals: thick burgers, spinach salad with the bacon dressing he loved, and lemon meringue pie. She had more time to shop, plan and fix favorite dinners since she only taught part-time this year.

Her husband Hank worked in commercial real estate with his uncle, Stephen in Orland Park, about a thirty minutes drive. He usually came home between 5:30 and 6:00 p.m. every evening, ready for his nightly cocktail. His idea of order meant a precise schedule followed every night. After she heard the garage door close, she poured the wine and set out the zucchini appetizers on the dining room table.

"Hi, hon. Come on in the dining room, cocktail hour is ready." She smiled as he walked up the stairs waiting to see if he noticed her new look. She had spent two hours at the beauty parlor, getting her hair cut and colored.

He sorted through the day's mail as he took the glass of wine, not looking up at her. "Something smells fantastic, bacon in a spinach salad?" He took off his jacket and draped it over a chair at the table, giving her a quick hug with one arm and still looking at the mail. Since they were both about the same height, a short peck on the check seemed so easy---no reaching up on tip toes like several of her friends did with their tall husbands.

"Yum," he said after the first bite of a zucchini tart. He then held up his wine glass to clink to hers, focusing on the display on the table and still not looking directly at her. "Cheers. What is all this on the table?" He picked up each of the choices she had left.

"Remember last spring I told you our block captain suggested a store for remodeling the bathroom called Better Baths and Kitchens? I went there to order new faucets." She took a sip of the Merlot and sat down holding a zucchini tart.

He looked at her closely. "Wait a minute, you cut your hair. Wow, you have lots of blond streaks. Really like this new look on you Lonnie, even though the length is very short."

"I'm so glad you like it, Hank. When the stylist suggested short, I seemed a little unsure. Even though the picture she showed me is the latest rage, I hesitated. It's called a shag cut and the sides and top are shorter than the back." She ran her fingers through her new do.

"After the appointment with the salesman, I went out to lunch and had it done afterwards. Then I hurried home to make the pie and get dinner started." She put her hand on his shoulder, giving his a loving squeeze and then smiled. "Can't wait to see my student's reaction when I go to school tomorrow." He put down his glass and gave her a hug, then picked up his jacket to go into their bedroom to change.

"I just have to turn over the burgers, baking in the oven. The salad

Greenebriar's Garbage

and pie are finished." She took her wine glass and went into the kitchen to get the silverware.

Later, as they sat down to eat, Lonnie planned her words carefully. "When I went to the store to meet with the salesman, he had been delayed. So another man came to help me."

"This is important because?" Hank questioned.

"He turned out to be one of the board members from Greenebriar, Doug Pulchowski. He's worked with several families on remodeling their kitchens and bath. He gave me a lot of information to help make some better choices. Remember we already picked out the faucets and toilet? We narrowed down the choices for tile, paint color, vanity and cabinets. I hope you like what I brought home."

Hank's body stiffened and he actually put his left hand on his knee for support. He took a large sip of wine. He knew this name. "I'm glad you narrowed everything to two choices, Lonnie. This way we can pick everything out tonight."

"Really Hank? Just in case something else needs to be ordered we'll have some more time to have everything ready for our anniversary party. Doug talked about how good this neighborhood has been for business. He's met a lot of the people from his volunteer board job as pool and clubhouse director. He gets called over to the clubhouse on the weekends when there is a party 'cause the music seems to always be too loud for some of the neighbors." She took another bite of salad and looked at him, pleased they could make these final choices so soon.

"Parties too loud . . ." He paused in mid sentence. "He has to go over there? I wouldn't have guessed this to be a problem." He took a sip of wine, than asked, "Police ever get called?"

Lonnie put down her fork "Yes. I seem to remember he did mention something about police coming over for those who refused to comply."

"What happened; did he say?" An idea formed as he asked this question.

"Guess the homeowner rules take precedence."

Hank knew he needed to make a phone call right away. "Lonnie, would you mind making the coffee and holding the dessert for a few minutes? I just forgot an important phone call I need to make before a client goes home."

She cleared the table, took everything into the kitchen and started the coffee. After the plates were into the dishwasher, she went back to the dining room to look at her choices.

Meanwhile, Hank went downstairs to his office and closed the door. He dialed a number from memory, known only to him. While the rings continued in his ear, a plan started to come to mind.

"Talk to me, Hank. I have only a few minutes." His Uncle Stephen's voice sounded hurried.

He lowered his voice a little. "You might remember a payment problem we've had for the past few months?"

Stephen knew exactly to whom Hank referred. "Yes. Has something happened?"

"Lonnie knows where he works and what he does in his spare time. We have a perfect out and can even use the clubhouse here where we live." His voice sounded sure of himself with the idea he had only thought of minutes before.

"Sounds like you might have a plan there, Hank. Let's meet for lunch tomorrow and you can give me your ideas." Stephen tapped his fingers on his custom-made oak desk, as a crooked smile crept over his weathered face, a little too tan for some.

Hank took off his glasses, wiped his forehead and continued. "This is just a far fetched idea, but I'm sure you or the rest of the boys can polish this up so we can get rid of this blackmailer."

"Call my secretary after ten tomorrow morning and she'll tell you the place I've picked for us to meet. This is something I don't want anyone else to hear now." He started formulating a plan to get rid of this cash flow situation.

"Great, see you tomorrow." Hank sighed and realized this could be the answer to their problem. He just had to get some more details from Lonnie after they picked out the choices for their bathroom.

CHAPTER 35
HANK

At lunch the next day, Stephen and Hank met at an out of the way diner in the next town. Hank heard how Doug started black-mailing his uncle while he and Lonnie were on their month long cruise. Hank worked hard to make sure his wife knew he worked in commercial real estate involving meetings and trips to Chicago. From the day they first met, he had decided what she didn't know would be best for their marriage. Even though he studied business and marketing in college, he did additional work for his uncle, involving dirty deals and underhanded schemes.

Hank remembered the rest of last night's conversation after they picked their final choices for the bathroom remodel. Lonnie asked him, "Why don't you come with me to the September board meeting? You could meet him." She gathered up the samples and put them back in the large box she brought home. "Remember when you went to the board meeting last fall and I couldn't go? We didn't know about him or the type of work he did." She stopped and took a sip of wine. "Several of the gals from bowling recommended him. Our neighbor, Joanne, told me the girls who were involved in that terrible accident, where a little girl was killed, were going to present their talk. Last week, we went to hear them, last week, at the August board meeting. Remember, I invited you but you couldn't come because of a scheduling conflict?"

"When are these meetings?"

"Always the second Tuesday of the month."

"I won't be able to come. Uncle Stephen and I already have a meeting set up with a potential client. You can tell me all about it when I get home."

Hank, standing only three inches taller in height than Lonnie, seemed tall compared to his uncle, who barely topped five feet five. His uncle reminded him so much of his father, Bradley Balliteria, who started this real estate venture and died in a car crash when Hank had been only fifteen. Uncle Stephen seemed to take over the father role for his brother's children. He had always been there for his sisters too. He usually acted as an authority figure, helping out their mom with major decisions. In fact, Uncle Stephen picked out the college Hank attended, Southern Illinois, as well as his major field of study, business, and even his fraternity, Sigma Nu.

They met at an Italian restaurant on the way to Joliet.

"If we can get this Doug over to a party at the clubhouse, we might be able to take care of him once and for all," Hank said.

While they savored their delicious lunch of homemade lasagna, garlic bread, salad and wine at Mama Mia's Italian Kitchen, they came up with several ideas, none of which sounded plausible at first. They continued to chew, drink and think, the good surfaced as the bad ideas sank. As they tossed around other possibilities, Stephen knew he'd have to run this by some others.

"Look Hank, this is really good work. Thanks for getting this information. I'll need to share this with the others and get back to you as soon as everything is finalized."

"I know you want me to have as little inside information as possible, just in case something ever happens, but I just feel so locked out of these decisions. After all, this is my idea." He took a small sip of wine to finish formulating his thoughts. "When can I be moved up to the inside when it comes to the planning?" Hank knew he might have stepped over the line on this one, but after five years of solid performances, he really thought he should be considered for an inside job now.

"Hank, you are right. We've really enjoyed watching you mature since you came on board during college. As you know, these decisions aren't made by me." He took a long sip of wine and ate an entire slice of garlic bread, wiping his chin to keep the butter from dripping on his pin stripe suit.

"What I'll do is present your idea, remind them of your loyalty and suggest the possibility of a promotion within. My guess is they will want to see how this plan of yours works. If everything is a go and there are no slip-ups, you'll get my vote for sure."

Hank sat up a little taller and smiled as broadly as possible, feeling quite happy about the possibility of a promotion. "Uncle Stephen, my devotion to you has never been questioned. You might remember, I've never argued with a single choice you guys have made or asked me to do." He took a large sip of wine to give him a chance to rethink his next sentence.

"Asking for a month off had been a difficult task, to say the least. I need to keep my new wife happy, as has been pointed out at several meetings. Home fires kindling with hot embers are a key to success, someone said."

Stephen drained his wine. "You are right Hank. Don't think this has gone unnoticed. Another reason why I pushed so hard for you to have this time off has been your constant loyalty. Even though we had a big project during your absence, one of your cousins stepped up to the plate and did a fine job." Stephen put his napkin on his plate, then snapped his fingers to get their bill.

Their waitress came up quickly and told them Mama Mia said lunch was on the house and to thank them for keeping the restaurant from closing. Hank, not aware of what she meant, looked at his uncle with a face full of questions. Stephen waved her away and said "Grazie."

As they stood beside their cars, Stephen said, "Give me some time to get this figured out, Hank. Just forget about it for now. I need you to straighten out some marketing management problems on a North Michigan Avenue property. If you call my secretary tomorrow, she'll have all the information you need to take care of this mess." He gave his nephew a strong bear hug and ended their conversation with words many employees love to hear, but rarely do

"Take the rest of the afternoon off and enjoy Lonnie. Be sure and give her my best." He drove away, waving his hand to a very surprised nephew.

CHAPTER 36
PROMOTION

The bathroom completion turned out to be everything Lonnie had pictured. The workmen finished four days before the anniversary party with their families. The celebration left her on cloud nine: happy with her choice of Hank, part-time teaching and coming clean with Doug. She continued to speculate on the possibility of Jenny Erthner as her daughter, but felt afraid. She just wasn't sure what she should do next with Doug. She kept telling herself to call the adoption agency, but just couldn't seem to get focused on this problem until after their party. She knew once school started she'd have less time, but decided this must be put on the back burner for now.

With Seth coaching Grant's team and a back deck to finish, getting ready for her reunion and the September board meeting seemed to take precedence in Sally's thoughts. Seth had most of the week off to tackle his practices and work on the deck. This month, he flew only on weekends.

Lisa agreed to watch the boys the weekend she flew to Panama City, since Seth couldn't change his schedule. Sally lost fifteen pounds and she felt pleased with her new look. She did feel a little nervous to see people she had never imagined she'd meet again once her family moved away from Florida.

Women's activities had been planned to start after the Labor Day holiday and Sally decided to add ceramics to her list of bowling and Women's Study Group. Her class at NIU extension in a nearby town only met once a week at night for three hours. Because she knew her job as board president would be over in November, she figured she'd just have a very busy few months. Luckily she had been able to enlist two other mothers to help with the soccer snacks and game carpooling. When

Seth held practice, Garrett and Brett always tagged along because one or two boys were always absent for some reason.

The day before Seth came home from his latest trip, he called in the afternoon. This was unusual for him unless there had been a flight delay. Sally panicked again when she spoke to him.

"Hi, Seth. Something wrong?" She tried to sound positive.

"Do I have some good news. Are you sitting down?"

Immediately she noticed an almost joyful sound in his voice, something she really had not heard in a while. This reminded her of their lack of laughter everyday and something she thought they should work on in their marriage. She sat down in a kitchen chair and looked into the back yard at their partially finished new deck, wondering what could have happened.

"Guess what I found out today when I went down to see job postings? Remember I'm in Atlanta now, so maybe this is a clue." His voice almost gushed with happiness.

"I really don't have a clue, Seth, so just tell me, since you couldn't wait until you came home."

"My bid for 727 co-pilot has been approved and I'll start my training after I finish my last trip this month."

She had not been prepared for this at all and had to take a deep breath before she could answer. She remembered how long his initial training had been almost . . . 90 days.

"Congratulations, Seth. I know this is what you've wanted for a couple of years. Moving up to the next plane is a great challenge. Isn't this one bigger than the one you're on now?" She tried to speak slowly and show support.

"No, it isn't. The reason I'm calling you today instead of waiting to tell you tomorrow is the training" He waited a second or two for her to digest this sentence before he dropped a heavy load.

"I'm listening, so just tell me."

He took a deep breath. "For co-pilot training, I'll be gone almost 70 days, depending on how I do on my written test and simulator check

A few seconds of silence ensued as Sally digested this latest information. *I'll have to do the next board meeting and annual meeting without him here to watch the boys; who will finish soccer and who will start hockey and what about the deck?* She ran through the upcoming plans for the next two months and realized she needed a specific start date before she could start to panic.

"Seth, this is what you have to do, so we'll just have to figure out who will do the things you have undertaken this fall." She started her deep breathing to keep herself relaxed.

"I'm sure I can get one of the dads to take over soccer for October. I'll just work hard every day to finish the deck. Since hockey is only on the weekends, I'm sure you can figure out a car pool if necessary."

"Well, sounds like you've already thought of everything. When did you find out?"

"This morning, right after we landed here in Atlanta. So, you're right, I've had a couple of hours to figure all this out before I called you. We have a three and a half hour layover here, so I just grabbed a calendar and looked at all the days I'd be gone."

"You'll be here for Thanksgiving, right? Remember we are having company from Milwaukee."

Another uncomfortable silence followed. "I don't think so; 60 days puts me through November. I probably won't be able to get two days off, but I'll sure ask. Everything will depend on what leg of the training I get, morning or night."

"Thanks so much for giving me a heads up on this one, Seth. I'll at least have tonight to look at our calendar and see what we have. Just be sure to drive home safely tomorrow and don't celebrate too much tonight after you land."

"Don't worry about me tonight. You know how strict Trans Air is on drinking. I'm so thrilled with this promotion, I'm sure I'll just fall asleep. Don't forget, this will mean a bigger paycheck."

She twisted the phone cord and looked at the calendar on the wall, with all the activities penciled in. Then she remembered her reunion and decided she'd just wait until he came home to get all the dates down.

"Here's another idea for spending money we don't have yet. Now we can replace this horrible avocado colored refrigerator, dishwasher and stove."

"Yes we can. I'll find out about the pay. I'm sure it won't start until after I finish and pass this training."

"I'll let you tell the boys, O.K? Thanks so much for giving me a heads up."

The conversation ended and she decided to have a glass of wine. Just as she started dinner, she wondered how much this new position would change his schedule every month. Knowing the boys would be coming home from Brett's any minute now, she thought: *I wonder how they will react to their dad becoming a co-pilot instead of a flight engineer. Will they even care?*

CHAPTER 37
REUNION AND AGENCY

Before she knew it, the Labor Day holiday arrived and her trip to Panama City, Florida, for her high school reunion, was down to a final countdown. Even though the September board meeting would be the week she returned, Sally had everything ready so she could now concentrate on her trip. She dutifully checked all possible flight schedules and the one with the most open seats left Thursday night. This would be the first time she had flown non-revenue by herself in several years. She flew to Atlanta, had a short layover and then took a smaller plane to Panama City. Landing at ten p.m., she found Karon, her friend from high school and junior college, waiting for her. Even at this late hour, she still looked quite chic with perfect makeup and short streaked blond hair. Of course, she wore the latest knit slacks and top in matching colors.

The weekend flew by, and Sally enjoyed seeing people she never imagined she'd see again. Her father had been stationed at Tyndall Air Force Base the start of her junior year. When they moved there, she had no idea how long they'd stay. She felt lucky now since she had gone on to Florida State in Tallahassee, only a short drive from P.C. Many weekends she'd been able to come back and visit her friend. When they drove out to the base, both Sally and Karon noticed the new buildings and which ones were gone, mainly the Teen Center where Sally spent many a Saturday night dancing with her base friends when she didn't have a date. The housing area looked quite different with large trees, only saplings when she had lived there. They found her house, now a different color and with an addition, a screened in back porch.

"I remember when you'd want to spend the night with me 'cause many of your dates didn't want to drive all the way out to the base to pick you up," Karon remarked, taking off her sunglasses and grinning at her flashback of sleepovers. "When you couldn't stay with me, Leona always volunteered her place. Since she lived with her mom, they had an extra bedroom. Do you remember when you stayed out past curfew with Greg and her mom locked up the house and you slept in their car?"

"Yes, I do. I'll never forget how shocked Leona's mom had been when she came out to get her morning paper and saw me sleeping on the back seat. Even back then, so many of my dates had to pay for their own gas. A trip out to the base and back took a half tank of gas."

"We sure had some fun times. I really did appreciate you and Leona letting me spend the night on short notice."

The funniest part of the reunion had been to see how many 'popular' people were now among the heavy set, had lost the most hair or just looked completely different with age. The two days passed quickly and Sunday morning, she flew back to ORD via ATL. Lisa came to pick her up, with a back seat full of bouncing boys, two who were really glad to see her.

"Mom, did you get to see any of your old boyfriends?" Grant asked, grinning from ear to ear with a large smile.

"Who told you I'd be seeing former boyfriends?" she asked playfully, tapping him on the shoulder. "I really dated just a few guys there since I only went to this school for two years. You know your granddad's rules were to be followed and not questioned. I really wasn't allowed to date much. He always seemed to have something going on at the Officers' Club and I'd have to stay home to watch my younger brothers and sister."

They arrived home safely and Lisa had already made dinner for them. After eating and getting the boys ready for bed, Sally unpacked her suitcase and looked through the high school directory souvenir booklet to see how many names she remembered seeing again. About nine p.m., Seth called, said he'd landed and would be home in less than two hours.

"How did you survive your reunion?" There seemed to be a little playfulness in his question.

"You were right, Seth. Even though a lot of people didn't look the same at all, I'm glad I went. The boys seemed to survive just fine with Lisa. Drive home safely now. I'll wait up."

He replied with his well known phrase, "Don't forget, no nightgown tonight."

Seth spent his days off planning soccer practices, finding dads who would help finish weekly practice sessions and coach the games for October. When this chore ended, he worked on the deck

Lonnie decided she just couldn't put Doug off any longer and made the difficult gut-wrenching decision to call the adoption agency near Joliet. She and Hank had spent a quiet Labor Day at a barbecue with their neighbors. She thought about this decision because this family had two toddlers and the family on the other side of them had a pre-teen and a teenager. Watching the teenage daughter play with the little ones reminded her again of how much she had missed. She knew this just had to be done and carefully arranged for the first day back at school to make this phone call during her extended lunch hour.

"Social services for families; how may I help you?"

Lonnie spoke slowly, yet carefully. "May I speak to someone about finding someone placed for adoption?"

"Yes, I can get you started. What year?"

"1963."

"Please hold. I'll connect you to one of our adoption specialists."

Just holding made Lonnie's nervousness increase and for a split second she considered hanging up. *You can do this now, Doug needs to know too.*

"This is Hazel Prestwick, How may I help you today?"

"Hi, Hazel. I want to find out what is required to find my daughter. I placed her for adoption through this agency in the summer of 1963. My name then was Lonnie Favero and the date of birth was August 17 in Demott, Indiana."

"Since the birth was in Indiana, I won't be able to help you, Lonnie. You'll need to contact them."

Trying to keep her composure, Lonnie explained the adoption went through their agency, even though the baby had been born in another

Greenebriar's Garbage

state. She almost had to convince the woman this had been the correct agency.

"I don't know what your rules are now," Lonnie continued, but I can assure you the baby came through this agency."

"Just a minute Lonnie, even if what you say is true, the birth year means this child is still a minor. There are strict laws in Illinois about disclosure. May I call you back?"

Once again, Lonnie felt a nagging pressure at the back of her neck and her stomach gurgled as she put her other hand on top of the pay phone for more support.

"No, I'll have to call you back. Why can't you just give me the information now? I am the mother who signed all the papers and I just want to find out who adopted my daughter." She took a deep breath, trying to maintain some sort of composure.

"This really isn't asking for much, is it?" She tapped her pink fingernails on top of the black telephone, remembering a similar conversation almost fifteen years ago. "I won't make contact if this is what you're worried about."

"You don't understand, even if I wanted to do this, the law is firm. I'm looking at the statute right now and this just isn't possible until she is an adult."

"Can you call the parents and tell them I'd just like to know how she is and where she is living?" She felt as though her frustration would come through in her tone, as her voice cracked and tears started.

"I don't have any leeway here, Lonnie. I must follow the laws. You can certainly put this in writing and we will keep your letter on file to show you tried to make contact. I'm so sorry, but I cannot help you now."

Stunned with this unexpected information, Lonnie hung up the phone without ending the conversation. She didn't understand why she'd have to wait when Jenny lived so close. As her shaking knees gave way, Lonnie slowly sank to the floor of the phone booth and sobbed quietly.

As she drove back to school, a plan formed quickly and she decided to act on this idea before she chickened out. To know the possibility existed of her daughter living so close made her realize she had to act now. She just couldn't give up. Like an overworked animal straining to pull a load, she just knew she could do this with one more step each day. She put a note in the principal's mailbox, seeking an appointment right after school.

Luckily for her, there had been a cancellation from a parent, and Lonnie received a note saying the principal would see her at 3:30 p.m. She felt nervous walking into her office, knowing this could really be just a long shot.

"Have you already found a speaker for the October teacher meeting?" She nodded her head as an informal greeting and blurted out her question before she took her seat.

"Lonnie, come in. Good to see you. Yes we already have a speaker lined up; what did you have in mind?" Her principal, Diana Haacke, PhD Education, Northwestern University, smiled at one of her favorite teachers. She took off her wire-rimmed glasses as she brushed a long strand of graying black hair off her face.

"You must remember we try to have our speakers lined up for each semester because of busy schedules and the need for planning in advance."

Lonnie sighed, momentarily forgetting about their schedule. Now she remembered it had been posted in the teacher lounge during the first week of teacher preparation in August. She explained about the teens presenting their speech on the auto accident at her subdivision board meeting.

"Maybe we could have them speak to the sixth grade class as a heads up to them about the problems when driving through areas filled with children playing."

"This is a good idea, Lonnie. Let me double-check with the PTA president who has scheduled all the speakers for teacher work-days. Maybe we can figure out a way to use this information in a positive light for the sixth graders if we can't change the speakers for our meetings." She stood up to offer a hand to Lonnie.

"You always seem to do just a little bit more, Lonnie. Maybe this part-time teaching is a better way to go then working full time. I remember how tired most of our working moms were before we came up with this idea of job sharing. I'll let you know what I find out."

Lonnie left quickly, pleased to have at least opened a door to get Jenny at her school, have a chance to speak to her, or maybe even work with her for this presentation. Pushing her hands into the deep pockets of her denim skirt, she felt quite accomplished with her day's work in getting Jenny into her life.

The September board meeting went smoothly with each temporary chairman giving their reports. Sally knew if they could just get through these next two meetings, she'd be home free with a new board getting elected at the annual meeting. The finances seemed to be on track for the barbecues, tennis tournaments and special fireworks on July fourth. The pool would close for the season next weekend and Emil had turned over his books before he moved. Doug seemed surprised to see how much more chlorine had been used this summer. .

The only concern had to do with hiring a new pre-school teacher. The lady who had been there for three years moved due to her husband's job transfer. The treasurer reminded everyone to start working on their financial reports so there would be time to go over them next month in preparation for printing the annual budget for the homeowner meeting in November.

At the Wednesday study group the next morning, a large turnout came once again to Pamela Cznarecki's house to hear her promote their continued reading of <u>The Power of Positive Thinking.</u> Many of the regular attendees had invited neighbors and friends to come to this meeting. Everyone picked up their snack and sat down.

"I'd like to open with prayer, ladies. . . .Who forgives all your sins and heals all your diseases, who redeems your life from the pit and crowns you with love and compassion, who satisfies your desires with good things so your youth is renewed like the eagle's?" Psalm 103:3-5

"Before we get started, I'd like to open our discussion with your summer reading to see how many of you were able to finish the chapters assigned."

Many of the women raised their hands, so Pamela decided to just go in order for each to have their say. She certainly didn't expect such an overwhelming vote of confidence in what this book offered.

--- "My favorite idea came from p. 131: 'Say to yourself, Worry is just a very bad mental habit. And I can change any habit with God's help.'"
--- "I like the idea of knowing there really is a solution for every problem. Sometimes with four little ones around 24/7, I get so overwhelmed with their demands, I forget to take care of myself."
--- "What helped me was listing everything on a piece of paper. When I saw each problem written down I could plan better."
--- "I identified with Dr. Peale's idea of believing and seeking the promise of the 73rd Psalm, 'You will guide me with your counsel.'"
--- "Keeping harmony in the family clicked for me. If I'm happy, this does affect everyone's day. When he said, '. . . deliberately speak hopefully about everything,' I realized I do control my children's attitude each morning by my cheerfulness."
--- "For me, holding on to the past has always been a problem. When he said '. . . cast out those old unhealthy thoughts and substitute for them new dynamic faith thoughts, I couldn't wait to read more.'"
--- "The ten rules on p.188 showed me what I needed to change, especially getting a correct mental attitude and learning not to put off tomorrow what I can do today. I did not pray regularly and I have seen how this works for me now."
--- "I can do all things through Christ hit the nail for me because Dr. Peale strengthened this with 'You are always watched over in danger. Live by a faith that will never let you down.'" (p. 311)
--- "For me, 'Developing strong mental shields to ward off the bombardment of negatives will always keep the positive principal going,' were key points for me." (p.406)

Pamela had not expected to hear so many positive comments

and reminded everyone motherhood did take a lot of self-control and patience. She let them finish their initial thoughts and then broke them up into five groups of four to discuss their ideas in more detail.

"Here is another idea to keep us on track: "Start children off the way they should go, and when they are old they will not turn from it." Proverbs 22:6

She ended their frank discussions with another great verse she found: Two are better than one, because they have a good return for their labor; if either of them falls down, one can help the other up. . . " Ecclesiastes 4:9

"Alright ladies, go out and make this another great week for you and your family."

The bowling league started up again with several new members thanks in part to a special ad in the monthly newsletter by the new social director, Nancy. She worked with Alexandra to make sure all the block captains met the newest homeowners quickly so they could start women's study, bowling and ceramics with as little delay as possible. Nancy felt these women would settle in a little better if they starting meeting their neighbors right away and were involved in all the social activities she had planned for the fall.

CHAPTER 38
FALL

The weather changed drastically the first week in October, and many moms had to scramble to find long sleeved shirts, sweaters, jackets and hats. The wind seemed to blow the hardest almost every afternoon when Sally and Lisa took their walk

"Sure like your new deck, Sally. Thanks for having us for dinner before Seth left so we could enjoy the results of his hard work. Even though we covered everything we could think of, Nate and I want to remind you again, you can count on us for any problem which might come up after Seth leaves for his training in Atlanta." She pulled her hat down to cover her ears, getting colder with each gust of wind whipping around them.

"Thanks so much Lisa; you and Nate are lifesavers for volunteering like this. The boys had a little difficulty saying good-bye to him, but he told me he'd see if we could get a family pass to come visit after his first 30 days of training. This sure would be a great surprise for the boys if he can get confirmed seats for us to fly to Atlanta."

"Are you ready for your next-to-the-last board meeting? Time sure seems to have a way of racing by when you are busy, doesn't it? I just can't believe what you've done in five months to get this place back on track, Sally. Who do you think will run for president?"

"I sure don't have a clue. I asked Alexandra to talk this up with her block captains to see if they could interest any of the new homeowners. I think we have 20 new families who've moved in since June."

"Sure didn't realize there were so many homes sold. I guess I don't pay attention to this anymore since Ingrid seems to be the realtor for most. Sure didn't figure she'd get any support after she resigned from the board."

"I'm with you on this one, Lisa. I've heard from several moms on Seth's soccer team how professional she is when it comes to listing and selling. Maybe because this is her income, she works better than as a volunteer."

The hour passed quickly because they walked a little faster, discussing how great the Feingold group had been for Garrett and how much better they were eating. Louise and her group were coming along with getting all the necessary information to get the speed limits lowered. Sally felt relieved after she bounced everything off Lisa, who had become a great listening walking partner and good friend. When she asked about the new fall T.V. shows and a couple of current movies, Sally's answer came as a surprise.

"I really don't watch T.V. at night. By the time the boys are in bed and I finally have a chance to sit down and relax, all I want to do is read and enjoy my cup of tea."

The wind started to get the best of them as they turned the final corner. They said good-bye and Sally went home to two little boys who were moping about and already missing their dad, even though they were watching their favorite cartoons. They would start their count down for the flight to Atlanta tonight.

The October board meeting went so smoothly Sally almost started to worry, thinking she had forgotten something. She continued to check her agenda as each temporary chairman gave their report. To her great surprise, there were only a small number of homeowners there and the complaints were from the newest members who did not know they moved into a neighborhood with monthly dues. The secretary, Leah, volunteered to contact Ingrid who continued to work as a realtor, and see what they could do about making sure all realtors, the realtor board, and licensing school knew about the subdivisions in the surrounding areas where rules and dues were a requirement, not an afterthought.

Doug thanked all those in attendance for supporting him coming back and agreeing with the previous board for approval to get his addition approved for the final inspection.

Sally couldn't help but notice a change in his behavior. He actually seemed happier. She wondered if this had been due to all the new remodeling jobs he had over the summer because of his ad in the monthly newsletter. What she didn't know involved his 'extra' income. He had been receiving a substantial sum since June when he started blackmailing the original owner of the property, Stephen Balliteria. This money had taken a big strain off his financial woes.

For the next four weeks, Sally planned, shopped, cooked three meals a day, cleaned up, and packed lunches to ensure they ate good food. The laundry pile never seemed to grow smaller, even though there had been one less person at home. Seth called regularly and the boys looked forward to hearing his voice. Grant happily told him practices were still good and they actually won a few more games. Sally spent most of her nights reading Mary Higgins Clark's latest book, listening to her favorite golden oldies radio station and once in a while catching Johnny Carson on *The Tonight Show.*

Lonnie felt real anguish knowing she would not be able to find out about a blood connection with Jenny Erthner soon. She knew she had to tell Doug but since their remodeling job had been completed, there really had been no reason to call him at work. Each week at bowling, she threw her ball as hard as she could to knock down all ten pins at once, taking out her frustration with the State of Illinois adoption laws. She kept trying to figure out a way to meet Jenny's mom, so she could pass along her idea of having her speak at school, opening up a door to finally meet.

Doug also felt anxious to hear from her. With fall soccer underway and both Jordan and Josh playing every week, he had made it one of his goals to help out when he could and go to every game. Marlene had been so busy getting all the contractors to build their addition, as well as supervising their work, she wanted to get a part-time job with both boys in school. Since Doug now had an additional income she knew nothing about, he encouraged her to continue to be a stay-at-home mom. He told her he had received a big bonus at work from all the new business he had brought in from his monthly ads in the subdivision newsletter.

Each week, he waited for Lonnie to call.

At the end of the month, Seth called with good news. Because his training had been going smoothly, he would be able to get the Thanksgiving holiday off. He told Sally to be sure and call Heinz, his best friend from the Air Force, to confirm he and his family could come down from Milwaukee.

"My bigger surprise, is you and the boys will be able to get guaranteed seats to fly here the second week in December. I know this will cut into Grant's hockey, but I figure missing one weekend won't hurt. What do you think?"

"Wow, this is good news. I think they will enjoy a short trip to see you. Have you any idea when you'll be finished?" She looked at the calendar, realizing hockey games wouldn't start until the second weekend in December.

"Garrett brought home a flier from preschool saying four year olds could start a Learn to Skate program. He really wants to do this. He is upset at having to wait another year to start soccer, so maybe this would be a good outlet for his energy."

"Great idea. Sally. I think this would be good for him. He's done so well with eating better, maybe this could be some kind of reward. If I had been there in October, you know I'd have let him come to practice."

She remembered Garrett's frustration at not being able to practice with Grant's soccer team anymore. She felt glad Seth agreed with her to add this new activity. Now the final item she had to add to her list included finding or making costumes for a Halloween party at the clubhouse.

Lonnie finally decided to take matters into her own hands by calling Jenny's mom and telling her about this idea of having Jenny speak to the teachers and sixth graders. Her principal said they would have a special meeting if the PTA president couldn't change the speaker for October. Anna Murphy felt her daughter had done enough public speaking, and really wasn't interested. Because Jenny had been in the room when the call came, she told her mom she would agree to meet Lonnie and speak at her elementary school the end of October.

Lonnie had to rethink this idea momentarily, the day Jenny came to her house. She felt so nervous and had to keep telling herself this would work if she just listened and kept her mouth shut. As Jenny sat down on a blue wing chair, Lonnie marveled at the resemblance between the three of them. She seemed to be a perfect blend of Doug's good features, beautiful black hair, a perfectly chiseled chin and Lonnie's high cheekbones and short nose.

"Would you like something to drink, Jenny? I have Coke, ice tea and cider."

"Thanks so much Mrs. Balliteria, Coke would be great."

She brought out the drinks and a plate of her oatmeal raisin cookies, a hint of cinnamon filling the air. "Please call me Lonnie,"

"When I heard you and your friends speak at the board meeting, I thought this would be perfect for the sixth graders. You really impressed all the homeowners with your candor." To calm herself a little more, she took a sip of Coke and a bite of cookie. "I can't imagine how difficult this has been for you."

"I really didn't want to speak anymore, Lonnie, but the idea of getting kids as young as sixth grade to remember this awful accident before they start driving seemed like the perfect final speech."

Lonnie took out a calendar to see which day would fit Jenny's schedule. She noticed a little worry creep over Jenny's face, with her eyebrows scrunched up as though she wanted to say something else.

"Look, I don't care what day you pick, since it will be after school. If you wanted to get me out of classes, then I'd have to get permission from my principal."

As they went over her speech, which she had typed on three pages, Jenny thought she wouldn't need to change much. "Kids just need to know a passenger can distract a driver with conversation and loud music."

"Were you talking about something which upset Gail, or just guessing who'd get to date the next hunk?" Lonnie tried to be funny, but saw right away this didn't go over well when Jenny's mouth formed into a frown.

Tears filled in Jenny's eyes as she looked straight into the exact same grey-green eyes on Lonnie's face. "I haven't shared this with anyone. Only Gail and Becky know what I'm going to tell you. You must promise me you won't tell my mom."

As her eyes widened with surprise, Lonnie decided this would be an occasion when she'd just listen and not interrupt. "Of course Jenny; you have my word."

"The accident is my fault." Her face looked so sad. "I told my friends I found out I'm adopted and they turned around to answer me when the accident happened."

A few tears slipped down her flushed cheeks. "Of course, I never dreamed in a million years my mom and dad aren't my real mom and dad." She took out a tissue from the box on the coffee table and dabbed her eyes. "I had to get some papers from our file cabinet. Mom said where they were and to just go get them. I happened to see a file in the back which had a label ADOPT in capital letters so of course, I pulled out this folder to see if maybe my little brother wasn't really my brother." She burst into tears.

Lonnie did not want to show any feelings so she looked down at the floor and breathed deeply. Her heart beat so quickly because she felt overjoyed with this news.

"There were two birth certificates inside, one with my name and theirs and the other with baby girl and parents left blank. ADOPTED had been stamped over this one."

She gobbled down her cookie and swallowed the rest of her Coke, dabbing at tears flowing down her cheeks. Slowly, she started to talk again.

"I just couldn't tell my mom what I found, so I thought maybe Gail and Becky would be able to help me decide what to do."

"You must know this accident isn't your fault. Your friend didn't have to turn around to look at you." Lonnie drained her glass of Coke to give her another minute before she spoke. "I certainly understand your confusion and wanting to get another opinion."

She stood up and walked over to the chair, giving Jenny a reassuring hug and another tissue. She felt overwhelmed with this information and knew she couldn't say anything today. She couldn't wait to call Doug and share this wonderful news.

CHAPTER 39
MURDER

Doug had called Sally to go over some key points for the board meeting on Tuesday night. He had a call on his other line and asked her to hold on.

"There is loud music coming from the pool patio speakers. My neighbor, Tom Tullis is calling to complain, the third person tonight. I'll have to call you back tomorrow unless I get out of there right away."

"Sure Doug. Sorry you're giving up another night at home with your family. Talk to you later."

Observing the site, Doug ambled up the sidewalk to the clubhouse, about ten p.m. Friday night, angry to have given up yet another night with his family. He reminded himself to take Marlene and the boys out to dinner tomorrow night. He pulled up the collar on his denim jacket and put his hands deep into his pockets, remembering how many Friday and Saturday nights he had given up for this volunteer position.

An outside light blazed from the building corner and barely lit part of the tennis courts where a foursome attempted to play in the dark. The entry door, standing wide open, had one of those large plastic garbage cans as a support to keep it from closing.

Loud rock music blared from two outside speakers and people were coming and going into the kitchen. The last group, three men, held a keg precariously and lifted it onto the counter where all kinds of snacks, soda pop and bottles of wine covered the rest of the existing open space.

He took a deep breath, walked inside and looked around for a familiar face. He stopped in his tracks, stunned to see Lonnie standing near the entryway. She looked like a little doll with a new short cut and blond streaks in her hair. Her perfectly applied makeup, not too much, not too little, accentuated her natural beauty of smoothly tanned skin with a smattering of freckles and grey-green eyes. She wore tight jeans and a long sleeved plaid blouse. In the dimly lit entryway, her cordovan loafers were perfectly polished, with just the right amount of shine. He had not expected to see her and put his hand on the wall for support.

"Hey Doug, what are you doing here? Do you know the Beals, our fantastic hosts?" She walked closer to him, giving his arm a squeeze.

"Can't say I do; where do they live?" He asked anxiously, continuing to look around. "I've had complaints on the noise and need to speak to your host. Can you show me who he is?" He took a deep breath. Seeing her again unexpectedly did make a difference.

"Sure. They live on Carver Court. But first, I want you to meet my husband." She turned toward the counter by the kitchen door and called, "Honey, come here for a minute. I want you to meet someone."

A man almost as short as Lonnie with reddish brown hair, dark brown rimmed glasses and bright blue eyes motioned for them to come over. He pushed up onto his tip toes to reach over someone and set down his beer, putting his left arm around her waist and extending his right hand, his wrist encircled with a heavy gold bracelet.

"Hi, I'm Hank Balliteria." He gave a firm handshake and then took a step back.

"Hank, Doug and I went to high school together, in Joliet. Can you believe I met someone from so long ago?" She smiled at her husband, and then gave Doug a look as if to say: 'Don't add anything, please.'

"Can't say I do. Several others drove over from Joliet; know anyone else here, Doug?" He appeared bored with the entire conversation and turned to pick up his beer.

"Don't know, Hank, really haven't paid attention to the guests." His voice sounded tense and he knew he'd better get control fast. "I'm on the board here and just came over to get the music level turned down a bit." He grabbed a bar stool and sat down, his knees now shaking. Hank gave off the-better-than-you attitude and Doug wanted to get away from him as quickly as possible; even though he recognized the last name, he only hoped there would not be a connection.

"Noise level? Doug, this party is just getting started. Are you going to spoil everyone's fun?" He took a long swig of his beer and looked around the crowd.

"Look, I need to find Mr. Beals." He looked at Lonnie as if to say, enough of this already.

Lonnie said, "His name is Mark and his wife is Hannah. He's the tallest guy in the group over there in the corner, with the blue oxford shirt and receding hairline. See him now?" She pointed to a group of men and one woman, standing in the corner.

"Yeah, I do. Thanks, Lonnie. Sorry, but I need to go." He stepped off the stool and said to Hank, "Nice to meet you." Then he nodded to them and walked away, breathing a large sigh of relief.

He passed the record player and immediately turned down the sound as an eight track popped out of the player. Shouts of "No" came from all four corners of the great room. Doug waved his hand in the air to grab their attention. "I'm from the board of directors here; there have been complaints on the noise. I'm only going down two levels."

Mark Beals walked over to Doug and asked, "Hey, what do you think you're doing?" His voice didn't sound friendly or caring.

"Hi, Mark. As I tried to say above the noise, I'm representing the board of directors and we have received complaints. Just need to turn down the volume a little."

"What do I care? I've paid my deposit and reserved this place with plenty of notice. Nowhere do any of your ridiculous rules mention anything about the music level." His tone became less friendly and more aggressive.

"Actually, it does mention this specifically. I didn't bring a copy of the CCRs, but I can tell you this has been brought up enough times when I've been called over here for many parties. I can look in the kitchen drawers to see if there is a copy for you to look at." Doug stuffed his hands in his pockets and looked around the room, the talking and shouting not quite so loud now.

"So what are you going to do if I refuse? Call the police?" Mark's voice level continued to rise and his face started to scrunch up in anger.

"Yes, I will and then this party will be over. You decide what you'd rather do." He kept his voice calm, yet authoritative, because every time this happened before the police said the rules had priority. He waited patiently, noticing how quiet the room had become now.

Someone yelled, "Turn down the music, Mark, nobody cares. Not worth the trouble."

After looking toward the voice, Mark composed himself and said, "Sorry, what'd you say your name was? Guess I've had one two many drinks tonight." He put down his beer. "Of course you are right; we don't want to bother our neighbors."

"Stay awhile." He put out his hand.

Doug shook it and said, "My name is Doug Pulchowski and I'm the director in charge of the pool and clubhouse, kinda like my second family. Thanks, I just might take you up on your offer." He looked around for Lonnie, then at his watch, wondering if Marlene would go to bed or wait up for him, yet again.

Two of the men who had been in the group with Mark walked over to them and made introductions. "Hi, I'm a business partner of Mark's, Matt Kerber, and this is a business associate, Stephen Balliteria."

As they shook hands, Doug looked at Stephen hesitantly. "Haven't we talked on the phone before? Your name sounds very familiar." He became nervous, suddenly realizing who this name belonged to, and leaned against the wall for support as his knees started shaking and his stomach churned.

Stephen smiled with a crooked mouth half open. His bushy grey eyebrows rose on an already wrinkled forehead. "Yes, we have. I'm one of the original owners of this land, one of the former garbage dumps of Chicago's trash. You have called me several times this past year. Hank is my nephew, you know, Lonnie's husband."

Doug couldn't believe how his luck seemed to be running out tonight. Another person he never wanted to meet. He started to sweat and tiny beads of perspiration dripped down the back of his neck. He kept telling himself: *remain calm*. He wiped off his forehead and neck with a handkerchief. He certainly never planned to meet the man he started blackmailing.

Greenebriar's Garbage

"Actually gentlemen, I need to speak to Doug alone, would you mind?" Stephen motioned to the two wing chairs.

Just before they sat down, Stephen asked, "Can I get you a beer, Doug? I need to freshen up my drink."

"Sure, Stephen, I could use one; thanks." He sat down and sank into the comfortable cushions. He looked around for Lonnie and only saw her husband, not knowing she had already gone home.

Stephen took out a small pill from his inside jacket pocket and dumped it into the beer can. He poured himself a stiff Scotch and water and walked back to Doug, giving him his beer before he sat down to take care of business.

"I'm glad we finally have a chance to meet, Doug; we need to discuss a few things." His voice, although calm, had a serious side as he looked through Doug and cracked a crooked smile.

"You will not receive a check this month or any other month, do you understand?"

His voice, strong and scary, sent a chill down Doug's back. He put his elbows on his knees, folded his hands and cupped them under his chin as he leaned in for the kill. "I've talked to the big boys and we've decided enough is enough. The body you found can never be traced to anyone." He looked deeply into Doug's troubled eyes with a threatening stare. "This dump site, one of many, many more, covered one square mile. Anyone could have dumped a body back then, in fact I know of several others." His eyebrows rose on his wrinkled forehead as he stared at Doug's rapidly blinking eyes.

Doug's insides felt like jelly, yet he had to put up a strong front. "Look, the police are still doing some kind of forensics study on the skeleton and I don't know how you figure no one will find out who it is." He took a large swig from his beer and reminded Stephen who held the cards as he pushed a shaky hand through his black hair, trying to get some kind of composure.

"You don't understand, Doug; we hold all the cards. These men I work for . . . you don't want to deal with them EVER." His voice did not crack as he held Doug's concentration by pointing a finger toward his chest. Then he looked over to the center of the room.

Doug decided to muster up all his courage and play his ace. "I didn't turn over everything to the police; there was a wedding ring left on a finger and there is an inscription which could probably be traced to some missing person." He took a large gulp of beer and then finished with, "Making it home from Vietnam in one piece did teach me some survival skills, Stephen."

Mark stood up and announced: "Party over. Dump your trash before leaving. Anyone who wants to continue can come over to our house. Right, Hannah?"

He looked over and his wife responded, "Sure, we can fix breakfast for all you brave souls who have to drive back to Joliet."

Doug looked at his watch; he couldn't believe it was 1:00 a.m. He felt worried about the direction this conversation seemed to be going, so he drained his beer and stood up to leave. Immediately he felt dizzy and fell back into his chair.

"O.K. there, Doug?" Stephen gave him a steadying hand to help him back up, knowing what he needed to do next.

"Man, I sure don't feel so good." He closed his eyes, his knees bent and he sank back down, deeper into the chair.

Stephen looked around, and played through the entire scene in his mind first:

He spotted Hank and nodded. Hank went into the men's room, unlocked the window and lifted it up ever so slightly, so as not to give notice to an open window. He thought he would drive Doug home, and walked over to Mark to tell him he'd be driving Doug home since he didn't feel good. He said they'd need a few minutes for Doug to be able to stand up and volunteered to lock up. Mark graciously accepted the offer as everyone helped pack up the food and drinks.

Immediately, Stephen realized this plan just couldn't work. If someone saw him walking Doug out to his car, he'd be questioned first because he drove Doug home. No one would understand how Doug managed to get back inside the clubhouse since Stephen would have locked the door as he told Mark he'd do.

He watched everyone leave the room as Doug sat in the chair his eyes still closed. Stephen turned off the lights in the great room and walked toward Hank, shaking his head. He whispered, "Follow my cues."

"Hey Mark, can we help you carry anything out?"

Hank walked over to the countertop and started putting the wine and liquor bottles into a large cardboard box with separators; he carried out this box to put in the Beal's car. Stephen covered the trash cans and walked over to the front door as everyone else carried out something. He quickly went into the men's restroom and left the window open, just a little.

"There's nothing left in here, Mark," he said. "I'll close up and follow you as soon as we get some cigarettes." He turned off the lights in the entry way, closed the front door and walked casually to his large black Lincoln Town car. He closed the door and started the engine.

Hank who sat slumped in the front seat asked, "What's going on?"

"New plan. Just give me a few minutes for everyone else to leave," he said quietly. "You get out of the car and go inside through the bathroom window, then open the front door just a little. I'll drive out of the parking lot, go down one street, turn around, turn off my lights and come back into the lot. Our excuse for coming late will be going to the gas station on the corner and getting a pack of cigarettes."

Hank knew the routine. He carefully opened the door as the last car pulled out of the driveway and crouched down, walking over to the bathroom window. He looked around to make sure no lights were on in any neighboring house. He climbed in the partially open window.

In less than three minutes, Stephen drove down the street and came back. He opened the front door, closed it and walked into the great room. Doug sat still as a dead animal, his breathing slow, yet regular. The pill had done its job and he was out cold. Hank came up behind them and looked at Stephen for direction, taking a heavy piece of wood Stephen had hidden behind his back and large pieces of plastic. Stephen turned on a small flashlight and wrapped a large piece of plastic over his clothes as Hank did the same. He lifted Doug off the chair folding him in half over his left arm, placing him on the floor on another piece of plastic. Stephen hit Doug's head as hard as he could. Hank dropped his body against a chair, which turned over.

They checked for any blood spatter where they stood, wrapped the wood in plastic and backed carefully out of the room, closing the bathroom window. On the way out the front door, Hank grabbed some paper towels to wipe off his hands, forgetting to make sure the door pulled shut tightly. Inside the large trunk of his car, Stephen took out a large plastic bag and put the wood, flashlight and pieces of blood covered plastic inside. He looked around carefully to make sure no window shades from neighboring houses had been opened since he arrived. They left with no lights on until they were two blocks away, driving to the gas station for their cigarette alibi. Then they went to Mark's house.

CHAPTER 40
PREPARATION

No one could believe a murder had taken place in their pristine subdivision. As news spread, the entire neighborhood felt the sadness and shock. Sally had the regular November board meeting to plan where they would finalize the annual meeting, only two weeks away.

Her first idea would be to tackle communication to all homeowners via the block captains as a way to ease everyone's worries. Her second idea involved Alexandra, the newsletter person. They planned what she could write in her column after the board meeting on Tuesday, only a few days away.

Her initial call to Marlene earlier in the morning, although sincere, had been too short. After they came home from hockey and lunch, Sally dropped the boys at Lisa's so she could call her again. She felt more in control and able to talk

"Hi Marlene, I hope you have a few minutes to talk. I felt so rushed this morning since I had to get the boys to hockey practice. Please tell me what I can do to help out." She sat in a kitchen chair, twisting the phone cord nervously, thinking how Lisa, once again, pitched in to keep the boys for a while as she made this necessary call.

As she spoke to Marlene, she felt an unspoken problem bubbling to the top.

"Look Sally, I really appreciate your gesture, but I have family who can help with the phone calls and funeral arrangements." She seemed to hesitate before continuing, letting out a large sigh.

"There's a problem with Doug's receipts for the pool. Paul called this morning while the policeman was here."

Sally sipped slowly, letting the flavor of this cinnamon flavored tea roll around inside her mouth, trying to give support by just listening.

"Paul and Doug were supposed to meet this morning at the clubhouse. He found some numbers not matching with lists of receipts in Doug's ledger. He called to change the meeting thirty minutes so I had to tell him what the police had just told me." She burst into tears and then tried to regain some sort of composure.

"What kind of problems did he find, Marlene? Did Paul say anything specific?"

Speaking in between long deep breaths and small sobs, she said, "Paul told me Doug's figures for his budget were way out of line and he was off by hundreds of dollars. They had planned to meet to go over the figures because Paul needed to have everything kosher for the annual meeting."

"Are you saying Doug's budget was wrong, or did he think there was just a mistake in adding?" She had several pictures in her mind: a contractor asking for kickbacks and Doug compiling or did he work out some kind of a deal with payback to him? For once, her worries seemed to overshadow anything else right this minute, wondering how liable the board of directors would be if anything could be proved. Her forehead creased with anxiety as she pondered what this outcome could become for the association.

"Oh Sally, what did he do? I never thought he could be involved in anything like this. I know he and his replacement, Emil, met a few times. Do you think he found something wrong with Doug's budget?"

Sally gasped as quietly as possible, not wanting to upset Marlene any more. *Someone thought they had a reason to shut him up permanently. Who would have done this, a contractor, a homeowner or someone else? What kind of information did they have against Doug?*

"Look, Marlene, I sure don't know what happened, but I'll call Paul right away. I just can't imagine Doug getting involved with anything shady." She looked out the kitchen window at a grey overcast sky as she chose her next words carefully.

"You take care of your boys now, Marlene and please put all this out of your mind. I will follow up on each and every possibility and let you know what I find out. You have enough to deal with today."

"Thanks so much, Sally. I just can't believe this is happening. When he hadn't returned by midnight, I should have called or gone over there instead of going to sleep. It's just that this has happened before, especially if the party was given by someone he knew and they invited him to stay." Her sobs changed to crying.

"Marlene, don't blame yourself. There is no way you could have foreseen this. The police will find the person responsible. Right now, you must stop second guessing what might have been."

They said good-bye and Sally called Paul. He had a little more information, which he shared piecemeal.

"Paul, after our regular board meeting this Tuesday, we only have two weeks to get this cleared up. Why can't you share anything with me now?"

"Look Sally, Doug might not have been one of your favorite people, but he was my friend and I want to doublecheck everything myself before everyone else finds out at the meeting Tuesday." His voice sounded stressed and his words came out very slowly. "I know if I just go over every purchase, I'll find something simple like transposing numbers, or forgetting to write down a few purchases."

She looked at the clock, realizing this conversation had gone on too long. "Alright Paul, you have a point. I'll give you until Tuesday. I really don't want to ruin Doug's reputation either and maybe you are right, just a simple math error."

Knowing how busy her next few days would be, Sally called Lisa and told her to send the boys home and asked her if they could cancel their afternoon walk. Sally knew there would be hockey tomorrow and then only one day to finalize everything for the board meeting. Since Monday had always been her day to stay home, plan meals, wash and clean up, she realized she'd have a full day to get everything ready. Even though she didn't like Seth gone for so long with his training, she felt glad he wasn't there to say 'I told you so.'

Only four days after Doug's murder, the board meeting started promptly at 7:00 p.m. Since the scene hadn't been cleared by the police yet, Sally had volunteered her house. Lisa agreed to make her delicious brownies and said she'd take care of drinks for all. As each person went over their budget and what they had done since June, Sally asked them if they would like to put their name on the slate for a permanent position.

Leah, the secretary, and the treasurer, Chris, both said no immediately. Alexandra, the block captain chair said she would consider running again. Nancy decided she really couldn't give both jobs her all, and she decided to stay on as a block captain and give up the social activities position. Karen, Mark and Patty said no. This left Doug's job, so they would need quite a few people to put on the nominee slate

Alexandra volunteered, "All the block captains have been talking to their neighbors and we do have some names to put on the slate. When we open up for nominees from the floor, I really think we'll get a few more, Sally."

"I wanted to thank you again for stepping up to help us out. Each of you has done a terrific job at such a last minute notification. I just can't tell you enough how much you've helped keep us on track." Sally looked at each one as she spoke sincerely.

The board's lawyer, Daniel, stood and asked each person to be ready for questions on how they spent the money allotted to them. "Since I've been on board, most homeowners don't seem to care one way or the other about how the board spends, as long as they are not impacted. This kickback and bribe situation has opened a lot of room for discussion, so just be prepared to let the police know you had nothing to do with anything before the June meeting. Be polite and refer anything legal to me."

Once again, the meeting ended in a record two hours. As they left, pleased with their reports, most felt prepared for the annual meeting in two weeks. Paul called Sally aside and told her he had not been able to finish checking Doug's receipts and wondered what he should do.

"I agree with Daniel's assessment of what might come. If no one asks a specific question, let's leave well enough alone for now, Paul. We can meet with the new treasurer if we have to. There is just no way you are responsible for Doug's budget, even though you were on his committee." She patted his shoulder.

Paul breathed a big sigh of relief. "Thanks so much Sally; I've spent way too much time worrying about these mistakes I just can't imagine what Doug did or didn't do with all these receipts. This murder has been too much for me to handle; I'm so sad. " He put on his coat and left with Lisa, who had no leftover brownies.

Grant's soccer team didn't make the playoffs, so he looked forward to starting hockey. The first day back on ice had been the morning Doug had been found.

Later, Sally went over everything in her mind, for the annual meeting, while taking out her frustrations at bowling where she threw the ball at all the problems standing in the form of ten pins. She and Lisa continued their afternoon walks, trying to figure out who would have wanted Doug dead. Since they had no idea about his backyard find or extra income, they just figured there must have been some contractor who wanted kickbacks and Doug wouldn't give in. Seth called nightly and talked over some of these concerns. Because of all these things, she decided not to go to the next women's study group meeting. She met with Alexandra and the block captains. There were still last minute decisions to be made for their final reports. After considerable thought, she decided this meeting would be more important. Of course, Lisa said she'd share what they discussed at the women's group, knowing they were still using the book about positive thinking.

The block captain meeting started at 9:00 a.m. at Alexandra's house. Vicki Stafford had a dilemma to share and asked for opinions on what to do. She asked everyone if they remembered when her neighbor's husband died of a sudden heart attack while on business in New York City last winter.

"I don't want to dwell on negative stuff, but my next door neighbor, Marie Martine really needs some support now. I know those of you who know her will make the time to call."

Seems both sets of neighbors socialized with weekly dinners at each other's homes. After Cindy's husband died so suddenly, this new widow always needed help with some new dilemma which came up at least weekly. There had been broken water hoses, doors coming off hinges, a garage door opener which stopped working and some plumbing problems. Since Marie's husband worked as a plumber, he always volunteered to go over and fix whatever broke. At first, they both would both go over together, and then Marie seemed to tire of the weekly calls. She stopped going over with him.

"Just three weeks ago, he went over on a Saturday morning and after two hours, Marie became concerned and decided to go over since she kept getting a busy signal on the phone. Imagine her shock when she went inside, heard some strange sounds and proceeded to the bedroom where she found them in a compromising position. Seems they had been having an affair for over two months and were in love."

Several of the block captains had heard rumors about this situation and proceeded to say what they had heard or seen.

Another block captain said her neighbor needed similar support because she threw her husband out after five years of marriage, two children and a life as 'celibate as a monk,' to share her quote. They were more like roommates than husband and wife. A month after he left, Lucy found out her loving husband had a boyfriend. Her priest didn't seem to be able to offer much support and she felt quite betrayed.

Comments were shared around the room and once again there came a familiar voice from the back. "I would like to recommend my husband, the divorce attorney, if you think a divorce might be coming," volunteered Helen Franks.

The next major problem centered on the newest homeowners who did not know they were moving into a neighborhood association and didn't understand about the dues and CCRs. Alexandra had continued working with Ingrid, the former board member who still worked in the real estate business. After a fast two hours, everyone felt ready for the annual meeting and once again, Sally thanked everyone for their continued support in keeping the neighbors informed.

CHAPTER 41
ANNUAL MEETING

Finally the big day arrived. Although Sally didn't feel nervous, she worried about having to answer questions from homeowners at the open microphone. Lisa called in the morning to say Nate decided not to go and would watch the boys, including giving them dinner. During his morning break, Seth called, giving her encouragement. He had simulator training this week.

"Great, Seth. After the meeting tonight I will be able to plan our menu since my spare time will not be working on planning meetings. The boys will be so glad you can come home." She put on the water for tea and took out some spiced tea mix, a gift from the block captains.

"I still can't believe someone decided death was the only solution to whatever Doug did." She felt stuck in a spider's web spun with worry. She continued to wonder how most homeowners would respond tonight. "The boys are going over to Brett's because Nate doesn't want to go to the meeting."

Sounding as positive as he could, Seth said, "I know you can do this Sally. Just relax and force yourself to speak slowly, one word at a time. You know how rushed your words are when you are stressed."

"You're right, Seth. I have all day to prepare and finalize my opening speech." She stirred the tea mix into the cup of hot water. "How's your training coming along?"

"The instrument panel on the 727 is quite different because a co-pilot position involves flying and landing the plane. When I worked as an engineer I only had to be concerned with the aircraft systems: fuel, electrical, hydraulic and air conditioning. Not so much more to learn, just a completely different concept. I've really missed flying. Right now I'm practicing landing and taking off in the simulator in three-hour shifts."

For a few seconds, she saw she had an easy day compared to what

Seth had to learn and practice. "Thanks so much for calling during your break, Seth. Call me tomorrow night when you finish your shift. I have women's group in the morning. I'm sure I'll be on the phone a lot tomorrow calling the newly elected people to answer their questions." She suddenly realized she really wouldn't be finished tonight

When the boys came home from school, Sally told them they'd be having dinner at Lisa's and would stay there during the meeting. They watched cartoons and ate their banana snack as she picked out her best knit pantsuit and white blouse. She carefully applied her makeup, putting on eyeliner as well as mascara and sprayed her hair so it wouldn't move. She dropped them off at five-thirty. Lisa gave her a ham and Swiss on rye and a cold Coke.

"I'll bring over some brownies for dessert when I get there about, 6:15."

She looked over at Nate, who had just started to chew a mouthful of spaghetti. "I appreciate you watching the boys tonight, Nate."

Looking at her boys, she smiled and said, "Best behavior tonight, right?" She gave them a hug as they nodded yes.

Driving over to the new elementary school gym where the meeting would start in less than one hour gave her those few extra minutes to compose herself. She chewed each bite of sandwich slowly. Looking at the houses she passed by gave her a small sense of relief, knowing tomorrow someone else would handle all the problems. Inside the gym, she looked at the tables where all the reports would be set out. Those who were interested could look at director's notebooks, secretary minutes and monthly treasurer statements. A notice had been printed in the October newsletter reminding everyone these reports would be available. No one really knew how many would be interested in looking at anything.

Daniel sat at the head table going over his notes. The janitor pulled out the last row of bleachers as most of the temporary board members were coming into the gym, putting down their reports and standing behind the table, ready for questions.

"Thanks for coming early. Please come up and take your seats at

6:25." She looked for Carole Anne, the block captain who had prepared the certificates of thanks for each replacement board member. She had also made name cards and had already placed them on the long rectangle shaped tables. Daniel motioned to her.

"Sure look nice tonight, Sally; how are you doing?"

"Thanks, so far so good. I'm a little worried about the types of questions we might get at the open mike session"

"Listen Sally, if there is a problem, just pass the question to me. I can legalize any sentence enough to pacify anyone."

"I just might have to take you up on this, Daniel. We'll see how everything goes." He smiled and gave her thumbs up.

At exactly 6:30 p.m., she opened the meeting by welcoming everyone. Then she asked for a moment of silence for Doug. After the introduction of each board member, they stood up as she gave out the certificates and thanked them again for their service to their community when needed. Two reports would be given before the open microphone session.

"My name is Leah Lansing. I took over the secretary position in June. Last year's minutes were placed on the table near the entryway. I can only answer questions from June through October. I recorded what happened at each meeting, who attended, and the vote for each motion. This is the seventh annual meeting since Greenebriar opened in 1971 because there wasn't a meeting the first year."

She sat down and the next person stood up. "My name is Chris Kolanos. I took over the treasurer position in June and can only answer finances from then 'til last month I have a degree in Accounting from DePaul University in downtown Chicago, and the financial statements on the back table are from last year's meeting 'til now."

He sat down and Sally continued. "Thanks Leah, and Chris. The microphone is now open for general questions." She felt relieved to see only five people standing up.

"Please introduce yourself and tell us how long you have lived here." She took a sip of Coke.

"My name is Mary Jane Trumps. I've lived here four years. I want to know how you are qualified to be President." She smoothed down her long blue sweater and put her well-manicured hands of bright orange nail polish into large pockets.

Sally looked straight at Mary Jane's frown and noticed her overly made up eyes with too much blue shadow on her lids; these eyes looked down at the mike as Sally started to speak.

"I qualified for this job by default. You resigned due to allegations of misuse in your position. Then the rest of the board resigned and left before the meeting ended, leaving Paul and me as the only two active members. Since Paul works everyday, he and Daniel voted for me to act as temporary president.."

Mary Jane's brown eyes blinked rapidly and her face flushed pink. Remembering Seth's advice, Sally continued her successful stare. She noted Mary Jane's discomfort as her flushed face changed to bright red.

"My only other qualification besides my concern for living in a well run, honest homeowner association, is my background as a teacher. I have a B.A. degree from Florida State University. In my education classes, we learned how to organize and disseminate information to a group of students. This is not a job I asked for or wanted."

Mary Jane turned and walked back to her seat without another word and the next person walked a little more slowly to the microphone. Sally looked over at Daniel who gave her a broad smile and another thumbs up sign.

"Hi. My name is Doris Dooley. My husband and I have lived here one year. This homeowner stuff is new to us because we didn't find out about this association until closing, too late for us to back out. What can this board of directors do to make sure all real estate people who sell houses here know what information a buyer needs to have?" She looked at each member. "This information is crucial to someone buying here."

Daniel called over to Sally. "I'll answer this one, okay?"

From then on, everything proceeded smoothly. Most of the other questions were from newer homeowners. Sally felt proud to announce the results of over a year's work to get the speed limits lowered. The new lower limits would take place in the spring. Then she called on Ingrid to report her results from contacting all real estate offices as well as the

Board of Realtors. She had to make sure training for those trying to get a real estate license knew the surrounding five townships and the five subdivisions in Eden were homeowners associations. After all reports had been given, Sally talked about the job titles and descriptions. She put up the large poster board Daniel had found from previous meetings which described each job.

"The floor is now open for nominations. Each motion must have a second. The person making the nomination will present a list of homeowner signatures." After those indicating an interest in running for a specific position were nominated and gave their speeches, there were some nominations from the floor. The secretary checked each signature page with her homeowner list to verify the names were correct before those placed in nomination from the floor could be accepted.

Anton Andreev stood up to the microphone and introduced himself. "I don't have any paper with signatures and I would still like to be nominated for the president's job. I could certainly do a better job because I've worked in the banking field for many years."

Daniel stood up immediately, telling Sally he'd take this one. "Excuse me for not letting you finish your speech, Mr. Andreev. The rules for this association are very clear. You must present a verified list of 30 homeowner signatures. Since you have no list, you can't be placed in nomination."

After the votes were counted, the new board stood up in front of over 200 homeowners who stayed until the end to see who would be representing them.

The president elect, Aubrey Autowski gave a better speech than the other two who were nominated from the floor. "My wife and I have lived here for seven years." He spoke clearly and listed his key points with emphasis on what he would do.

"My goals for improving this board of directors are four in number: 1. I will make sure there are no kickbacks of any kind, ever. 2. I will find an independent accounting firm to go over our books. 3. I will make sure the new treasurer follows current accounting procedures. 4. All bids will be published in advance in our newsletter. This will give any homeowner who works in the same business, or knows anyone who is qualified, to be able to bid for the contracts necessary to run this association honestly." He smiled at the crowd and then turned to the board seated at the table.

"We owe a great debt of gratitude to Sally, Paul and Daniel for handling all the problems when everyone else resigned as well as to the eight brave neighbors who stood up for what is right, by volunteering to finish the jobs vacated. Vote for me and I'll make you proud of our neighborhood again."

After the meeting closed at 9:30 p.m. Sally asked all newly elected board members to come up front.

President, Aubrey Autowski	Clubhouse/Pool, Harvey Cooper
Vice President, David Guilaroff	Clubhouse rental, Rick Mateus
Secretary, Alice Dratch	Social, Julie Ellis
Treasurer, Whilden Voorhis	
Grounds/Maintenance, Steve Connor	
Block Captains, Alexandra Hyatt	
Membership/Newsletter, Joan Gerberding	

They were given their packets of information. Sally then invited all temporary and newly-elected members to come to a Christmas party at the clubhouse in place of the December board meeting. She asked each to bring hors d'oeuvre to share.

She and Lisa drove home together. Sally felt very pleased with the outcome, yet relieved the burden had been lifted off her shoulders by ten other homeowners. She now knew any complaints, critiques or comparisons would fall on the new board members.

Lisa said, "Now you can really enjoy the holidays, well, except for Doug's murder, of course. I guess this will be a noose around our necks until solved."

They woke up Grant and Garrett and Sally drove them home, each falling into bed. Seth called and they had a good conversation, sharing their day.

The next morning after the boys were fed and off to school, Sally checked with her next-door neighbor and Lisa so they could walk down to the women's group together.

After getting their food, Pamela divided them into five groups of four. She gave out Bible verses and asked them to discuss how this thought would be helpful to improve their attitude during the Thanksgiving and Christmas holidays. They had fifteen minutes for discussion. Then they should be ready to share one of two key points with the rest of the group.

Group one had Philippians 4:11-13. ". . . I am not saying this because I am in need, for I have learned to be content whatever the circumstances. I know what it is to be in need, and I know what it is to have plenty. I have learned the secret of being content in any and every situation. . . .I can do all this through him who gives me strength..."

Group two had 2 Corinthians 1:4. ". . .who comforts us in all our troubles, so that we can comfort those in any trouble with the comfort we ourselves have received from God."

Group three had Ephesians 4:29. "Do not let any unwholesome talk come out of your mouths, but only what is helpful."

Group four had Hebrews 13:2. "Do not forget to show hospitality to strangers, for by so doing some people haves shown hospitality to angels without knowing it."

Group five had Ephesians 4: 2. ". . . Be completely humble and gentle; be patient, bearing with one another in love.

After a most encouraging sharing from most of the women, Pamela ended with Hebrews 3:13. "But encourage one another daily, as long as it is called "Today . . .

Then, she wished everyone a very Happy Thanksgiving, Merry Christmas and Happy New Year, reminding them the next meeting would be in January, 1979.

Sally continued to prepare her menu after she spent the rest of the day calling each new board member and making sure there were no questions for now. She also called Marlene to tell her Paul had not been able to find out anything about the discrepancies with Doug's budget and just handed over everything to the new person

Marlene, still sounding distraught asked Sally again, with sadness in her voice, "What do you think he could have been involved with to have this happen?" Her voice sounded almost hoarse. "I've decided not to say too much to the boys. My parents want us to come back to Joliet for the next school year, so I will start cleaning out all Doug's things and talk to Ingrid about putting the house on the market next spring."

Sally took a deep breath to keep calm. "Maybe with one of the new ideas Aubrey came up with, an accounting firm will be able to figure out what happened to Doug's budget. Meanwhile, please try not to worry and just let the police find out who did this."

Wanting to offer support, she tried to be as positive as she could. "I hope this move will work out best for you Marlene. Of course, we'll be sad to see you go, but you must consider what is best for your boys. Have a safe trip to Joliet for Thanksgiving with your parents."

The bowling teams went out to lunch after their final game for the year. They voted to have the week of Thanksgiving and all of December off. Everyone picked a name to receive a five dollar homemade gift or a food item with a recipe. Sally decided to share the spiced tea recipe and found a fancy jar to wrap up this delightful drink.

CHAPTER 42
HOLIDAY

To everyone's delight, Seth arrived home to celebrate Thanksgiving with his best friend Heinz and family. Everyone went to the skating rink on Friday. The adults had more trouble learning to stand up on skates, and falling down gave the children something to talk about on the drive home. They had leftovers for dinner and before she felt ready to let him go, Seth had to leave. After dinner he drove away, followed by their company. He reminded them he'd see them in Atlanta in less than two weeks.

The next morning Sally dutifully took Garrett to start the learn-to-skate classes. She found a pair of used ice skates at the same store they bought skates for Grant. His hockey team had a tournament for the Thanksgiving holiday in Milwaukee. Because they had company, he didn't go. While the class kept the little kids busy, he just skated around on the rest of the rink.

On Sunday morning, snow floated to the ground in large fluffy piles, sticking on impact. By eight a.m. over three feet covered everything in sight. After Sunday school and church, the boys were going over to stay with Brett.

"Mom we learned something neat in Sunday school class today," Grant said as they were driving home. "I even have this idea on a special piece of paper to practice saying when I have a bad day."

Once again, Sally looked at her seven year old with new interest. Watching him grow up continued to present daily and weekly challenges. If only he could go to Sunday school every week instead of going to hockey practice from December through March, she'd feel more content about them learning this sport.

"Our teacher gave us a fancy piece of paper and we had to copy this Bible verse from Proverbs 12:25. "Anxiety weighs down the heart, but a kind word cheers it up."

"Can you tell me what this means to you?"

They spent the rest of the drive home talking about being nice to others and how some days other kids at school were mean to him and others. He really seemed to understand how much people do respond to a kind word and how he felt when others didn't say anything nice, but bullied him.

After the boys were dropped off, she and Lisa shopped 'til they dropped, finding all the Star Wars toys not available last year. The cookie exchange went well with the block captains and the Christmas party on Tuesday night felt relaxing for Sally. She did not have to plan anything anymore. The new board members were a friendly group, several of them living there since the beginning, and willing to share how much this neighborhood had changed. Most asked some basic questions after they had looked over their folders with their job descriptions and notes from the last two years of meetings. They ate, drank and socialized. Only once did they stop when someone asked for a prayer for Doug and his family. Since she had nothing new to report from the police, they wished each other a Merry Christmas before leaving.

On Wednesday, Sally and the boys drove out to O'Hare for their short trip down to Atlanta to visit Seth. The boys really enjoyed sitting in first class, although they were concerned about having to wear nice clothes. One of the company requirements included wearing a tie. They were given confirmed seats for both the flight down and home as one of the benefits from Seth's job. The flight went smoothly and they waited for him to finish his day's shift of flying in the simulator by enjoying the indoor pool at their hotel. He had been able to get permission to take them over to the training building and show them the simulator, in-between the morning and afternoon shift. The boys really enjoyed sitting in the captain and co-pilot seats. Seth showed them all the switches and dials on the panel. He reminded them to ask the captain to see the cockpit on the flight home to see if they could notice the difference from one airplane to another. Sunday came too quickly, and they flew home, happy for the chance to see what their dad did while he had been gone all these weeks.

There would only be one week left before the Christmas break and Seth assured them he'd pass on the first go round of tests. This would be the first Christmas he'd be home in over four years. They had even talked about trading in their two-door Cutlass for a four door car since they'd continue with carpools for several years to come.

Seth had one more surprise to pass along to Sally. During his final week of training, he met a fellow pilot who'd been scammed by a builder. Seems this man required a very large down payment and then skipped town, never to be found. His five acre parcel in Harvard, on the northwest corner of Illinois, had to be sold. Seth planned to drive everyone out there after the first Saturday hockey game. He just knew this would be a perfect place where they would live and raise the boys, "out in farm country with lots of peace and quiet and no homeowner association."

Lonnie had difficulty enjoying Thanksgiving with her family. She felt so guilty because she never had the chance to tell Doug her idea after she met Jenny. Now he was dead and would never know Jenny could be their daughter. Her husband Hank had received a large bonus from work and they would be leaving for a two-week vacation in Mexico during her Christmas break from teaching. She did feel encouraged with her initial meeting with Jenny. Her plans were to get to know her and see where this took them. Maybe she'd be able to work out something with her mom and dad in the New Year, 1979.

CHAPTER 43
ANSWER

The police force had their work cut out for them. There were over 75 people at the party where Doug lost his life. To get the names of all attendees from the Beals took more time than this small group of officers could handle. The party hosts were certainly helpful, but neither Hannah nor Mark were sure of all those who came. They found out a few people brought along unknown guests, bringing the total number to be interviewed to well over 100.

Finally, Sam decided to call on the Joliet force for extra men to help with the interviews. With all the guests who worked, setting up interviews became a hindrance with the holidays and so many people going out of town. With each new day, to make an appointment and expect these people to show up became another matter for Sam to handle. This problem caused a great deal of anguish for Marlene, who waited patiently for some news. She tried hard not to call Sam every week.

He sat at his desk, overflowing with signed statements from the party goers, and reminisced about going over to Doug and Marlene's house, that fateful Saturday morning, over a month ago He remembered the scene as if it were yesterday:

Two small boys attempted to play basketball with a shortened pole and smaller hoop. The taller of the two wore a soccer uniform. He guessed their ages between seven and nine. He asked to speak to their mom.

"Wow. You are a real policeman."

Then a car pulled up beside the driveway and a horn honked.

The front door opened and a short plump woman with streaked blond hair stood between the door and step. She looked haggard as though she hadn't slept much. Her eyes were puffy and her face a little red. Her plaid robe hadn't been tied completely and she wore only one red slipper.

"Thanks for taking the boys to the soccer tournament, Melissa. I'll be

over later." She called out to the boys as they walked toward the car; they wondered why they needed a ride to the game.

"Behave now for Mrs. McCall. Good luck Jordan; will get there as soon as I can. Josh, don't worry about the policeman. I'll explain later." Then she noticed Melissa's daughter, Janice sitting up front. She waved to her and then motioned for Sam to come inside. She looked at him with a scared and unsure face, full of questions.

"She grabbed his arm and asked, almost in a whisper. "What happened? Where is Doug? Tell me, please. I just can't wait another minute."

Sam stepped inside a large living room scattered with stacks of files on the coffee table and end tables. The morning newspaper had been opened and spread out on the blue and white checked couch. All the lamps were on, as well as an overhead light in the adjoining dining room. A radio played classic oldies. He introduced himself.

"I need to talk to you about Doug, Mrs. Pulchowski. Can you sit down and tell me what happened last night?"

"Please call me Marlene." She did not sit down. "Doug had a phone call about loud noise at the clubhouse. As he's done so many times before, he told me he'd check it out and be home as quickly as possible. If he knew who hosted the party he would stay sometimes. When I woke up at five a.m., he wasn't here."

"You went to sleep and didn't notice he wasn't here until five a.m.? What made you wake up?" Sam had taken out his small notebook and started scribbling notes.

"I don't know; I can't remember right now. Please, Sam tell me what happened." Her hands were shaking as she searched his solemn face for an answer. He just figured she had an inkling of bad news coming when he saw her hands shaking.

"I have some very bad news, Marlene."

She started crying immediately and he helped her sit down. She grabbed a tissue from a Kleenex box on a table near the couch.

"The cleaning crew found your husband's body this morning when they went in to clean up from last night's party. He had been struck on the head. Please accept my sincere condolences."

Marlene cried out. "Oh no, not Doug. Oh no. I just can't believe this." She burst into tears. He put his arm around her shaking shoulder and tried to comfort her. She sobbed uncontrollably as he kept his arm around her. A few minutes later, he removed his arm and she stopped crying momentarily.

"Who can I call for you?"

"What?" She stared out the window. " Please,just tell me what happened."

"Tell me, Marlene, who called Doug to complain?"

She just stared at him, her eyes opened wide, still in shock. "I usually have to get up early with the boys on week-ends for their soccer games. Doug has to, I mean had to, work most Saturdays. He knows most of the people who have parties and after he gets everything calmed down, he just stays a little while." She stopped to take in a large breath and sobbed little more heavily now.

The phone rang and Sam looked at her. "Please let me answer this for you."

"No, I'm alright; probably just one of my nosy neighbors. I really should take it so no one can guess why you're here right now." She stood up slowly and Sam offered her an arm to walk to the phone.

"Oh hi, Paul." She repeated his sentence for Sam to hear as she motioned for him to come into the kitchen.

"You were supposed to meet with Doug this morning to go over his budget and you'll be late?" She looked at Sam who shook his head yes.

"I have some very bad news I'm going to ask you to keep quiet for a while. There won't be any meeting this morning; Doug is dead." She started sobbing. "A policeman is here now and he might need to talk with you since I'm just too numb." She passed the phone to Sam.

"Hi, this is Sam Gregorczyk. To whom am I speaking? Yes, Mr. Hoffman." Sam opened his notebook to a new page. "I'm going to need to ask you some questions this morning. Oh, you have soccer too? Well, how about this afternoon? No I haven't talked to the association president;

Greenebriar's Garbage

who is it? No, I'll get the number from Mrs Pulchowski." He paused for a minute, forming his next question. "May I have your cooperation, Mr. Hoffman? This is very important. Do not tell a soul about this until you hear from me again. Can I count on you?"

He hung up the phone and looked at Marlene who continued to cry. "How can I find out who had the party last night?"

"Nancy would have the list. Do you want me to get her number for you?"

She walked over to a desk next to the kitchen and pulled out an association phone book. She found the page and showed him Nancy's number.

Sam called her and found out the Beals were the hosts.

"I'll leave you to your calls Marlene. But don't hesitate to call me if you need some help." He gave her his card with the precinct number. "I'm going over to see Sally Williams next to give her this information if you don't mind. Then I'll go over to the Beals. Do you know these people?"

"Yes, I know Sally and you can count on her to keep this information quiet until you give her the O.K. I'm sure the Beals will cooperate too; their son plays soccer and they are probably at the tournament, so if they aren't home, maybe you can call them later, Sam. Thanks for your concern now. I just need to figure out what to do first. When will I have a chance to see Doug? Should I find a funeral home first?" She sat down in a kitchen chair and started crying again.

He stood up to go and she continued to sit there, in a complete stupor.

"Maybe you can contact some family first to give you some suggestions for who can help with the phone calls and picking a date for the funeral." He put on his hat, and stood up to leave.

"Then I would recommend a funeral home because they will be the ones to collect the body. Will you have the funeral here or at his home town?"

She shook her head with a no and motioned for him to leave.

He let himself out.

The ringing of his phone brought him back to reality. He shook his head as if to clear his previous thoughts. It rang for a third, fourth and fifth time. Finally he picked up the black receiver and answered.

"Officer Gregorczyk, Eden Police." He heard sniffles and a deep sigh.

"Hi, Sam. This is Marlene. I need you to come over as soon as you can. I found something in the back of Doug's desk drawer addressed to you."

"Just a minute, Marlene." He looked at his desk stacked with paperwork and decided he could finish in the afternoon. Maybe this information would be a key.

"Can you give me about fifteen minutes? I'll just clear up something here and sign out. See you in a few."

He stacked the papers in some form of order and told the secretary where he'd be, grabbing his hat on the way out. Sam walked outside to a cold snowy day, trying to imagine what she had found. He then wondered if he should tell her about the skeleton Doug found last spring. He drove over slowly, pondering his choices. He knew if he told her, another Pandora's Box would be opened and he'd have a lot of explaining to do. He had promised Doug he would not tell. Yet if this information could be a key; shouldn't she know? He kept going over the possibilities and wondered if this decision would be best made by his supervisor, the chief of the force in Joliet.

While he rang the doorbell, he still felt undecided about what he should do. *The chief's been doing this a lot longer and probably knows some unwritten rule on this, I bet.*

"Good morning Sam. Come in."

Marlene looked so much better today. He hadn't been able to go to the funeral in Joliet, and still remembered her image from the fateful morning he gave her such bad news. Her hair had gone from bright blond to darker shades of blond and brown. Her nicely shaped eyebrows showed off her blue eyes. She had on a dark blue sweater and jeans Instead of standing hunched over, she stood straight and tall, showing off her 5'8" frame.

"When I started clearing out our desk, Doug had two drawers just for his stuff. Imagine my surprise when I found this envelope with your name. What do you think is inside?"

Sam took the small manila envelope, feeling some type of cardboard or covering over whatever had been placed inside.

"Thanks so much, Marlene. I really do need to get back, so I'll call you later." He walked back toward the front door when she put out her arm to stop him.

"Aren't you going to open it here, Sam? I'd really like to know now." Her face looked at him with an undefined look of don't make me wait any more for an answer.

"I must follow procedures Marlene and open this at the station with a witness. I'll call you as soon as I can this afternoon. Thanks again."

He couldn't get out the door fast enough. He waved goodbye from inside the car as he drove slowly over snow packed streets, not yet cleared. He went straight to the Winchell's doughnut shop for coffee and a glazed bear claw.

As he sat in his car, sipping his coffee, he wondered what could be in this envelope. He took a couple of bites of his favorite morning treat and decided to drive back to the station as quickly as he could. So many questions floated through his mind, he wished for a definite answer inside this enclosed heavy paper. Snowflakes started to fall and he decided to drive a little more slowly; he didn't want an accident with this valuable information in the seat next to him.

Once inside his office, he locked the door and opened the envelope, without calling for a witness. Two cardboard pieces slipped out with a wedding ring taped to one of them, FMD, 6-28-59, Love Always, SMD.

CPSIA information can be obtained at www.ICGtesting.com
Printed in the USA
LVOW12s0048220115

423810LV00001B/16/P

9 781490 842424